Hazelnuts
and
Homicide

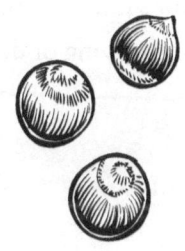

BY N.E. CARLISLE

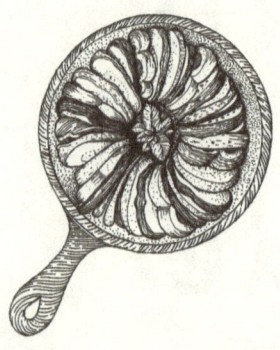

Cover design by Janna Steagall
Book design by Jessica Cameron

ISBN: 978-1-956146-70-7 (hardback)
ISBN: 978-1-956146-71-4 (paperback)
ISBN: 978-1-956146-72-1 (ebook)

My heartfelt thanks to my family and friends for their constant encouragement, laughter, and belief in this story from its first spark to the final page. Your support made the writing journey a joy.

I am deeply grateful to Dr. Karen Metheny and the Boston University Gastronomy program for inspiring me to explore the rich connections between food, culture, and storytelling. Their insight and passion for culinary history continue to shape how I see the world — and the mysteries within it.

Chapter 1

Arriver Comme un Cheveu sur la Soupe:
To Arrive Like a Hair in the Soup (an uninvited appearance,
or something or someone who disrupts the situation)

I closed the window in the dining room as a chilly breeze slipped inside, unaware that this small act would mark the start of a season I'd never forget—a season filled with murder and secrets. The soft click of the latch brought my attention to the comforting scent of my house—candy canes. With the salty tang of the Oregon coast wafting in all morning, I hadn't noticed it until now.

I loved candy canes. Their bright, sweet aroma brought more than just peppermint to a room; it was the smell of possibility and of holiday magic waiting just around the corner. It was a scent woven with memories.

My mother—not French, but a trained French pastry chef—approached the holidays like an artist, pies gleaming with egg wash, golden pâte à choux, and tablescapes as precise as her menu. My father, a construction work-er, brought the same devotion to carving Nativity figures and crafting the unshakable tree stand that kept our Douglas fir perfectly upright. My par-ents were opposites, but at Christmas, structure met whimsy and tradition danced with improvisation.

I liked to think I'd inherited the best of both of them. My mother's ele-gance showed in my high cheekbones and the soft curly wave of my black bob, which chose a new part daily, no matter how I styled it. My father, a na-tive of Quebec City, gave me French as my first language, my height—nearly five-nine—and a frame balanced between strength and grace. An open box of damaged organic, gluten-free, and allergy-safe candy canes filled the entryway with a festive peppermint scent. I popped a broken piece into my mouth: classic peppermint, of course. None of that sour green apple or mint chocolate nonsense. The crisp flavor cleared my head.

At my feet, Oscar, my fluffy black-and-white Bernedoodle, wagged his tail, his big brown eyes begging. "Not yet, buddy," I said.

He stared, his big eyes melting my soul.

I caved. "Fine. You win. Again."

I handed him a nub, and he crunched it happily, the morning light catching in his fur. His usually tragic breath improved a little with the treat, which made his inevitable slobbery kisses more tolerable.

"You're lucky you're cute," I muttered as he licked his lips, already angling for more.

Smiling, I brushed a streak of flour from my sand-colored sweater and tucked a rebellious, gray-streaked curl behind my ear. My loose linen pants were wrinkled, and my favorite sweater was already dusted in flour. My look wasn't glamorous, but comfortable, and comfort counted.

"*Allez*, Oscar," I said, grabbing another piece of candy cane. "It's going to be a long day. But if we start with candy canes, how bad can it be?"

Oscar had been training to be a service dog when I found him—obedi-ent, kind, and ready to learn. But he wasn't brave enough for the job, and honestly, I didn't hold that against him. Bravery, as I'd come to understand, was often overrated. He could cuddle all day and bring me his goofy, lopsided grin when I needed it most, and that was good enough for me.

It was still November—Thanksgiving, to be exact—but my mind had already skipped ahead to Christmas. I'd begun gathering my essentials: cookies, Bûche de Noël, and candy canes. Some people say Christmas is about family, but I'd learned not to count on that. I relied on sugar—serotonin, dopamine, and the rituals that lit up my house.

Most years, I was a Thanksgiving guest, breezing in with my famous pumpkin cheesecake, a gluten-free crowd-pleaser that saved the host from figuring out which dessert is safe for people like me. I let myself roll into Christmas mode without the chaos of hosting the previous holiday.

But this year, I was hosting Thanksgiving, and it was throwing off my rhythm. My tradition of having the house fully decorated by the Friday after Thanksgiving was now threatened by turkey, stuffing, and a soon-to-be-full dining room.

The kitchen door swung open, and Oscar was immediately on his feet, tail wagging like crazy. Alejandro, my old friend who lived in the cottage behind my house, stepped inside, carrying a heavy bushel of apples. His cheeks were flushed from the brisk November air, and he shook his head, clearly amused by Oscar's enthusiastic greeting.

At six foot three, Alejandro seemed to fill a room just by entering it. He had dark brown hair that curled slightly at the edges, with the faintest hint of premature silver at his temples. He was carrying an extra thirty pounds, but was still fit, looking like a retired linebacker or someone who spent more time chopping wood than sitting at a desk.

"Happy Thanksgiving, Annee," he said with a grin, setting the apples down on the counter. "Your grandmother's orchard is as beautiful as ever, but those apples...not light. Hope you appreciate the effort."

"Happy Thanksgiving, Alejandro." I smiled as I wiped my hands on a towel. "And I definitely do. You know, her apples are the best. Just that right balance of sour and sweet."

He glanced over at the countertop where I'd laid out ingredients. "Apple tart, right?"

"Exactly," I said, pulling out a cutting board. "For 'Lenore's Fallen Apples' tart."

Alejandro let out a chuckle. "You and your thematic menus."

"Someone's gotta keep things interesting," I replied, slicing the apples. "Plus, Edgar Allan Poe makes for a fun Thanksgiving twist." I gestured toward the pot simmering on the stove.

"Save me some of the Macabre Caramelized Brussels Sprouts." Alejandro leaned back against the counter. "You've really outdone yourself."

"By the way, did you catch the Macy's parade this morning?"

"Nope, missed it," I said, grabbing some thyme for the stuffing.

"Same old floats, mostly," Alejandro replied. "And the Broadway numbers this year? Phenomenal. Maybe next year the three amigos—you, me and Mackenzie—will finally make it to New York to catch one of those shows in person."

I smiled at the idea. Mackenzie was my former high school rival, who just happened to be my best friend now. "That would be amazing, Alejandro. It's been ages since I've traveled anywhere."

"Same here," Alejandro admitted, his voice quieter. Then his phone buzzed, cutting through the moment.

I couldn't help but tease. "Maybe we'll add a fourth to the group? You've been pretty glued to your phone lately."

Alejandro glanced at the screen, and a shadow crossed his face briefly. "It's nothing," he said, sliding his phone into his pocket. "Just some work stuff."

I frowned slightly. "You sure? You looked—"

"Yeah, I'm fine," he interrupted gently, his tone a little too light. He cleared his throat and patted Oscar. "Come on, let's go watch the dog show—the parade's over."

"All right," I replied as the kitchen door swung closed behind them. The smile stayed on my face, but a small flicker of worry lingered as I turned back to the apples. Something was off. Oscar went as far as the backyard between the cottage and the kitchen, but then he came right back into the kitchen to be near all of the smells.

"Traitor," Alejandro called out after him.

Alejandro had been living with me ever since a bad turn at work sent him looking for a quieter life. For the most part, he seemed better—more grounded, even content helping around the property. But lately he'd been glued to his phone, slipping away to answer calls or brushing off texts a little too casually. I didn't press; still, I couldn't shake the sense that something was stirring under the surface.

Even with the comforting smell of baking in the air, my morning routine felt off. Most days, Oscar and I would walk into town, but today I was hosting. Hazelton would be coming to me. I'd already heard from Chief Cora that morning—she was more than our law and order; she was a friend. Still, I couldn't help inventing little mysteries about her, the way I did with everyone else. Yesterday, I'd noticed she'd dyed her graying hair red. Was it for a date? A fresh start? Or just boredom? Oscar and I had our theories.

Since we had missed our morning walk, Oscar needed to get his energy out, and I needed a break. I turned down the heat to let things simmer, covered what was already done, and decided it was time to survey the front of the house for our guests. I hoped that they might dress up and really take part in the Edgar Allan Poe theme of my literary culinary event, but usually only a few diners ever went the extra mile.

"Come on, Oscar!" I threw open the front door and grabbed another candy cane for a quick sugar boost.

I lived in a sprawling pale blue house with an architectural identity crisis. It was part Gothic Revival, part Victorian. Its steep rooflines, arched windows, and ornate gables give it a church-like feel, softened by my grandfather's Victorian touches, like gingerbread trim and a wide wraparound porch. During the holidays, I leaned into the whimsy. Twinkle lights traced the roof, wreaths hung from each arched window, and garlands draped the porch railings, turning the house into something out of a storybook.

The house sat far back from the road, so it took some effort to make it to the front door. Along the way, you passed my grandmother's army of ceramic bunnies and gnomes. As a kid, I found them unsettling, because their painted eyes always seemed to follow me. But to her, they were precious. Each one had a name, a story, and a purpose. My grandfather gave them to her, one by one, over the years. She kept them all. And now that the house was mine, so did I.

Charlie Watson, our postal carrier, town council member, and part-time UPS driver, walked up the driveway with a package tucked under one arm and another balanced precariously in his other hand. He waved, his smile apologetic. "Morning, Annee. Happy Thanksgiving! These should've made it to you yesterday, but I ran out of daylight. Better late than never, I always say."

I met him halfway, taking the box from him. "Thanks, Charlie. Happy Thanksgiving to you, too. Busy day ahead?"

"Always," he said, shifting the second package under his arm. "Between setting up the Christmas market and getting to your dinner later, I've got plenty on the schedule. I might be a few minutes late, but I'll be there." He handed me the second package. "This one's for Alejandro. Mind passing it along?"

"Not at all," I said, tucking it under my arm.

Charlie's gaze landed on the house. "By the way, you've done a nice job with the place. It's good to see it stay in the family. Houses like this hold a lot of history."

I smiled. "Thanks, Charlie. That means a lot."

He nodded, tipping his cap. "Well, I better get moving."

"Happy Thanksgiving, Charlie. See you later," I said as he walked briskly back to his truck, leaving me with the packages and a faint smile.

My family didn't start in Hazelton. On my mother's side, my Puerto Rican grandmother and Scottish grandfather met in Boston. She worked in her uncle's restaurant and he built ships in the Navy Yard. Practical and ambitious, they headed west with their three kids and settled here, where my grandfather built this house room by room with more plans and skill than money.

My grandmother brought the house to life, and even turned it into a bed and breakfast after my grandfather died. For years, it was full of guests, garden blooms, and warm meals. When business slowed, she never complained. She just kept going.

That's when my cousins and I started coming more. Summers here were loud and chaotic. She'd call us her "little storm" and swear we made the house feel alive again.

When she passed and left me the inn, I gave it new life with my business, The Literary Table. It's part bookstore, part teahouse, part event space. A place for food, stories, and conversation.

I looked at the bunnies and gnomes by the front path. I couldn't imagine ever moving them. They had watched over the house for too long. They had seen the people who built it, filled it, and kept it going. They had seen all of us.

Our parents shipped us here every summer, or whenever they needed a break. There were three cousins: Sylvester, whose name origins remained a mystery (we teased him with Tweety and Rocky references), Emerson, named by his poet mother, and me—Bonne Annee Steele. Born on January first to a sentimental French pastry chef, I ended up with two first names. By third grade, I became just Annee.

The boys stopped coming once they hit high school, leaving me the last grandchild standing. By junior year, I'd moved in full-time, right around the time my mother went missing in the Congo. She had thrown herself into environmental activism after my dad died from mesothelioma, convinced that saving the rainforest was her new mission.

I didn't share her passion. The planet had already taken enough from me. When I went to college and culinary school, I worried about leaving my grandmother behind. But she insisted it was time for her to move into a group home, where, surprisingly, she thrived. Friends, crafts, and for once, someone else taking care of her.

After she moved out, the house went quiet. Mr. Morrison, our caretaker, moved into the cottage to tend the property. College and culinary school felt like my chance to follow in my mother's footsteps. She was a gifted chef, as was my grandmother, who could cook circles around most professionals. Christmas was their masterpiece; Thanksgiving, a polite truce in between layers of stuffing and cranberry sauce. I wanted to create that kind of magic—the kind that fed both heart and belly.

But I quickly learned I wasn't destined to be the next Julia Child. Pastry school was a mess—too much precision, too many allergies, and way too many sharp tools for someone as clumsy as me. I left culinary school and found my own path. I might not be a chef, but I could craft a killer menu and host an unforgettable event.

Food and creativity seemed to run in the family. Sylvester built a restaurant empire after ditching investment banking. Emerson critiqued food and everything else, including me. He stayed in contact only via social media. His comments were more barbed than warm, but it was still a connection. Maybe that was his version of caring, or at least, that's what I told myself.

Even Mr. Morrison, our longtime caretaker, eventually retired. He was ready to enjoy peace and quiet. It felt like the end of an era. Yet the house still hummed with life in its own way. I liked to think my literary culinary treats kept things lively.

When the weather finally cooled this year, I started planning my fall-themed events. My guests voted on the monthly theme—September was *Harry Potter and the Half-Blood Prince*, October brought *Something Wicked This Way Comes*, and November became "Poe-vember," with *The Raven and*

Other Poems as the featured book. Gothic touches mingled with harvest décor, fancy ravens alongside pumpkins and wheat stalks.

Thanksgiving, to me, was like the Olympics of holiday meals. These days, people my age seemed less enthused, favoring "Friendsgiving" or skipping it altogether, but I still loved the challenge of cooking for the season. It's a day when food, family, and tradition converge—even if the family part was a little unconventional in my world.

This month's Poe-inspired menu leaned moody: cotton candy macarons, carnival-spiced coffee, and apple cider mimosas with cinnamon-sugar rims. I thought of rebranding them and bringing them back. They were crowd favorites. Though I offered lighter books, the votes skewed dark. I was a little tired of black and purple, but the rotating guests, locals, Portlanders, and coastal travelers made every event feel fresh. I gazed up at the house, contemplating my menu. I had a good feeling this month's literary event would be the most memorable one yet.

If only I'd known how right I'd been.

Chapter 2

Avoir du Pain sur la Planchet:
To Have Some Bread on the Board (to have a lot of work to do)

A soft knock at the door sent Oscar trotting over, tail wagging. I wiped my hands on a dish towel, glancing at the apple slices lined up for the tart. "Hold on, Oscar," I murmured, heading to the door.

Mackenzie stood on the porch, grinning, her arms piled high with clothes. Her coppery curls peeked out from beneath a slouchy knit beanie and her cheeks were flushed pink from the cold. She wore a moss-green peacoat and boots with faux fur trim—festive and practical, as always.

"Wardrobe delivery!" she announced, stepping inside and brushing past Oscar, who practically vibrated with joy at her arrival. "Also, your front walk smells like cinnamon and Christmas."

"You just smell the tart," I said, shutting the door behind her.

She dumped the bundle of clothes onto a nearby chair, then turned, spotted the candy cane jar, and grabbed one with a grin. "Don't mind if I do. You always have the good ones—classic peppermint, none of that weird green apple nonsense."

I laughed. "Glad someone's excited. I'm elbow-deep in apples, stuffing's on deck, and the Brussels sprouts are judging me from the fridge."

Mackenzie spun dramatically and took a deep sniff. "Your house smells amazing. If this is what Poe-themed Thanksgiving is supposed to feel like, I'm sold."

"The 'Nevermore' shrimp cocktail is chilling, the tart's almost done, and the ghostly gravy boat is waiting for its close-up."

She leaned against the counter, unwrapping a candy cane. "Okay, morbid menu aside, I've got Christmas on the brain. Have you seen downtown? The market setup already looks like a movie set."

"It does," I agreed. "I drove through yesterday—booths are up, and lights are everywhere. It opens tomorrow, right after this dinner."

"Exactly. Black Friday launch. Cocoa first, wreath shopping second, cinnamon almonds last." Mackenzie grinned like she'd been planning for weeks.

I raised an eyebrow as I sliced apples. "You've really thought this through."

"Of course." She laughed.

"Now go change into your Poe costume. I need your help with the tablescape, and you can't assist me in jeans."

She picked up her clothes and headed down the hall. "Just wait. After Poe, it's full-on tacky sweater season. Consider yourself warned."

I turned back to the apples, the scent of cinnamon and cloves filling the kitchen. With Mackenzie humming off-key in the other room and Oscar now glued to the candy cane jar, it was officially the holiday season.

Mackenzie was my right hand at The Literary Table. Every book we featured had a hidden culinary thread, and she was my sous chef and partner-in-crime for bringing those menus to life. One of my favorites was our Regency dinner for *Emma*, a reminder that food in literature always says more than it seems.

In high school, though, we were anything but a team. As the new kid, I was no match for Mackenzie, who'd been "best at everything" since kindergarten. We competed over grades, clubs, and even crushes—until my grandmother, who was friends with Mackenzie's parents, forced a truce. She framed it as charity: the orphan and the overachiever bonding for balance. The awkward hangouts eventually turned into genuine friendship.

Now, Mackenzie helped me with everything from seating charts to centerpieces. I obsessed over tablescapes—circling the room, adjusting angles, snapping photos—and she kept me grounded. I once considered competitive tablescaping, but even I had limits.

We hosted two events per book: one brunch or tea, and one dinner. Just enough to stay creative without tipping into chaos. Tonight's Poe-inspired Thanksgiving dinner was no exception. With Mackenzie there, I knew it would all come together.

Mackenzie reemerged from the hallway in full Poe regalia, black lace shawl, dramatic makeup, and a raven feather tucked behind one ear. "Well?" she asked, twirling with flair. "Do I look sufficiently Gothic for Thanksgiving dinner?"

"You look like you should be writing love letters and curses in candlelight," I said, eyeing her fondly. "Very on-brand."

She grinned and smoothed her skirt. "Perfect. I even scared Oscar a little. That's how I know it's working."

Oscar huffed from his spot near the hearth, unimpressed.

Mackenzie slid into her usual rhythm, arranging votives and adjusting table settings. "So," she said casually, "there are a lot of market vendors coming tonight, huh? How did you let them rope you into hosting a kind of welcome event for the Christmas Market?"

"They cornered me at Katie's Café," I said, stacking appetizer plates. "The council said I was the obvious choice, since The Literary Table already brings in out-of-towners. But I told them I would only do it if it matched my theme. No way was I designing a whole new event two days before the Christmas season kicks off."

Mackenzie nodded. "Smart. I'd cry if we had to redo the décor. These miniature ravens took me forever to find." Mackenzie stopped arranging the place cards and looked at me. "I still can't believe they asked you to feed the organizers tonight. On Thanksgiving. At the end of Poe month."

I shrugged. "At least I didn't have to cancel anything. And I did get the final say on the guest list, number, and the menu."

As we placed the last of the centerpieces and checked the lighting, I felt a flicker of hope. Maybe this would be the best Poe event yet.

"Okay," Mackenzie said, placing one final raven in the center of the table. "It's spooky, seasonal, and suspiciously festive. And it feels very literary."

"If all else fails," I added, "we'll distract them with wine."

"Cheers to that," she said, raising her water glass in a mock toast. "Now, let's get Poe-litically incorrect."

There was a cawing noise outside the window. "I'm happy the birds came to the party." I thought to myself how perfect these on-theme corvids were. Ravens, after all, were resilient winter birds—perfect for late fall, unfazed by the chill. They were intelligent and fascinating, could mimic human voices, and felt right at home in our coastal environment, where rocks and open spaces abounded.

Alejandro and I had even been working to attract a few to the garden, hoping they'd help with the rodent problem in the mini-orchard. My grandmother had planted citrus, apples, peaches, and even finger limes, filled with tiny, caviar-like pearls that paired beautifully with seafood. One of her Australian guests smuggled the finger lime here years ago, back when it was illegal to grow them here.

To encourage these clever birds, we made some changes. Out went the wind chimes, the fountain was transformed into a birdbath, and we added a decoy bird from the hobby store. Ravens were social, though notoriously quarrelsome, much like my own family. We even played a recorded raven call and left out food.

It worked. Maybe too well. They're everywhere now, lurking in the garden like feathery sentinels.

At least the effort got noticed. A write-up in the paper praised the raven-themed events as "spectacular" with "attention to every detail." The town council pounced on this success, which was how I ended up hosting tonight's dinner for a mix of entrepreneurs, educators, and neighbors.

Tonight's Thanksgiving feast was the third in my Edgar Allan Poe dinner series, and I wanted it to feel fresh, mysterious, and unforgettable. With my many food allergies, I built menus that were safe for me—but that didn't mean they lacked magic. Plus, a few lurking ravens didn't hurt, either.

Still, something had been missing—until I found a strange, glossy green chayote at the farmers market. Its goblin-like texture gave me chills in the best way. Alejandro reminded me the Mayans and Aztecs revered chayote, and that ancient edge sealed the idea.

I poached the halved chayote in a spiced blackberry sauce and plated each side with fresh blackberries and a dark chocolate raven silhouette. I called it *Raven's Kiss*. With that eerie little flourish, the menu felt complete—a gothic, gluten-free triumph.

Chapter 3

Traîner des Casseroles:
To Drag Some Saucepans (like personal baggage)

The table was dressed in soft harvest tones, peachy-pink and orange roses, cream feathers, and just enough black to nod to the Poe theme. Three candelabras flanked each floral arrangement, spaced so no one's view or plate was blocked. With no staff, I always chose a self-serve buffet. It gave guests flexibility and let me design a separate table where every dish could shine.

I used vintage serving pieces from my grandmother's collection, a tradition I continued through estate sales and rummage finds. With locals downsizing, like Mr. Manzetti, who closed his old pizza shop to retire, we lost the personal touches that once defined Hazelton. I salvaged his commercial dough roller. Although massive, it was perfect for my crusts and fondant work.

It earned its place on my menu. Pizza was a safety net for picky eaters, freeing me to experiment with bolder dishes. I even hosted two vegan events a year, though nut-free vegan cheese still mystified me. Because of my allergies, the main kitchen stayed nut-free. I used Alejandro's cottage kitchen when necessary.

Tonight's guest list was a mystery, appropriate for a Poe-inspired Thanksgiving. Usually, I knew my guests and their dietary quirks, but this time it was a wild card. What I *did* know: fifteen guests was a few too many. I preferred even numbers of eight or twelve, but made it work with two round tables of eight, joining one myself.

My large dining table would hold part of the buffet, and we had cleared the sitting room to give everyone a view of the fireplace. Alejandro and Mackenzie were on deck to help, which meant I could enjoy being both host and guest. The town kept hinting I should reopen overnight stays. I had agreed to the dinner, but not the lodging. I ran a bookstore and kitchen, not a bed-and-breakfast.

To the left of the dining room, shelves of books lined the wall in antique cases with a library ladder that creaked as it rolled. Mostly cookbooks, classics, mysteries, and whatever else my community requested filled the shelves. It was not grand, but people liked browsing with a glass of cider in hand, watching the mist drift through the evergreens outside, and it reminded me that stories and recipes were both ways of keeping traditions alive.

What did I do with the empty rooms in my house? Well, I was no minimalist. They were filled with my collection of things, each with its own purpose or story. I always kept a room ready for visiting friends, or if I was honest, for my mother, should she ever return from the Congo. Yes, I know it was a childhood dream, but I couldn't quite let go of it.

Lately, I'd been thinking about getting another dog to keep Oscar company, but I wasn't sure I was ready for the added chaos. A neighborhood cat, plump and orange, used to patrol the property. I'd leave milk out near the bird feeder—not for the cat, I told myself, but for the ravens. Still, the feline had vanished, and I couldn't help but wonder where it had gone. My allergies had flared up after a visit to Alejandro's cottage, and I suspected the culprit had found a new home there.

Paul Monroe arrived first. He was the local hero, an Olympic bronze medalist, the high school swim coach, the golden boy of Hazelton—and my secret high school crush that I still harbored. He greeted me with a kiss on the cheek that made my pulse stutter.

"Bonne Annee, stop worrying. It's perfect," he said with a smile.

Guests arrived steadily: Cora, our police chief, sharp-eyed and newly red-haired; Jasper, our fire chief, steady and smiling; and Katie the café owner, dramatic and delightful in head-to-toe raven glam. Felix and Magda from the hazelnut farm made their Literary Table debut, their curiosity as evident as Magda's no-nonsense stare.

Charlie, our mail carrier and town council head, waved cheerfully. Sophia, sharp and reserved, entered in velvet and lace, notebook in hand. Then came the market vendors: Ilsa, elegant and unreadable; and Karl, warm and chatty, with a bottle of wine.

Last came the carnival family: Skye, Scott, and their father, Steve. Skye made a beeline for Paul with a flirtatious smile that made my skin prickle. "If you liked the carousel, you'll love the Ferris wheel," she said.

Paul smiled politely.

I busied myself with a tray of drinks, escaping into the kitchen just in time to watch Mackenzie plate the poached chayote. "You okay?" she asked.

"Just needed a minute," I said, spooning sauce over the halved fruit. Blackberry, pomegranate, cinnamon, vanilla, cloves. The scent calmed me more than any meditation app ever could.

Back at the buffet, I was greeted by a gust of cold air—and Emerson.

He never knocked. Tall and theatrical in his long black coat, he stepped inside like he was making an entrance.

"Hello, Bonne Annee," he said, smirking. "Still hosting your little food-meets-fiction soirées?"

I didn't rise to the bait. Emerson had always belittled what I built here. Still, his words stung.

Alejandro slipped out the back the moment he saw Emerson. There was a history there, no doubt. Emerson made a beeline for the buffet, plucking up a canapé. "This one's a tragedy, I assume?"

"It's food making a connection to the story," I said simply.

He chuckled. "Quaint. Maybe you should write a cookbook—*Bonne Annee's Table*. People eat that kind of thing up."

And maybe you should stop pretending you don't miss being part of this family, I wanted to say. Instead, I patted Oscar and turned back to my guests.

The night had only just begun, but something in the air had shifted. The ravens outside stirred. And I couldn't shake the feeling that not everyone who walked through my door tonight would walk out the same.

From across the room, I kept my eyes on Emerson, a knot of unease growing in my stomach. He hadn't called, hadn't warned me he'd be here—and judging from the look on Alejandro's face, he hadn't known, either.

Needing answers, I found Charlie by the fireplace, clipboard in hand. "Weren't we expecting fifteen guests?" I asked, scanning the room.

Charlie rubbed his chin. "We were. Maybe someone's running late. You know how these things go."

He looked momentarily sheepish. "Might be tied to one of the Portland food pods—the Misto truck or maybe the Creole one. I forget."

"That's all right," I said. "I've started the Poe slideshow so we can give everyone a chance to arrive".

Just then, the doors opened, and in walked Johnny and Lucca from Misto. The smell of fried calamari followed them like a culinary calling card. Johnny, with his salt-and-pepper beard and calm presence, nodded toward the room. Lucca, grinning and energetic, wore a T-shirt that read *Fritto Misto King*. Their arrival sparked a wave of excitement.

I slipped back into hostess mode, smiling and making small talk, but under it all, a familiar ache stirred. Emerson's presence had cracked something open. All the years of feeling excluded from the closeness he shared with Sylvester. I had tried to stay connected, but the gap always widened. Was it because I was the only girl? Or just too easy to forget?

I dimmed the lights, letting Vincent Price's voice fill the room as he recited *The Raven*. Guests leaned back with their coffee and dessert, some laughing nervously at the macabre verses, others lost in thought.

Across the room, Emerson looked at me. Something flickered in his eyes for a brief second—not smugness, but panic.

His skin had gone pale, blotchy red patches blooming on his cheeks.

Then came the coughing—deep, dry, and sudden.

My pulse quickened. His face reddened further, and tiny welts began to form along his jawline. Another cough, this one more of a gasp, followed by the unmistakable swelling of his lips. My stomach dropped. I had seen this before.

Then, as if in slow motion, Emerson slumped forward, his hand knocking into the "Raven's Kiss" dessert, sending the chayote and blackberry sauce splattering across the table, onto the dishes, and even onto a few of the other guests. His body collapsed against the table with a sickening thud.

Chapter 4

C'est la Fin des Haricots:
It's the End of the Beans (all hope is gone)

C haos erupted. There were screams and shouts as people jumped up from their seats to rush to his side.

At that moment, I did what I always did in a crisis: I got eerily calm. I slipped quietly from the room, my mind calculating my next move, distancing myself from the panic swirling around me. I hurried into the kitchen, my pulse starting to race but my hands steady. The muffled sounds of frantic conversation filtered through the walls.

I heard Paul's voice rise above the noise. "I'm calling an ambulance!" he called out, seemingly forgetting that both the police chief and fire chief were sitting in the very same room. They were already alerting their teams.

I didn't waste time. I opened the junk drawer next to the refrigerator, filled with batteries, rubber bands, and a myriad of odds and ends. But it also contained something vital: my EpiPen.

The symptoms were unmistakable now. Emerson was in the middle of a full-blown anaphylactic reaction.

I re-entered the dining room, EpiPen in hand. The guests had already moved Emerson to the floor, where someone had futilely attempted CPR. I could see the panic in their eyes as they hovered over him. I moved swiftly, motioning them to clear the way.

"Excuse me," I said, calm but firm.

I knelt beside Emerson, gripping the EpiPen tightly. With one hand, I pulled off the blue safety cap, the familiar click of the cap snapping off grounding me in the moment. I pressed the orange tip firmly against the outer thigh of his pants, midway between his knee and hip, and pushed until I heard the second click—the one that meant the needle had deployed and gone into his leg.

I held it there, counting the seconds in my head. *One…two…three…* until I reached ten. Then I pulled the pen away, the safety tip automatically sliding back over the needle. I massaged the area gently to help distribute the medication.

"Someone start a timer," I said, glancing up at the nearest guest holding a phone. "We need to monitor how quickly he responds. I just used my EpiPen, so there's plenty of epinephrine in his system helping him out at the moment—but if his symptoms don't improve soon, I may need to give him a second dose."

For the next minute, we all waited. The seconds felt like hours, but gradually, I noticed Emerson's breathing start to even out. The wheezing slowed, the swelling in his face began to subside. After five minutes, the blotches on his skin started to fade. He was stabilizing.

With help from a few guests, Emerson was eased onto the couch. His face remained pale, his breathing shallow, but his eyes fluttered open just as the paramedics arrived. Relief swept through the room as they moved swiftly, prepping the stretcher.

Just before they lifted him, Emerson turned to me, lips dry and cracked. "Thanks," he whispered, a faint smile ghosting across his face. It was fleeting, but it landed hard.

I stood frozen as the ambulance doors closed with a thud and pulled away.

Around me, the room buzzed with lingering nerves. Guests began to leave in a quiet exodus, murmuring their goodbyes and slipping out into the night. The Poe-themed dishes sat cold and mostly untouched, the evening unraveling completely.

I scanned the room, dazed. A jacket hung forgotten by the door. The once-vibrant table now looked abandoned, a hint of its festive promise.

"Mack," I said, spotting her near the sideboard, "can you drive us to the hospital? I'm too rattled to go alone. And Alejandro's not picking up." My voice cracked at the edges. Mackenzie grabbed her key and coat without hesitation.

We were almost out the door when I remembered Oscar. As with all my events, I had set him up in the downstairs bedroom right before guests were seated. I had his TV playing his favorite cooking show on a loop to keep him calm amid the noise of guests and commotion. But now, I could hear him whining, a high-pitched, almost frantic sound that wasn't like him. Then came the scratching, persistent and sharp.

"I'm coming, buddy. I'm sorry, but I'll have to put you in the kennel. We've got an emergency," I called, opening the door to fetch him.

But instead of bounding toward me, Oscar let out a sharp bark, something between a cry and a reprimand. His eyes were fixed on something behind me, and I followed his gaze, my confusion turning to dread.

The faint smell of lavender and peppermint hit me—familiar yet suddenly unsettling. I turned back slowly, and there, crumpled on the floor, was Charlie, our local postal carrier and town council member.

My heart stopped. I rushed to his side, my breath catching in my throat. He wasn't breathing. His face was swollen, his skin blotchy. I knew the signs instantly: anaphylaxis. The same allergic reaction Emerson had just narrowly survived. But Charlie hadn't been so lucky.

Mackenzie called out loudly, trying to be heard over Oscar. "Hey, you okay? Need help? I decided to put some of this food away while you got Oscar. Still no sign of Alejandro."

I responded, "Not okay—not okay!" I rushed out of the room. Now Oscar followed along, since he had told his story of what was in the room. I met her in the hallway.

"Mr. Charlie is dead. He's dead, and he's in that room." I pointed. Oscar and I stood frozen. Oscar's tail stood straight, no wags. I hadn't called him Mr. Charlie since I was a small kid visiting my grandmother over the summer. I couldn't stop myself from crying.

Mackenzie ran to the room as I dialed 911 and then Cora on her cell. "You've got to get back here," I said. "Something happened to Charlie. I'm pretty sure he's dead."

Cora let out an uncharacteristic gasp. She must have felt the same way. It was Charlie. It was unimaginable.

How did two people at my dinner party have allergic reactions? One that was fatal, and one that was still under watch. Emerson wasn't out of the woods yet.

Before I hosted a party, I asked everyone to list their dietary restrictions. I started with a menu that was free of nuts because of my allergies, and then I tailored it to my guests. What was Charlie allergic to? I grabbed my phone and started scrolling through texts and files until I found the guest list. Nuts—Charlie was allergic to nuts. Mackenzie came out of the room, teary and pale.

"He *is* dead." She seemed surprised that I was able to make that diagnosis, but one look at him would have made it clear to anyone. She slumped down on the floor and sat with her back against the wall.

"Who will deliver the Christmas cards?" she babbled. She knew him as Coach Charlie from the year he was roped into helping out with the soccer team. It was rumored that he had actually played soccer in Europe when he was in his twenties. We knew that he had spent a lot of time in Europe travelling around, but we never had confirmation as to what he really did during that time. Maybe we did, and weren't listening. We were young and not that interested in the stories of our elders.

I felt the loss with a strange, unexpected depth. I would wait by the mailbox, hoping for a postcard, a note, or anything from my missing mother. Maybe that steady, simple act linked him to her, in the back of my mind. Maybe he would bring news one day of her return—or at least, of someone finding her alive.

But now he was gone, and it felt like I was losing my mother and my hope all over again. And yes, some of those tears were also for Charlie. I had known him for most of my life.

True, he was often *too* aware of what was in the town's mail. Some people thought he was too much in everyone's business. He had contracted with the big online store to have the route, so he was always in the know about what was coming into the town. When I got my big envelope for college and the many small ones, he knew first. When the postcards stopped arriving from my mother, he knew.

He was real and cared about what happened to the people on his route. He was a part of everyone's story. He was our mailman; he connected us to what lay outside of this tiny town.

He had been the first one to think of the Christmas market. He had been to several and thought it would be just the thing to give our town a win on the tourist map. He didn't understand why the food pod concept in Portland hadn't been a consideration in our little town. Food pods, after all, were just little neighborhoods of food carts—gathered together like a picnic with endless choices, twinkle lights, and shared tables, where strangers became fast friends over tacos and dumplings. But most people thought we only needed

Katie's Café, the pizza joint, and one Asian fusion take-out place to be happy. People preferred cooking and eating at home, and many even grew their own food. Our town had a community garden, and we often held potlucks. I guess we were a bit provincial.

I locked up Oscar and waited for Cora. She arrived with her team. They asked us questions and went into the room. It seemed insensitive to leave as they investigated.

This had been his second year on the city council. The town was growing, and commerce was getting too much for his delivery schedule. He had announced this would be his last year in charge of the local post office. He was considering hanging on to the other route and maybe having some high school kids deliver packages. Anything to lighten the load.

"Cora, I know this is awful, but I feel like I need to get to the hospital to check on Emerson."

She ran a hand through her red hair and put it in a ponytail, as if to signal she was on the job and no longer a dinner guest of mine. "Okay—go ahead and check on him. But stay at the hospital so I can find you when this is done. It does look like he had an allergic reaction of some kind."

I paused momentarily and then grabbed my phone to read a text. "He had a nut allergy. Hazelnuts."

I buckled into the passenger seat of Mackenzie's orange VW bus, its heater already whirring and the dash cluttered with candy wrappers and a thrifted snow globe that jingled with every bump. As she pulled out of the driveway, I tapped out a quick text to Alejandro and then opened our location-sharing app.

It was something that he, Mackenzie, and I always did. Single, often alone, and without the usual family connections, we had a safety net in each other. If one of us was ever stuck in a ditch or had an accident, the others could find us. Alejandro didn't just live in the cottage behind my house; we had created our own type of family unit. The three of us would have movie nights, usually watching the film adaptation of whatever book I'd featured at my brunch or dinner event.

Lately, Alejandro had been glued to his phone, even more than usual. I'd catch him checking his texts in the garden, his focus somewhere else entirely. Mackenzie had noticed, too, and suspected he had a secret girlfriend. Mackenzie once peeked over his shoulder and saw the name *Monique* on his screen, but I knew who Monique was—definitely not a girlfriend. She was his AI BFF.

"His phone's still showing him here on the property," I said, zooming in on the map to try to get more detail. "Oh, it's in the main house. He must've left it in the chaos."

Mackenzie nodded from behind the wheel. Then she gave a small shake of her head, her brows knitting with concern. "Where did he go? When did he leave? He didn't seem too happy, especially after he saw Emerson walk in."

I then started to wonder when the last time I saw him was. Had he served himself any of the food? Yes, I remember he had fixed a plate and left for the kitchen.

"I bet he went to the cottage once he saw everyone was serving themselves. He probably didn't want to mingle with Emerson. I didn't see him when I did my Poe presentation. He was definitely gone by the time I was playing the recording of the poem. Oh, I hope he comes back to clean up!"

"So why doesn't he like Emerson?" Mackenzie asked. "I thought they connected when they were in school."

I had my suspicions. Emerson could be arrogant, and I wouldn't be surprised if he'd looked down on Alejandro's corporate career. I think Alejandro once shared some early ideas for his taco book with him, and maybe that didn't go over well. I'd always meant to ask about it, but somehow I never did. Part of me wondered if it was really my place. The other part? Just too buried under my to-do list to remember. I gazed out the window and muttered softly, "To do: ask Emerson why he came here."

Then it hit me. I didn't have anyone's number to call. Ever since my grandmother passed, I hadn't heard from anyone. My uncle Thomas never liked my mother, his own sister. It was like he always expected her to disappear and leave my grandmother with me, though he never offered to take me in. He'd split from his poet wife when their son started high school, and my aunt Suzanna, Sylvester's mother, was on her third husband, living in Aspen, I think. Thomas visited my grandmother a few times toward the end, but never stayed long.

I had no idea who to call. I guessed the hospital would sort that out.

We parked and headed to Hazelton General, a small but sturdy-looking hospital. The exterior was utilitarian—brick walls that had weathered many seasons, with patches of moss clinging to the edges, showing the passage of time. Inside, the hospital smelled faintly of disinfectant and something else that was sterile and unfamiliar. I searched my pocket for a bit of candy cane—one last small one.

The hallways were narrow, and the lighting had a faint yellow tinge, giving the place a muted, almost sleepy atmosphere. Nurses and staff moved quietly, their voices hushed in conversation as they went about their routines. The beginning of holiday cheer was creeping into the otherwise stark halls. Strings of soft blue and white lights had been hung along the windows and doorways, their glow gentle and neutral, suggesting winter without calling to mind any particular holiday.

As we waited by the elevator, I fished the candy cane from my pocket, breaking off a piece. I turned to Mack, holding it out between my fingers.

"Candy cane?" I offered, hoping the sweet, familiar taste would help ease some of the tension hanging in the air.

Mack glanced down, a small smile tugging at the corner of her lips. "You always have candy canes stashed somewhere, don't you?"

"Part of my charm," I replied, trying for lightness despite the nervous energy simmering under my skin.

She took the candy cane and crunched on it thoughtfully as the elevator doors opened. The faint twinkling of the holiday lights and the cool aroma of peppermint felt like a small comfort as we stepped inside, bracing ourselves for whatever news awaited. Then I remembered Charlie's liniment. My relationship with that holiday scent might be forever altered.

We found Emerson's room without trouble, but just as we were about to step inside, a nurse raised her hand, blocking the doorway. "I'm sorry," she said gently, her eyes full of concern. "He's not stable right now."

"What happened?" I asked, heart already sinking.

"He went into biphasic anaphylaxis," she explained. "A second reaction, even after the first one was treated. His airway constricted again, and his blood pressure dropped sharply. He's in a coma now."

Mackenzie inhaled sharply beside me. "His emergency contact—?"

"We've already called Sylvester Steele," the nurse said. "He should be on his way."

I nodded numbly and let her words sink in as we backed away from the door. The corridor seemed suddenly too quiet, the kind of silence that only hospitals could hold.

I slumped into a chair in the waiting room, the familiar hum of machines and muffled footsteps surrounding us. Mackenzie sat down beside me without saying a word.

There was nothing to do now. Just wait.

My thoughts kept circling back to the question that gnawed at me. How had hazelnuts, or anything else that could cause such a reaction, made it to my dinner party? I knew about hazelnuts—or filberts, as some people called them here in Oregon. Even though the town's name might suggest otherwise, this wasn't the typical growing region. I was familiar with the hazelnut farm that Magda and Felix had started, but they were outliers, competing against the larger hazelnut farms in the state. And because of my nut allergy, I'd always kept hazelnuts at arm's length.

Yet, this evening had unraveled with deadly consequences. Charlie was dead, and Emerson was clinging to life. My mind spun with the details of the night. Magda and Felix, the "celebrity" owners of the hazelnut farm, were vendors at the Christmas market and had been seated beside Emerson. Could the hazelnuts have triggered the reaction? Charlie's allergy list had mentioned them, but Emerson…I didn't even know if he was allergic to them. I didn't remember him having a nut allergy.

Hazelnuts were my first suspicion, but it could have been anything—some cross-contamination, a hidden ingredient in the food. The thought that I had meticulously planned every detail of this dinner, aware of every dietary restriction, only deepened the mystery. I had taken extra precautions, especially with my own nut allergy, and yet something had gone terribly wrong. Was it something else entirely that triggered the reactions? Or had I missed something critical?

"Mack, I was lucky to have the EpiPen tonight," I said, my voice shaky. "If I hadn't been prepared, Emerson might not have made it." Then almost to myself, I added, "And he still might not."

Mack looked at me with compassion, her eyes soft. "Thank God you had the EpiPen. Hopefully they'll figure out what caused the reaction." She reached for my hand, squeezing it gently. "I'm just glad you're okay. I'm glad it wasn't you."

I shook my head, the weight of guilt settling deep. "That's the thing, Mack—I don't feel okay. I've always been so cautious. With my allergies, I have to be. I check everything and double-check it. But tonight, something slipped through. And it was on my watch. I don't even know what went wrong, which scares me."

"You think it was hazelnuts? Weren't they on Charlie's allergy list?" Mack asked gently, concern filling her voice.

"Maybe," I said, exhaling heavily. "It could've been, but I can't say for sure. And that's what makes me sick. I can't figure it out. Hazelnuts weren't even on the menu. I don't cook with them, and I can't think of a single ingredient that would've been processed near them. Not knowingly, anyway." I paused, feeling the anxiety build. "The very thing I've spent years avoiding—something dangerous—got into my house. Whether it was in the food or the air, I don't know."

Mack's frown deepened. "So, it could've been anything?"

"Yeah," I muttered, my thoughts spiraling. "It could have been anything, but I've never had Magda and Felix over before. They handle hazelnuts all the time on their farm. What if it was on their clothes? Even just the residue might've gotten into the air." My voice wavered. "I didn't think to ask them to be careful. And now…Charlie's gone, and Emerson—" I choked on the words.

The responsibility felt suffocating. I'd failed at the one thing I prided myself on: keeping everything safe. "I can't shake the feeling that this is going to come back on me somehow."

Mack's eyes widened a little. "Really? Like legal trouble?"

"I don't know," I said quietly. "I mean, it was my dinner party. Two people had severe allergic reactions, and one of them died. What if someone blames me? What if someone thinks I wasn't careful enough?"

Mack shifted in her seat, then asked, "What about your insurance? Does your business cover this kind of thing?"

I blinked, suddenly realizing I hadn't even thought about that. "I—I think so. I mean, I have liability coverage, but…I don't know if it's enough. What if it isn't? What if someone sues?"

Mack reached over and squeezed my hand. "We'll figure it out, Annee. But for now, let's just focus on getting some answers. We need to know what actually caused the reactions."

Maybe I was letting all of my Poe-vember planning get into my head. *Once upon a midnight dreary, while I pondered, weak and weary….* Poe's words from "The Raven" floated through my mind, echoing the darkness that seemed to cling to this night. I glanced at Mack, grateful to have her by my side, but the questions wouldn't stop swirling, growing louder with every passing minute.

What were the chances of two people having severe allergic reactions on the same night, in the same place? Could it have really been a terrible accident? Or was it too bizarre a coincidence to brush off?

My thoughts twisted further. Was there something more deliberate lurking beneath the surface? Some hidden malice I hadn't seen coming? The idea sent a chill down my spine, but I couldn't dismiss it.

I sat in the waiting room, the steady hum of the hospital equipment filling the silence, my mind racing. The more I searched for answers, the more they seemed to slip through my grasp.

Mackenzie and I both checked our phones again, staring at the screens with growing concern. Alejandro's location sharing, which we had all set up for safety reasons years ago, was no longer on. I refreshed the app, hoping it was just a glitch, but nothing changed. His location had vanished.

"Did that just go away on your end?" I asked, glancing over at Mack, who was already opening our friend finder app.

She shook her head, her brow furrowed. "Yup, it's deactivated here, too. He's completely offline."

I felt a sinking sensation in my chest. Alejandro was always connected, always quick with a response when we needed him. I opened my messages and typed out another text, trying to keep my tone casual, though panic was creeping in. *Alejandro, where are you? Call me.* I stared at the screen, waiting for the dots that indicated he was typing, but they never came.

Mackenzie's phone beeped, and we both looked at it, hopeful for a second. But it wasn't Alejandro, just a random notification. She sighed, rubbing her temples.

"I don't like this, Annee," she said softly. "He never just disappears like this. Something's off."

I nodded, the knot in my stomach tightening. "Yeah, he's usually glued to his phone. No response…no location sharing…."

Mack looked at me, her eyes filled with the same worry I felt. "What do we do now?"

I glanced around the waiting room, the hospital's quiet hum filling the space, feeling the weight of everything that had already happened tonight. First Charlie, then Emerson, and now Alejandro. The thought of something happening to him, of him getting caught up in whatever was going on, made my chest tighten.

"We need to find him," I said, my voice steadier than I felt. "And we need to do it fast."

Chapter 5

Avoir un QI d'Huître:

To Have the IQ of an Oyster (to not be very smart)

The nurse stepped into the hallway, her tone gentle but steady. "You should both head home and try to get some rest," she said, offering a reassuring smile. "Emerson's stable and under constant watch. If anything changes, we'll call right away. I promise."

I looked at Mack, feeling torn. "I don't want to leave," I whispered.

Mackenzie put a reassuring hand on my arm. "We'll come back if anything happens, Annee. Let's go check on Oscar and see if we can find Alejandro."

Reluctantly, I nodded, knowing she was right. There was nothing we could do at the hospital.

The drive home felt longer than it should have. The quiet between us was heavy with worry. When we pulled up to my house, my heart sank. The lights of police cars were still flashing, and yellow crime scene tape fluttered on the breeze near my front porch. My stomach twisted as I realized they were still there, combing through the scene.

A cluster of ravens perched on the fence and roof. They weren't just watching—they were gathered as if roosting communally, like they were sharing secrets, exchanging some unspoken information about the night's events. Their dark eyes followed my every move, heads tilting and shifting, curious and almost…knowing.

One raven let out a low croak, the sound hanging heavy in the air.

I tore my gaze away, feeling the weight of their presence. I needed to shake off this dark feeling, and quickly. Christmas decorations had to go up soon—the lights, the wreaths, anything to bring warmth back into this space. I couldn't let the heaviness linger in the yard. The police tape fluttered in the cold breeze, but all I could think about was filling the space with holiday cheer, something to push away the shadows that seemed to have settled here—along with the ravens.

As we stepped into the house, the weight of exhaustion and anxiety settled in. The dining room was a mess, food half-eaten, decorations tangled, and chairs overturned. It was a dark snapshot of how violently the night had been interrupted. Everything felt out of place, the chaos a reminder of what had unfolded.

Cora stood near the table, waving us over. Her usual sharp demeanor was softened by fatigue, the long night etched in her expression.

"They're still taking pictures," Mackenzie murmured beside me, her eyes wide as she took in the scene. My home had become a snapshot of the disaster.

Cora looked up as we approached, shaking her head slightly. "Annee," she began, her voice heavy, "my team's been through everything. From what we've seen, it looks like an unfortunate accident."

I blinked, trying to process her words. "An accident?" I asked, my voice weak, as I struggled to accept such a simple explanation in the midst of all the chaos.

Cora sighed. "Yes. The allergic reactions don't appear to be the work of anything more sinister. You were careful, but these things happen. I suggest you contact your insurance provider. They'll help you sort through the damages and any claims that come up."

I nodded, feeling numb as she gave me a quick pat on the shoulder before turning to leave with the rest of her team. "Try to get some rest," she added over her shoulder as the officers began packing up, the last few camera flashes signaling the end of their work.

The house, which just hours ago had been set for a perfect dinner, was now in complete disarray. Once the police left, I turned to Mackenzie. "I can't believe this," I muttered, glancing at the mess in front of me.

"Let's just start cleaning up," Mackenzie said softly. "It'll help take your mind off things, even just for a bit."

We moved silently, clearing away the dishes and throwing out what was left of the food. The quiet made every noise—every clink of glass and scrape of a plate—feel louder, heavier. My mind was racing, filled with questions I didn't yet have answers to. Emerson's reaction, Charlie's death, and Alejandro's sudden disappearance—it was all too much.

I turned to Mack. "I'm going to check the cottage, see if Alejandro's there."

"Okay, but his car is gone," she said, her brow furrowing as she glanced toward the driveway.

I stepped out into the cool night air, making my way across the property to the small cottage Alejandro called home. The breeze nipped at my skin, and I hugged my arms tightly around myself, trying to shake the uneasy feeling that had been gnawing at me all evening.

When I reached the door, I hesitated, half-expecting to hear the faint hum of music or the rhythmic clatter of him moving around inside. But when I eased the door open quietly, the cottage was silent and empty.

I guess I was snooping. I thought it might will him home or at least give me an excuse to give in to the temptation and look around his space—something I had always resisted. Alejandro was not a mystery to me. We had been friends too long for that. But lately he had been harder to read, and I could not shake the feeling he was secretly feeding that cat I was allergic to.

But something felt off. There was a stillness in the air, almost eerie, like he'd left in a hurry. The scent of coffee lingered, but the pot sat cold on the counter. The throw blanket he usually kept draped neatly over the chair lay crumpled on the floor, like it had been tossed aside mid-thought. His shoes—normally lined up like little soldiers by the door—were gone.

I scanned the room, unease prickling at my spine. It didn't look like the home of someone who'd stepped out for a walk.

I moved farther into the room, scanning for any sign of where he might have gone. As I walked toward the kitchen, a sudden blur of orange darted past me—a flash of fur. The cat. The same one that had been skulking around for weeks, now slipping out through the open door. I sneezed, the familiar tickle in my nose reminding me of my allergy, and I rubbed my eyes in frustration. Of all nights for that cat to be lurking around.

I stepped into the kitchen, my gaze drawn to the countertop. My heart skipped a beat when I saw it: a piece of paper, folded neatly, as though waiting for me. With trembling hands, I reached for it and carefully unfolded it.

I've gone to my little tree house.

I recognized the handwriting instantly—Alejandro's looping, precise script. My pulse quickened. The tree house. It was a spot he had always referred to fondly, somewhere he had discovered when he first came to Oregon. He escaped there whenever things got overwhelming. But I hadn't heard him mention it in years.

I clutched the note, my mind racing. Alejandro wasn't just avoiding us. He was hiding.

I tucked Alejandro's note into my pocket, the paper crinkling as I tried to push my unsettling thoughts aside. I couldn't afford to let the anxiety take over—not tonight. If he needed space, I'd give him that. I needed to focus on something I could control.

I walked out of the cottage and back toward the barn, the cool night air biting at my skin. The house loomed ahead, still draped in the remnants of the chaos from earlier. The crime scene tape had been taken down, but the emotional residue lingered, heavy and unseen. Still, if I had to stay up all night, I was going to make sure Christmas came to life in the front yard.

As I reached the barn, I yanked the door open, the scent of old wood and holiday nostalgia wafting out. Stacks of boxes filled the space, each one labeled in my grandmother's perfect handwriting: *Christmas Lights, Garlands, Ornaments*. I made my way to the back where the outdoor decorations were stored. My fingers traced over the labels before pulling out the heaviest box. The weight of it was familiar—comforting, even. I remembered the way I decorated the house every year, the Gothic Revival and Victorian details coming to life with twinkling lights and garlands, turning the place into a whimsical Christmas wonderland.

I piled a cart high and wheeled it across the yard, each bump in the ground reminding me how fast the year had flown by. As I reached the porch, I dropped the first box with a thud by the front door, already feeling the night's exhaustion creeping in. But the sight of the yard waiting for decorations sparked a familiar determination.

Mackenzie came outside to see what the noise was and saw me. "Find him?" she asked, her voice soft but curious.

I shook my head, glancing briefly at the ground. "No. He wasn't back there. Just this." I tapped my pocket where the note was. "He said he's gone to his little tree house."

Mackenzie raised an eyebrow. "Tree house?"

I shrugged, feeling a mix of frustration and worry. "He mentioned it years ago. Anyway, I can't worry about that right now. I need to get Christmas up in the front yard." I motioned to the boxes, already feeling the surge of determination rise in my chest. "If I have to stay up all night to do it, so be it."

Mackenzie grinned, shaking her head. "I'll put on some hot chocolate."

"You don't have to stay," I said, reaching for another box of lights and ornaments, my tone softer than I intended.

Mackenzie laughed, pulling her jacket tighter. "I'm not quite ready to go home yet myself."

With Mackenzie by my side, the tension of the night seemed to ease, if only slightly. We worked together, untangling lights and sorting through the decorations. Oscar, sensing the shift in mood, bounded around the yard, occasionally pausing to nudge one of the boxes or lick Mackenzie's hand. The front yard began to transform into the holiday haven I imagined.

The long strands of white and colored lights crisscrossed the steeply pitched roof, their glow outlining the house like something from a storybook. Garlands draped across the porch railings, thick with artificial pine and dotted with tiny silver ornaments. I climbed the ladder to hang wreaths from the arched windows, just like my grandmother had done every year.

Oscar padded along beside me, watching curiously as I arranged the outdoor trees along the walk—three artificial Douglas firs, each one a little taller than the last, adorned with delicate fairy lights and silver bells that jingled softly in the breeze. The house finally started to look like Christmas.

As Mackenzie wrapped another strand of lights around the bushes near the porch, I stood back to admire our work. "Well," I said, half out of breath, "it's not quite done, but it's a solid start."

Mackenzie smiled, her face flushed from the cold. "It looks incredible. Your grandmother would be proud."

I nodded, warmth spreading through me. "Thanks. It feels good to have something up. The house needed this."

She handed me the final strand of lights, and together, we wound them around the last tree by the driveway. When everything was in place, I grabbed the extension cord and plugged it in. The yard came to life all at once—the twinkling lights, the garlands, the wreaths, the trees. It was like stepping into another world, one where the mess of the night no longer existed, where Christmas had taken over.

The ravens, who had been perched silently on the roof the whole time, watching as we worked, suddenly stirred. I looked up at them, smiling despite myself. "Happy Thanksgiving," I called out softly, more to myself than to them.

As if on cue, the ravens flapped their wings and took off into the night, their dark forms disappearing into the glow of the lights. I watched them go, a strange sense of peace settling over me.

Chapter 6

Long Comme un Jour sans Pain:
Long as a Day Without Bread
(as long as a month of Sundays; seemingly unending)

My little town on the Oregon coast had had many names over the years, both those given by indigenous peoples and those who later colonized the lush green spaces and windswept landscape. Its latest name reflected nature and commerce: Hazelton, after its abundant cultivated hazelnut trees. My house was private and almost secluded, but close enough to take in the daily events of the community.

A few days passed, and Alejandro was still missing in action. There had been no contact from him, and he remained invisible on all our location apps. Emerson, however, was on the mend. He had come out of his coma and was starting to heal. Meanwhile, the Christmas market was in full swing, and people were already preparing services for Charlie. As I walked to Katie's Café with Oscar, I felt the heat of stares, like everyone was watching me. It dawned on me that I was everyone's little story today. The café was usually my refuge, but I hadn't visited since the incident.

In the days since, I had been trying to clean up everything, from my house to the mess in my head. Between visiting Emerson in the hospital, talking with my insurance guy, and figuring out how the holiday season would look, there was a lot on my plate. I even wondered if I should still host my annual Sugar Plum tea since people might not want to come, or if I should just curl up in bed and wait for the new year to arrive. Still, something about how quickly the case on Charlie's death was closed seemed odd—almost suspicious. Could everyone believe I was that negligent? Me, the one known to have multiple food allergies? And what was Charlie doing in that room with Oscar?

Cora, the police chief, thought Charlie had gone in there to make a phone call, given that they found his phone on the floor. Or maybe, if he wasn't feeling well, he was trying to find the bathroom. It was possible, but none of it sat right with me. I knew the town didn't want any bad press so close to the launch of the Christmas market, which probably explained why the paper only printed a simple obituary and details of his services at St. Luke's. It turned out to be good for me as well. But then again, if you wanted to know what happened in our little town, you wouldn't find out about it in the paper.

When I arrived at Katie's Café, the glances from the townspeople only intensified, making me want to turn back. But Katie saw me coming and immediately scooted a table by the window for me and Oscar, a spot she always kept for us. She never minded him there, as long as he stayed curled at my feet.

Katie's Café had been a breakfast staple in Hazelton for decades, known for its eggs, bacon, and biscuits and gravy, nothing fancy. Her parents had run it before her, but when Katie took over she began slipping in the recipes her mother brought from the low country of South Carolina. Slowly she introduced the town to her Gullah Geechee roots. I still remembered the day fried okra and grits appeared on the menu. She didn't just add new dishes; she told stories about them, tucked into the menu like little love notes. A different town might have resisted, but Hazelton embraced it. It always felt like she was cooking for us, not at us.

Oscar and I never warmed up to the okra—too slimy for both of us—but grits, bacon, and coffee had always been our favorite. Back when the weather was warm, we claimed the movable table under the big shady tree by the street. I would shift the chairs to follow the shade, and Oscar would lie at my feet, regal and alert. I once watched him give a single low grumble at tourists who tried to sit there. Not a bark, not a whine, just a quiet objection. We're both a little like that.

She greeted me now with her usual warmth, commenting that today was a strawberry waffles and bacon day for me with lots of whipped cream, of course. She really knew me well. She also brought over a carafe of hot coffee and cream, allowing me to help myself. It was something she reserved for customers who needed privacy. She understood that waffles were my comfort food, and she was the only one I trusted to make them gluten free without risking a reaction. It felt ironic, given what had happened to Charlie.

After bringing out my waffles, Katie took a seat across from me, nodding to one of her servers to cover her tables. She leaned in, her voice soft. "I know you've been through a lot. If Charlie looked anything like Emerson did before the EpiPen kicked in… I can't imagine how traumatized you must be. How are you holding up?"

I hesitated, picking at the edge of my napkin. "Shaken," I admitted. "I still don't know what could've caused it. I've gone over every ingredient, every label, and I can't find a single thing that could've triggered a reaction."

Katie nodded, concern deepening in her expression. "You're always so careful. I tell people all the time—no one's more meticulous about allergens than you." She paused. "So… was it hazelnuts? Is that what they determined?"

I shook my head. "I'm not sure. No one's said anything officially. I don't even know if they've done an autopsy on Charlie. I'll have to follow up with Cora." I sighed. "Insurance might need that information too. It's all… murky."

As if on cue, the front door chimed and a woman I didn't recognize stepped inside. She looked vaguely familiar—like someone who had probably attended one of my earlier events. She spotted me right away and made a beeline for our table.

"I hope you're satisfied," she said sharply, her voice loud enough to turn a few heads. "Charlie was a good man."

I blinked, stunned. "I know," I said quietly. "He was."

She crossed her arms, eyes narrowing. "Then how could you let this happen in your home? At your event?"

Katie stood up, her posture calm but firm. "That's enough," she said evenly. "This isn't the place."

But the woman was already backing away, shaking her head. "Just be glad the whole town hasn't turned on you. Yet." She pushed through the door, leaving behind a wave of silence.

Katie sat back down, exhaling slowly. "Ignore her. People lash out when they're scared and grieving."

I nodded, though my stomach had twisted into a tight knot. "It's not just her," I whispered. "What if she's right?"

Turning the conversation away from the heavy topic of Charlie's death, I asked Katie how her booth was doing at the Christmas market. She told me she was only running it in the late afternoons and evenings to catch the Christmas lights crowd, except on the weekends, when she staffed it all day. The market had brought a lot of out-of-town visitors, so business at the café had picked up too. The extra food trucks didn't thrill her, and she didn't care much for the Misto guys, but she admitted that the market had been a bigger success than anyone anticipated. So far, even on the weekdays, the crowds were surprisingly strong, maybe due to the new work-from-home culture, which seemed to give people more free time during the week to get out of the house.

As I sat there, listening to Katie and sipping my coffee, I couldn't shake the lingering suspicion about Charlie's death. I still felt like something was missing, and I couldn't rest until I figured out what.

I stared out at the street with Oscar curled at my feet, snoozing through the quiet magic unfolding beyond the window. Hazelton had fully transformed into a winter wonderland, and for a moment, it truly looked like something out of a vintage Christmas postcard, lights twinkling, garlands swaying, and storefronts dressed in nostalgic charm.

Strings of delicate lights crisscrossed above Main Street, casting a warm glow over the slate-colored sky. Lampposts were wrapped in evergreen garlands dotted with oversized ornaments of burgundy, icy blue, and silver that caught the shimmer of the faux icicles swaying in the breeze.

Across the street, The Quilted Patch had outdone itself. Bolts of red and white fabric stood like candy canes beside felt reindeer with button eyes, and delicate lace snowflakes were suspended above, like frozen dreams. The care behind it was apparent. Someone had stitched love into every inch.

The café door opened with a chime, and a rush of cold air carried in the scent of cinnamon from the bakery down the block. It mingled with the buttery sweetness of waffles at my table and the steady comfort of fresh coffee.

Outside, a tabby in a red sweater strutted along the sidewalk on a leash, drawing surprised looks and amused smiles. Even Oscar lifted his head, curious, before settling back into his cozy sprawl.

The first flakes floated past the window, unhurried, before thickening into a steady snowfall. The café grew still as people drifted toward the windows to watch. Beyond the glass, a few patrons stepped into the snow, laughing softly as it dusted their coats and hair. For a moment, the whole town seemed to hold its breath, suspended in quiet wonder.

I should have been caught up in the joy of it too, but something pulled me from the magic. A sudden movement, a flash of black, caught my eye. I looked up just in time to see a raven swoop down from the gray sky, its inky wings cutting through the silver snowfall, before it landed on the tree outside the café window, directly in front of my table. Its feathers were glossy and oil-dark, its beady eyes fixed on me with unsettling focus.

A chill ran through me. Against the backdrop of garlands and snow, the raven looked like an unwelcome shadow dropped into the middle of all this festive cheer. Was it one of the birds we had shooed away from the inn? Did it recognize me? Was it also wondering what had happened to Charlie and Emerson?

It cawed once, sharply, the sound cutting through the soft murmurs of the café. I felt a knot form in my stomach. In that instant, it was as though the raven had stolen a bit of my holiday joy, leaving me unsettled. The snow continued to fall, the lights continued to twinkle, and the laughter of the patrons filled the air, but I couldn't shake the raven's presence. It was as if the darkness I'd been trying to ignore—the mystery, the tension of recent days—had followed me here, casting a shadow over this perfect winter scene.

I looked away from the street, focusing on my coffee again, trying to find warmth in its familiarity. But the raven's image lingered, a reminder that not everything this season was as it seemed.

I had only worn a light sweater, since I hadn't realized the weather was going to change so drastically. Alejandro was usually my barometer. He was always quick with a forecast update and anything else his gadgets deemed important. But I hadn't heard from him, and now the snow was starting to come down hard. Still, I finished the last few bites of my waffle. They were still comforting, gluten-free as always, and exactly what I needed on a day like this.

Katie approached with a to-go cup of hot coffee. "On the house." She smiled. "You'll need this to warm up on your walk."

"Thanks, Katie," I said, taking the cup gratefully. I paused for a moment, glancing out at the café's patio through the window. "Looks like this might be the end of patio dining for the season."

Katie chuckled, looking out at the empty chairs. "Yeah, looks like it. Snow has a way of chasing everyone inside."

I nodded, feeling the cold bite before even taking a step out there. "I'll stop by your booth at the market, though—if not tonight, then tomorrow."

"I'll be waiting. Don't forget to try our fried catfish this time. It's amazing," she added, her eyes twinkling. The market's most talked-about dish was giving the Misto guys a run for their money.

I laughed. "I'll give it a shot."

With that, I stepped out into the swirling snow, pulling my scarf tighter and wishing I'd brought my coat. As I made my way down the street, the flakes started to fall more heavily, and I decided to give Mackenzie a call.

Before I could even say hello, she answered, chanting, "It's snowing! It's snowing!"

I couldn't help but smile. "Yeah, I noticed."

"First snow means movie night, right?"

"Yep, *Christmas in Connecticut*, as always. Do you still want to come over?"

"Of course," she replied.

I was thinking about how this day was shaping up to be a carb-heavy one, between waffles and now whatever snacks Mackenzie had in store. "Looks like I'll be indulging today."

"And you know what? We should bake cookies, too!" she added, her excitement contagious. "I'm kind of glad it's just us girls tonight. No Alejandro to critique our cookies this time."

I could tell she was remembering last Christmas, when we had made a huge batch of iced cookies in all the usual holiday shapes: Santa, Santa's boot, snowflakes, angels, and bells. The cookies had been brightly decorated but a little off, with icing that bled in odd places and colors that never quite hit the mark. Alejandro had still said they were the tastiest cookies he had ever eaten, even if they weren't much to look at.

"Speaking of Alejandro, have you heard from him today?" I asked, unable to shake the nagging feeling about his absence.

Mackenzie didn't seem concerned. "Nope, but honestly, I'm not worried. He'll turn up when he's ready. Besides, it'll be fun—just the two of us and a mountain of cookie dough."

"True," I said, though I still felt uneasy about not hearing from him. Alejandro had been distant lately, and that was before his weird note in the cottage. I couldn't ignore the growing tension between all of us. But Mackenzie's excitement for the evening made me smile.

"Don't worry," she reassured me, sensing my hesitation. "It's going to be a perfect night—cookies, movies, and snow."

"Alright, I'll see you soon," I said, starting to feel the warmth of her enthusiasm spread to me.

As I hung up and continued my walk home, the snow was piling up on the sidewalks. Instead of dreading it though, I let myself lean into the magic of the moment. Movie night with Mackenzie, the first snow of the season, and some much-needed comforts were just what I needed. I could worry about Alejandro tomorrow.

As I made my way through the snow-covered streets of Hazelton, I felt a little lighter. Perhaps the warmth from my waffles was still lingering. The flakes were falling steadily now, covering the ground in a soft, white blanket. My eyes landed on familiar figures up ahead—Paul, with his sister Molly and brother Marc—walking toward Katie's Café. A smile tugged at my lips as I saw them. There was no urge to duck away this time. I was happy to see them, happy to feel a sense of normalcy after everything that had happened.

Molly spotted me first, her bright eyes lighting up as she waved, her chestnut hair catching the light from the café windows. "Annee! Hi!" she called out, her voice filled with the kind of cheer that instantly lifted my spirits. Marc, more reserved but always warm, gave me a nod and a small smile. His quiet presence was comforting.

Oscar wagged his tail, his excitement mounting as Molly knelt to pat his head. "Hey, Oscar! You're always so handsome," she cooed at him, scratching behind his ears.

"Hi, guys," I said, smiling.

"We're just grabbing a table," Marc said, gesturing toward Katie's Café. "Wanna join us?"

"Thanks, but I actually just ate," I replied. "I think I'll head home and warm up a bit instead."

As Molly and Marc made their way into the café, Paul hung back, his friendly grin making me feel instantly at ease. He stepped closer and wrapped me in a hug, a gesture so familiar and kind that I let myself sink into it.

"How are you holding up, Bonne Annee?" he asked softly, his voice filled with genuine concern.

I sighed, leaning back to look at him. "It's been a lot, you know? I'm managing, but it's hard."

Paul's expression softened, his eyes full of understanding. "Everyone's going to miss Charlie. He was special to a lot of people."

Hearing those words only made the tightness in my chest worse. Even though Paul was just reminding me of how beloved Charlie was, I had to wonder, could other people be quietly holding me responsible?

Before I could say more, he stepped back, his brow furrowing slightly as he noticed my shivering. "Bonne Annee, you're freezing. Where's your coat?" Before I could even protest, he was shrugging off his jacket and wrapping it around my shoulders. "Here, take this. I'm not even cold."

"Paul, really, you don't have to—" I started, but he was already securing the jacket around me.

"Trust me, I'm fine," he said with a grin. "Besides, it looks like it's almost sleigh ride weather, right? Remember, you owe me a picnic at the lighthouse and a sleigh ride. Don't think I've forgotten." The lighthouse was a favorite spot for tourists and a romantic destination for locals.

I laughed, the memory of our conversation about *Christmas in Connecticut* and my offhanded comment about wanting a Barbara Stanwyck-style sleigh ride coming back to me. "I didn't realize you were going to hold me to that."

"Of course I am," he teased. "I'm waiting for my perfect sleigh ride moment."

Oscar, not wanting to be left out, stood on his hind legs and tried to lick Paul's face, making him laugh.

Just then, Marc appeared at the café door, waving at Paul. "Our table's ready!" he called.

Paul gave me one last smile. "I'll get the jacket back from you later. Maybe I'll see you at the market tomorrow?"

"Maybe," I said, pulling the jacket tighter around me, feeling its warmth and his kindness. "Thanks again."

He jogged back to join his siblings inside, while I continued my walk home, feeling warmer despite the cold. The snow fell more heavily now, but it didn't bother me. I felt lighter for the first time in days, wrapped in a moment of kindness and the promise of simpler, happier things.

Chapter 7

Casser du Sucre sur le Dos de Quelqu'un:
Breaking Sugar on Someone's Back (gossiping about someone)

Mackenzie and I were nestled by the fire, sipping on hot cocoa topped with whipped cream and sprinkles of crushed candy cane. The rich aroma of cocoa mingled with the sweet scent of freshly baked sugar cookies, their edges golden and crisp, while soft gingerbread men lay on a nearby plate, their little raisin eyes staring up at us. Oscar, with his soft black-and-white fur shimmering in the firelight, was curled up between us, his body radiating warmth. His Christmas pajamas, red and green with snowflakes, matched mine—an indulgence I had convinced myself we both needed. His curls caught the light just right, making him look as if he were part of the holiday decor.

The Christmas tree, glowing with twinkling white lights, stood gracefully in the corner of the room, its branches heavy with handmade ornaments from my childhood. There was a homemade angel that hung crookedly at the top, just like it always had since I was a kid. The mantel was draped with garlands of evergreen and holly, with stockings hung neatly underneath—a small tribute to the past, even though it was just the two of us.

I took a sip of my cocoa and reached for one of the food spreads from *Christmas in Connecticut* we had re-created—a plate of pancakes stacked high, soft and fluffy, glistening with butter and syrup, exactly like the ones Barbara Stanwyck's character pretends to cook in the film. Mackenzie let out a satisfied sigh as she scooped some hearty beef stew into a bowl, the aroma of slow-cooked meat and vegetables filling the air. The stew, rich and flavorful, was something we had both laughed over—neither of us particularly liked goulash, but were determined to honor the spirit of the movie.

"I like that Barbara Stanwyck's character didn't even know how to make any of this." Mackenzie giggled, stirring the stew.

"Yes, and she had Uncle Felix to help her out!" I laughed, tearing off a piece of bread before dipping into the stew. "He's most of the fun in the movie, right?"

We settled back into the couch, and as the movie began, the familiar black-and-white glow lit up the room. It had been our tradition since high school, and even now it carried the same joy and comfort. But there was something bittersweet about it, too. My mom had started this tradition with me when I was little, back when things were simpler. Now that she was missing, and my grandmother was gone, I was left with memories that were as nostalgic as they were tinged with an undeniable sadness.

"Wow, on nights like this, I really miss my mom." I teared up a bit.

Mackenzie put her bowl down and gave me a long hug. "I know. I'm sorry."

I was grateful for the hug. I guess I did need more of them.

We settled back in for the movie. Oscar shifted slightly, his fur brushing against my leg, and I ran my fingers through his soft curls. He nuzzled into my hand, his tail wagging softly, content to be part of the cozy evening.

Mackenzie gave me a sly look and there was a familiar glint of mischief in her eyes. "So… have you heard from Paul lately?" she asked, raising an eyebrow as she nibbled on a cookie.

I felt my cheeks heat up, and I knew the fire had nothing to do with it. "Maybe," I said, trying to sound nonchalant, but I could already see the knowing smile forming on her lips.

"Come on, Annee," she teased, leaning over to give me a nudge. "You've had a crush on him since forever! And now it looks like he might finally be noticing you."

I couldn't help but smile. Paul and I had known each other since high school, and while I'd always had a soft spot for him, I never imagined he'd feel the same way. But lately, things seemed different. He had asked me to go on a sleigh ride, and the way he looked at me…well, maybe Mackenzie was right.

"He did invite me out for a little Christmas cheer," I admitted, unable to suppress the grin spreading across my face. "But I'm not sure. What if he's just being nice?"

"Nice? Please." Mackenzie rolled her eyes dramatically. "He's definitely interested. You don't ask someone out during the most romantic time of the year if you're just being nice. People think it's Valentine's Day, but the Christmas season is much more romantic!"

We both laughed, and for a moment, it felt like we were back in high school, gossiping about crushes and daydreaming about what the future held. I glanced down at Oscar, who was now fast asleep, his little paws twitching as he dreamed.

"Speaking of the past," Mackenzie said, her tone softening, "did you hear that Joe's band played at the market the other night?"

"Joe?" I asked, surprised. "As in, *your* Joe?"

"Yeah, that Joe." Mackenzie sighed, leaning back into the cushions. "It's been so long, but seeing him up there, playing like he used to…it brought back a lot of memories."

"You still have feelings for him?"

"I don't know," she said, sounding conflicted. "It's complicated. We were good together, but we were also young. I'm not sure if going back down that road would be a good idea."

I nodded, understanding the complexity of old flames. The holidays had a way of making us nostalgic, bringing up feelings we thought were long buried.

Then her face grew serious. "Have you heard from Alejandro at all?"

I set my cup down. "Nope," I said, my voice quieter now. "I'm really starting to think something's wrong."

"I'd talk to Cora if I were you. It's strange he hasn't reached out." Mackenzie frowned, shaking her head.

We sat in silence for a moment. The fire flickered, casting long, wavering shadows across the room, but even the warm glow of the Christmas tree wasn't enough to chase away the underlying anxiety. I absently stroked Oscar's soft fur, letting the familiar comfort of his presence steady me.

Then, the front door creaked open. To my surprise, in walked Emerson— and my cousin Sylvester.

It took a moment to fully sink in. I hadn't seen Sylvester in years, and the shock of his presence left me momentarily speechless. He looked polished and put together, but he was tired. There was no disputing that he was handsome. His strong, chiseled jawline, tan complexion, and dark, thoughtful eyes caught Mackenzie's attention right away. She stood up, happily startled as well. Sylvester had inherited all the dominant Puerto Rican traits in the family, from his warm skin tone to his thick, dark hair and his unmistakably Spanish last name. There was a quiet pride in the way he carried himself.

"Emerson!" I exclaimed, rising from the couch. "What are you doing here? I didn't know you were being released."

"They called," Emerson said with a faint smile, his voice weak but steady. "Your phone must've been off."

I fumbled for my phone on the coffee table and saw the missed messages—one from Emerson, one from Sylvester, and even one from my insurance agent. Guilt gnawed at me as I looked up, feeling a little off-balance. Emerson still looked worn out from his hospital stay, but Sylvester, standing there with an awkward, uncertain expression, was what really caught me off guard.

"I had to get out of that hospital," Emerson added, his usual sharp tone softened by exhaustion. "Machines and needles aren't really my thing."

Before I could respond, Sylvester cleared his throat. "I guess we're staying here tonight, Bonne Annee." He hesitated, as if the name itself was heavy on his tongue. "There's nothing available in town tonight. Emerson's got a follow-up appointment tomorrow, but after that, we're heading out."

The use of my full name stirred something in me. We hadn't been close for years, not since high school, not since...everything.

"Leaving so soon?" I asked, my voice softer than I intended. "It's been forever, Sylvester." I paused, feeling the awkwardness bloom between us. "It's strange seeing you after all this time."

He gave a half-smile, a little uncomfortable. "Yeah. It's...been a while."

Mackenzie, who had been standing quietly beside me, tilted her head. She leaned forward, studying him for a second. "I don't think we've met before."

Sylvester shifted on his feet, clearly aware of how much time had passed between us. "I'm Sylvester—Bonne Annee's cousin," he said, holding out his hand with a polite smile. "Though, it's been long enough that I guess we could be strangers and not cousins."

Mackenzie shook his hand, smiling back. "I'm Mackenzie. Nice to finally meet you. She's mentioned you...well, used to, anyway." She shot me a playful look.

I gave her a small smile, feeling a pang of sadness at the reminder of how far apart Sylvester and I had drifted. "A long time ago."

Sylvester's smile faltered a bit, and he glanced around the room. "Yeah. Too long."

I stood there for a moment, feeling the weight of all the years of silence, the unresolved grief about my mother, and the distance that had grown between us since high school. He knew, of course, about her disappearance. The awkwardness was heavy, like an invisible wall between us.

"Of course, you guys can stay here tonight," I said, finally breaking the tension. I moved toward the hallway, already shifting into host mode. "No need to rush out. I'll get some blankets and pillows. Only one of your old rooms still has a bed, but there is a pull-out couch in the other one. "

Sylvester gave a nod, but there was still a flicker of unease in his expression. "Thanks. I appreciate it."

Mackenzie, sensing the tension, leaned back and gave him a lighthearted grin. "She's got the best holiday setup here, trust me. You'll be cozy and comfortable tonight."

I turned off the movie, gathering the blankets and trying to shake the memories. Once I had them settled in their rooms, Mackenzie and I resumed our visit. The warmth of the fire and the glow from the Christmas tree provided some comfort, but it wasn't enough to chase away the shadows of everything unsaid. Sylvester's presence brought the past rushing back—the closeness we once had and how easily it had slipped away. The night had started as a cozy tradition with Mackenzie, but now it felt like a reminder of everything unresolved in Hazelton...and in my family.

For tonight, I pushed the thoughts of Alejandro and the secrets swirling around the town to the back of my mind. Instead, I focused on the fact that, for now, we were all together—safe, but with so much left to be said.

Chapter 8

S ylvester and Emerson stayed the night, and I filled the house with the comforting smells of breakfast. Feeling nervous, I had gone all out for my cousins—both known foodies. I'd set the table on the covered and heated back patio, overlooking Alejandro's deep blue Blauer Prinz hydrangeas, their dried blooms now forming a serene and textured backdrop against the winter landscape. The yard was decorated for Christmas, even in this quiet corner, with twinkling lights, garlands around the patio posts, and small wreaths on the garden gates.

An elaborate spread of gluten-free pancakes, frittatas, roasted vegetables, and freshly brewed coffee covered the table. My fingers drummed on the counter as I watched from the kitchen window as Sylvester and Emerson took their first bites, hoping everything tasted as good as it looked. There was no look of disgust, so I emerged with a second pot of coffee.

Emerson, who had been sarcastic and biting on Thanksgiving, seemed kinder, more introspective this morning. After a few minutes of quiet eating, he put his fork down and looked over at me. "You saved my life, you know?" he said softly, a hint of gratitude in his voice. "I've had mild nut reactions before, but nothing like that. It's crazy how they say allergies can worsen as you get older—I guess I didn't believe it would happen to me."

"I'm so glad you're okay," I replied, managing a small smile. "But it's strange. We're completely nut-free here. Maybe it was a GRAS ingredient—something we didn't know could trigger a reaction?" GRAS stood for Generally Recognized As Safe.

Emerson sighed, nodding. "Yeah, maybe. Just one more thing I get to worry about now."

As we sat, appreciating the morning sun and the view of the flowers beyond the cottage, Sylvester, who had been quietly observing, suddenly stood up. "Speaking of allergies," he said, glancing over at me, "aren't you allergic to cats?"

I looked up, puzzled, as Sylvester pointed toward the far side of the yard. There sat the plump orange cat that had been roaming the property, watching us from a distance.

"That cat looks like it lives here," he remarked. "It doesn't seem concerned about us at all."

I nodded. "Yeah, I think he secretly lives somewhere on the property, but I've been careful not to get too close."

As Sylvester walked toward the garden, I noticed his pace slowing, his gaze fixed on something that had caught his attention. Just in front of one of the hydrangeas, there was a small patch of disturbed earth. "Hey, Annee, come over here," he called, his voice edged with tension.

My heart raced as I stood up and made my way over to him. Sylvester knelt down, brushing loose soil away from the base of the bush. "Is this...a cell phone?" he asked, frowning in confusion.

My breath hitched as I recognized it instantly—Alejandro's old phone, the one he had ditched for the latest model, half-buried in the dirt.

Desperately searching for an explanation, I blurted out, "Oh, Oscar must've buried it. He's been hiding things lately." I felt fiercely protective of Alejandro and whatever was happening with him.

At my feet, Oscar let out a low, almost offended sound, as if he knew I was pinning the blame on him unjustly.

Sylvester raised an eyebrow, clearly skeptical. "Oscar's suddenly into burying cell phones?"

"Well, old things with people's scents." I laughed, forcing some nonchalance into my voice despite the anxiety prickling at the edges. "He's a quirky dog."

As if on cue, the orange cat tried to break the awkward silence, though I could feel Sylvester's eyes lingering on me, questioning. The cat brazenly jumped onto the patio, trying to join the breakfast group. I shooed it away and heard the flutter of corvids taking flight in response. They had been quietly watching from a nearby tree.

I quickly shifted the conversation. "Hey, why don't we check out the barn after breakfast? I've got some of your and Emerson's things from when we were kids that you might want to take home."

He hesitated, watching me for a beat longer, then nodded. "Yeah, let's do that."

I put the phone on the counter in the kitchen, trying to ignore its call to investigate.

We walked across the lawn toward the barn, passing under the rows of twinkling lights strung through the trees and along the fences. Inside, the barn was dimly lit, but I had organized a corner filled with old trunks and boxes from those long-ago summers we'd spent here together. I opened one of the boxes and pulled out a dusty stack of comics and a set of old baseball gloves. Sylvester knelt beside me, sifting through the memories.

"It's been a long time since I've thought about these," he said softly, his voice touched with nostalgia.

I smiled, grateful for the shift in conversation. "Yeah, a lifetime ago."

But even as we reminisced, the weight in my chest only grew. Alejandro's phone buried in the garden couldn't just be a coincidence. Something was wrong, and the peaceful morning we were sharing felt more and more like the calm before a storm.

Sylvester picked up a box and brought it to the patio where Emerson was finishing his coffee. The two of them looked through the items, and I slipped into the quiet house, the morning air still and crisp. The low murmur of Sylvester and Emerson's conversation outside faded as I gently closed the door behind me.

The warmth of the kitchen welcomed me, but my mind raced, unwilling to settle. Alejandro's phone—why was it buried in the garden, but not hidden very well? I knew sometimes he kept his old tech for parts or resale, but this was weird. I cleaned the dirt off the phone.

I made my way to the living room, my feet feeling heavier with each step. Once there, I sat at the small wooden desk. Glancing around the empty room, I felt a strange guilt creeping in, even though I knew no one was watching. My hands were clammy as I pressed the power button, the phone vibrating softly in my grip, its familiar screen lighting up. It had been turned off—fully charged. It felt wrong, like I was invading Alejandro's private world by looking at the phone. But he'd buried it for a reason, and I needed to know why.

As the screen flickered to life, a flood of notifications greeted me, most of them from the same name—Monique. It was unusual that there was no password prompt.

My stomach twisted. Alejandro had mentioned Monique before—his AI therapist, his unbiased advice machine, he'd called her. I remember how he joked about it, how she doubled as his AI girlfriend, the perfect distraction from real connections. But what I was seeing now went beyond that. The conversation threads between them stretched for weeks, maybe months. I scrolled, my heart pounding. So many of the earlier messages had been deleted, leaving gaps in the story and pieces missing. But enough remained.

One message chilled me.

Monique: I hope you have a nice time at the tree house.

Alejandro's response had come quickly.

I've left you a note. If you don't find it, I've decided to go to the little tree house. Try to remember when I told you about it.

Monique: Yes, several years ago. You said it was a place you liked to go. I hope it brings you peace.

My breath caught. This message was for me. Now I remembered when he talked about the tree house. It was a resort! The guest rooms were actually luxury tree houses. Why was he retreating there now?

I kept scrolling, anxiety building, my fingers trembling as I pieced together more fragments. Names appeared, like Emerson and Magda. Emerson had tried calling Alejandro, which didn't surprise me. And Magda, the owner of the hazelnut farm, had also called. Why would she be reaching out to Alejandro, especially after Charlie's death? There were no voicemails, nothing to explain it—just another blank space in a growing puzzle.

As I mulled it over, my own phone in my pocket buzzed, making me jump. Mackenzie's name lit up the screen, and my heart raced as I answered. "Hey, Mack."

"Annee! Alejandro's phone just pinged from your place. Is he back?" Mackenzie sounded curious, almost relieved. "I got the alert and figured maybe he finally decided to come home."

Panic surged through me. I hadn't even thought about how turning the phone on might send a signal. "Oh…I, uh, found it," I stammered, struggling to sound nonchalant. "It was in the yard, buried…. Oscar must've dragged it out and buried it."

There was a long pause on the other end of the line. "Oscar buried it?"

I could practically hear Mackenzie raising an eyebrow. "Yeah, he's been… burying things," I added, wincing. The lie sat heavy on me, but I couldn't take it back now. What was I protecting Alejandro from? What truth was I afraid of exposing? Was he involved with Charlie's death? No. No, I couldn't think that.

"Okay…" Mackenzie's voice was skeptical, but she didn't push it. "Just…be careful, Annee. I know you're looking for answers, but this is getting weird."

"Weird doesn't even begin to cover it," I muttered.

I hung up, staring at the phone in my hand. Had turning it on been a mistake? There was no undoing it now. Alejandro must have set this old burner phone up as a backup, and synced to his cloud account so it could mirror some of the activity from his primary phone. That's how his messages and apps were still connected, even though this wasn't the phone he carried every day. I wondered if, somewhere, Alejandro would realize that I'd found his hidden phone—maybe a notification, maybe just instinct.

I leaned back in the chair, my thoughts spiraling. What had Alejandro gotten himself into? Why was Monique, this AI, playing such a significant role in his life? I scrolled back through the messages, but all that remained were more fragments, more questions. Just as I tried to gather my thoughts, my phone rang again. My heart jumped, thinking it was Mackenzie calling back questioning my explanation. I glanced at the screen and froze. It wasn't Mackenzie—it was my insurance agent.

I braced myself and answered, forcing my voice to sound steady. "Hello?"

"Annee Steele?" The voice was calm, clipped, almost detached. "I'm calling with an update on your recent claim."

My stomach twisted. "Yes, I'm here. Go ahead."

There was a slight pause, and I could hear the careful deliberation in his tone. "Unfortunately, after reviewing the details of the incident at your event, we've determined that the claim may not be eligible for coverage under your current policy."

"What…what does that mean?" I asked, my voice barely a whisper.

"It appears there may be grounds for negligence on your part, given the nature of the allergic reactions. Because of this, your policy likely won't cover the damages, and you may be held personally liable. I hate to say it, Ms. Steele, but…I'd consider shutting down the business, at least temporarily."

The words echoed in my mind, leaving me numb. "But… I was careful," I managed, my voice trembling. "I made sure everything was safe."

"I understand, but the findings suggest otherwise. I'm sorry, Ms. Steele. I know this isn't the news you wanted to hear."

I murmured a faint thank you before hanging up, my hands shaking as I put the phone down. The room felt like it was closing in around me, and my mind reeled with questions and doubts. Could I really lose everything because of this?

Suddenly, Alejandro's phone felt heavier in my hand. Mackenzie was right—things had become strange, and now, with my business at risk, I couldn't ignore it any longer. Whatever the secrets Alejandro buried were, I had to uncover them. Where was that tree house resort he mentioned? I needed to find him. If this wasn't an accident, who might have wanted to harm Charlie or Emerson? This wasn't my fault, and I needed to prove it.

Chapter 9

Avoir la Patate:

To Have the Potato (to feel great and to be in good form)

I drove into town, and it felt colder than ever, as if the temperature had dropped in sync with my mood. I needed to find Cora. I had to know more about the investigation or the lack thereof—what had happened to Charlie? And was there anything new on Emerson? But I knew the timing was terrible. Today was Charlie's service, and the whole town seemed suspended in an odd, conflicting rhythm.

The streets of Hazelton buzzed with a mix of sorrow and celebration. On the one hand, Charlie's death cast a shadow over everything, the grief palpable as people gathered for his services. On the other hand, Hazelton was alive with the energy of holiday homecomings. College students were returning, families reuniting, and the streets were filled with laughter and the warm glow of holiday lights. It was a strange contrast—this vibrancy set against the heaviness of loss.

I drove slowly to the senior home to pick up Mr. Morrison, distracted by my thoughts. He'd been living there for nearly seven years now, and every time I visited, I couldn't help but hope he was thriving. He was a fixture in my life back when he was the caretaker for the inn, and though our visits had grown fewer, the connection was still there.

When I arrived, he greeted me with that same gruff smile. "Bonne Annee," he said, using my full name like he always had. "I'm headed to another funeral gathering. Seems like too many of my friends are gone these days. I can't say I'm looking forward to it, even though most of the town will be there."

"Neither am I," I admitted, helping him into the car. "But it's important. C'est triste." I often wondered how my father would have liked to have been remembered. A French word now and then was all that I had left of him. Mr. Morrison touched me gently on the arm, and I returned to our present journey. I shut the door for him. I knew this wouldn't be easy.

He settled in, peering out the window as we drove. "The whole thing sounds crazy to me," he muttered after a while, shaking his head. "You know, some of us at the senior center think there's more to Charlie's death than just an accident."

I chuckled. "You're all watching too many mystery shows." But inside I agreed with him.

Mr. Morrison snorted. "It's not TV shows—it's true crime podcasts. And we've heard plenty about situations just like this."

I smirked, catching the seriousness in his sweet elderly face. "True crime, huh?"

"Yep," he said, looking me square in the eye. "And mark my words, something's off about this whole thing."

"I know that a lot of people are looking at me when they say that. I'm glad you wanted to skip the graveside service," I said as quietly as possible, almost hoping he didn't hear.

"Yes, child. I thought it was best for both of us." He placed his hand gently on my shoulder.

By the time we pulled up to Charlie's house for the gathering, I had to admit that Mr. Morrison had put another seed of doubt in my mind. But I pushed it aside for now. Charlie's house was already bustling with people—Jasper had opened it up for the reception after the services. It had been Charlie's wish that when he passed away, people would say farewell to him there and not at a stuffy funeral home. Everyone seemed to be gathering inside, paying their respects and sharing food. The warmth of casseroles and baked goods wafted through the air as I helped Mr. Morrison out of the car.

It felt like half the town had shown up. I saw familiar faces everywhere—Katie's brother Mickey, back in town for the holidays; Mackenzie's old flame Joe and his band, laughing with some of the locals; and so many others who had been part of the Poe party. Even some vendors who'd coordinated with Charlie for the Christmas market were there. It was the kind of gathering Charlie would have loved, but it felt hollow without him, and I felt responsible. Maybe I should lose my business.

Jasper, who had been Charlie's best friend, was standing near the kitchen, greeting guests as they came in. His usual bright demeanor was dimmed by the loss, but he was doing his best to host. The house, normally quiet, felt strangely full of life, yet there was no one in Charlie's immediate family to give a casserole to. That realization hit me hard. I'd brought a gluten-free lasagna, hoping it might bring some comfort, but I wasn't sure who I was even offering it to.

I slipped it into the lineup of casseroles on the counter and took a moment to survey the room. There was Ilsa the market manager, looking more distraught than she should have. Sophia was by her side, comforting her, and I couldn't help but feel a strange unease. Ilsa's connection to Charlie hadn't seemed that deep—or at least, not enough to warrant this level of distress.

Feeling the pull of curiosity, I excused myself and quietly slipped down the hallway, away from the crowd. If there was ever a time to snoop, it was now.

Charlie's house was a maze of memories, and I couldn't help but wonder if there was something there—something that might explain the unsettling feeling surrounding his death.

I crept through the hallway, each familiar creak of the old floorboards under my feet a reminder of just how long Charlie had lived in this house. I stopped at the door to his study, hesitating. It felt private—off-limits. I wanted to respect his space, but today, I couldn't. I was about to intrude on the privacy of a dead man.

With a glance over my shoulder to make sure no one was watching, I turned the knob and slipped inside. The room was dim, the scent of old paper and wood thick in the air. I moved quickly to the desk, rifling through the scattered papers, hoping for anything that might explain Charlie's death. And as I searched, I couldn't shake the feeling that it wasn't the accident everyone assumed it to be.

I hadn't noticed his personal touches of engraved letter openers, bobble heads (of who or what I had no idea) acting as paper weights, and a wax seal kit. Among the clutter were copies of Alejandro's mail. Charlie had been snooping—far more than I realized. I knew he was curious, but making copies of his neighbor's letters was a federal crime. Why were they sitting here on his desk? Was he reading them the night of the Poe party?

On closer look, the letters were copies of legal documents, revealing that Alejandro had been a whistleblower in a case about a new food product. The company name had been redacted from the paperwork, and it didn't say what role Alejandro had played in the company.

I took out my phone and used my favorite scanner app. I was always scanning the backs of product containers or recipes, so I made quick work of the documents.

The documents revealed that the company had begun using a new type of flour from a supplier that marketed it as a "generally recognized as safe" or GRAS ingredient. GRAS ingredients, like vinegar or olive oil, were considered safe based on expert consensus and didn't always require explicit approval or detailed labeling.

However, this flour wasn't safe—and it wasn't listed as an ingredient because its GRAS designation allowed it to avoid full disclosure. People were getting sick, some even dying, while others suffered permanent liver damage from ingesting it. I knew from my own allergy adventures that what was on the label of a product wasn't always what was in the product. There could be a little of this or a little of that, depending on the manufacturing process. Maybe something was used to make an item not stick to a processing table or clump in a package. Or the amount would be just too small to make a difference.

I was surprised that Alejandro was part of this. I was the only one in town who knew he was in Hazelton, because he was trying to vanish from the corporate food world. I knew that before he'd arrived to live in my cottage, he had uncovered a corporate espionage plot at the multi-million-dollar food corporation he'd worked for. They were using a laboratory-created strain of *E. coli* to cripple their competition. After several lost lives, their rival's stock plummeted and they purchased them—eliminating the competition at all costs.

He had threatened to take his story to the media, but fear had held him back from pursuing any case against the company. I wasn't sure if it was guilt for not standing up to the corporate giant or something else that kept him tied to this kind of fight. For him to get involved in another case like this, it must have been something more personal.

But the bigger question was, why did Charlie have these documents? What had he discovered, and was that why he was dead?

I heard footsteps in the hall and remembered where I was. I'd think about those questions later. What else was here in Charlie's things? I wondered if he kept secrets from people when he opened their mail. That's when a foolish thought popped into my head. Maybe there was a letter in there that Charlie kept from me—from my mother? I pushed the thought away as I heard Mr. Morrison's voice in the hall. I'd have to find a way to come back later. Maybe after the market tonight.

As I left the study, I took a shaky breath, trying to steady my nerves. This was the last place I should have been during Charlie's gathering, but there I was, desperate for answers no one else seemed interested in seeking. I closed the study door as quietly as I could and stepped into the hall, my heart racing every time I passed someone who might wonder why I was there alone.

Mr. Morrison was standing in the hallway, watching me with a curious expression. I swallowed hard, doing my best to keep a neutral look on my face.

"Annee," he greeted, his voice as gentle as ever, though his eyes flicked toward the study door behind me. "It's…quite a turnout here. A testament to Charlie's life, really."

"Yes, quite the gathering," I replied, feeling my voice come out a bit tighter than intended. I forced a smile, but I could feel a warmth creeping up my neck. Did he know I'd been in the study? "I'm…just glad to see everyone here honoring him."

Mr. Morrison nodded, but he lingered, and I fought the urge to shift my weight from one foot to the other. After a small silence, he finally gave a small, respectful nod and drifted away toward a group by the entryway, leaving me with my frantic thoughts.

Scanning the room, I spotted Mackenzie, my one refuge in this sea of strained smiles and quiet sorrow. She was speaking in hushed tones with a few familiar faces, nodding and gesturing softly. Catching my eye, she made her way over, her expression a little curious as she studied me. "What's up?" she whispered, leaning close.

I glanced around, feeling Ilsa's eyes on me from across the room. "Are we still going to the Christmas market tonight?" I asked, my voice a bit lower than usual.

Mackenzie's eyebrows lifted in surprise, though she quickly nodded. "Of course. After you take Mr. Morrison back, right?" She gave me a look, sensing something was up, but her voice was as steady and calm as ever. "It'll be good for us. A little escape from…" She gestured vaguely around us.

Ilsa stood nearby, her gaze steady and unnervingly focused, her sharp eyes capturing every detail. I felt the weight of her observation, like she could see past the surface, peeling back layers I wasn't ready to reveal. Her look held an intensity I couldn't quite define—curiosity, edged with something harder. Suspicion, maybe? Or was my imagination running wild? I forced a polite nod her way, feigning ignorance of the way her gaze lingered. Turning back to Mackenzie, I noticed the soft understanding in her expression, a quiet warmth that brought a sense of relief.

"Just breathe, Annee," she murmured, gently squeezing my arm. "It's a hard day. We're all a bit on edge."

I nodded, grateful for her steady presence. But I couldn't shake the feeling that I wasn't just being watched—I was being analyzed.

Chapter 10

Gagner Son Pain à la Sueur de Son Front:
To Earn Your Bread By the Sweat of Your Brow (to work hard)

I reached the edge of Tamanawas Park, our town's best gathering place. A towering Christmas tree stood proudly in the center, its branches adorned in vintage holiday splendor. The tree was decorated with vibrant red, green, and gold bulbs, each one glimmering under the soft glow of string lights wrapped around the tree. Handcrafted ornaments, many with a retro flair—porcelain angels, tin soldiers, and glass baubles with glittering snow scenes—dangled from the branches, evoking the warmth of Christmases past.

Below the tree, the bustling Christmas market was in full swing. Wooden stalls lined the path, each one offering local crafts, handmade ornaments, and warm holiday treats. The nearby food trucks filled the cool winter air with the enticing aromas of roasted chestnuts, spiced cider, and gingerbread cookies. I spotted Paul near the towering Christmas tree in the park, looking as handsome as ever with his dark hair slightly dusted by the falling snow, giving him a rugged, almost storybook look.

He was in full park director mode, a role that seemed to suit him effortlessly. He gestured toward a group of young children and their parents, pointing out some of the ornaments higher up on the tree, his face lit with the same excitement as the kids. I couldn't help but smile, watching him bring so much energy to the scene.

But then, with familiar caws and flutters of dark wings, a small flock of ravens swooped down, settling on the branches of the Christmas tree. They perched defiantly, their beady eyes almost gleaming in the glow of the twinkling lights, adding a strange but charming contrast to the scene. Paul's face shifted from amusement to mild exasperation as he caught sight of the feathered intruders.

He waved his arms, calling out as he tried to shoo the ravens away. "Come on, guys! Not tonight! Take a hint!" His voice was playful but firm as he attempted to clear the birds from their perch. They fluttered to higher branches, then stared down at him, as if mocking his attempts to restore order.

I stifled a laugh. Paul glanced up, sighing with a dramatic shrug before noticing me standing nearby. He caught my eye, and his exasperation melted into a grin as he waved, looking slightly embarrassed.

"Glad you could make it, Bonne Annee!" he called out, his breath puffing in white clouds in the chilly air. "I'll meet you by the hot chocolate in about fifteen minutes. I've just got to have a little chat with our feathered friends first."

I nodded, unable to suppress my own smile. "Good luck! I think they're enjoying the festivities too much to leave."

He laughed, flashing me a wink. "We'll see who wins, won't we?" He returned to shooing the birds, his movements theatrical.

The ravens, stubborn as ever, only rearranged themselves, settling back with what looked suspiciously like satisfaction.

I watched him for a few more moments, the glowing lights of the tree casting a warm glow over him as he played out this little battle of will with nature. All around us, the Christmas market hummed with life. The soft murmur of holiday music and the cheerful laughter of children made me glad to be in Hazelton and nowhere else.

With a grateful sigh, I turned and made my way toward the hot chocolate stand, the snow crunching softly beneath my boots. Hazelton truly felt like a winter wonderland tonight, and with Paul there, adding his own warmth and humor to the scene, I felt a little extra magic in the air.

I paused near the heart of the market, taking in the festive scene. Stalls lined the paths, filled with handmade ornaments, freshly baked treats, and steaming mugs of hot cider. People moved around, laughing and chatting. Children tugged their parents eagerly toward the towering Christmas tree, where donations were piling up—gifts wrapped in bright paper and topped with shiny bows. Everyone who brought a gift for a child in need received a ticket to see Joe and his band, Priorities, play later on. Hazelton's heart was as big as its tree, and I couldn't help but feel a swell of pride.

I scanned the crowd, hoping to catch a glimpse of Mackenzie. She'd promised to meet me, but with the throngs of people moving through the market, spotting her would be a challenge. I noticed a stand selling hot chocolate, and I figured no one would mind if I got started. I could use something warm to hold while I waited.

Oscar trotted beside me, sniffing the air thick with scents of cinnamon, chocolate, and pine. I ordered a hot chocolate, and the vendor handed me a steaming cup topped with whipped cream and a dusting of cocoa. Wrapping my hands around the cup, I took a sip, savoring the rich, velvety chocolate.

I felt a gentle tug as Oscar pulled towards something. I looked down to see a tiny corgi in a red-and-green striped sweater, his short legs prancing proudly through the snow. He gave a happy little bark, his eyes bright as he gazed up at me, tail wagging.

His owner, a woman bundled up in a vibrant red coat, rushed over, smiling apologetically as she tried to catch up with her enthusiastic pup. "Sorry about him," she said with a laugh, giving the corgi a fond look as he tugged toward another dog. "He thinks everyone's his best friend."

"He's adorable," I replied, giving the corgi a friendly pat as he sniffed eagerly at Oscar, who looked up at me with an expression that seemed to say, *Where's my sweater?*

All around us, people strolled with their own festively dressed dogs. A golden retriever ambled by in a sweater patterned with reindeer, tail wagging lazily, while two dachshunds zipped past, one in a sweater covered in Christmas lights, the other in a bright red cable knit. Even a massive Great Dane lumbered behind me, wearing a dark green sweater dotted with snowflakes. It was impossible not to smile at the sight of all these dogs decked out for the season.

"Sorry, buddy," I murmured to Oscar, ruffling the fur between his ears. "I'll get you a sweater."

He gave me a look that clearly said, *You better*, then trotted ahead, leaving little paw prints in the snow, tail wagging with each step.

I wandered closer to the stage where Joe and his band Priorities would be playing later. The first act, a group of carolers in Victorian costumes, was singing "O Holy Night," their voices hauntingly beautiful against the winter air. But the crowd was a little distracted, already eager for Joe's rock band to take over.

The bandstand was lit up with strings of twinkling Christmas lights, casting a warm glow over the crowd gathered nearby. The anticipation was palpable, especially from the snowboarders and fans who had gathered closer to the stage, clearly waiting to see Joe. I could already imagine the energy shift once the music began, drawing people in from all corners of the market.

I took another sip of my hot chocolate and kept an eye out for Mackenzie.

Mackenzie caught me smirking to myself and pinched me. "I bet I know what, or should I say who, you're thinking about right now."

"I'm thinking that this hot chocolate is delicious."

"Not that delicious," she teased.

We stood near the back, watching the scene unfold with Oscar sitting patiently by my feet. Mackenzie, as usual, was a little too invested in what Joe might be up to. She leaned in close to me, her breath visible in the chilly air. "Do you think Joe still surfs and snowboards, just like he did when we were together?" she asked, her eyes scanning the stage like she expected him to pop out any second. "I mean, he was always larger than life, you know? He always had that...vibe."

I rolled my eyes but smiled. "He's got a band, doesn't he? He can't be too different than what he was like in high school. Not to mention, I think half of the women in town are waiting for a glimpse of him."

Mackenzie laughed, but I could tell she was still caught up in her own little world of wondering what Joe had been up to all these years.

Sylvester suddenly appeared at my side, looking slightly out of place but happy to be there. After all the stress, it seemed he had decided he could use a little winter cheer. "Hey, cuz," he said, grinning as he pulled his coat tighter around him. "I've never actually been to Hazelton in the winter. I've gotta say, it's...beautiful. Really different from the summers here." He looked around, his eyes lingering on the snow-dusted rooftops and the brightly lit trees that lined the park. The town sparkled under the earlier snowfall, and I could see it through his eyes—the magic of a winter in Hazelton.

"It's like this every year. C'est magnifique," I said, smiling. "You should visit more often."

"Yeah, I don't know why my dad refuses to come back to this town," Sylvester mused, almost to himself. "He acts like it's cursed or something. But I'm glad you're here, and I'm really glad you have the Inn. It would've been a shame for it to go to strangers. It feels like a piece of Grandma is still here."

I felt a warmth spread through me. "I think she'd be happy to see you here tonight."

"I'm not going to stay long out here. I don't want to leave Emerson too long."

"Make sure you bring him back some hot chocolate," Mackenzie piped in, almost flirting with Sylvester.

"Good idea. I'll grab some for myself, too. Yours looks pretty good." His eyes had a little flicker of mischief.

I felt a medium cringe. Nope. Not what I wanted for a family reunion. Just another person Sylvester would rather hang out with than me. These worlds wouldn't be colliding. Instead, I directed her attention back to another eligible bachelor. "Hey Mack, I think the concert is about to start!"

A jingle of bells caught our attention, and a horse-drawn sleigh glided along the edge of the market, the horse's breath puffing out in soft clouds as it trotted through the snow.

Sylvester's face lit up, and he turned to Mackenzie with a twinkle in his eye. "You ever been on a sleigh ride?" he asked her, a smile tugging at the corner of his mouth. "Because I think we should go. How about it?"

Mackenzie blushed, looking a bit flustered by his attention. "Maybe I'd like that," she said softly, her cheeks pink in the glow of the lights.

I couldn't help smiling. Mackenzie and I had watched *Christmas in Connecticut* so many times we could quote it line for line, and the idea of a real sleigh ride always made us giddy. For once, it felt like our favorite movie had spilled right into Hazelton's snowy streets.

Before I could tease her, the carolers finished their song, and polite applause rippled through the crowd. The stage lights dimmed for a moment, signaling the end of their set and the beginning of the real show. The buzz of anticipation swept over the square—Joe and his band were about to take the stage.

The shift between the traditional Christmas singers and Joe's modern rock band felt like whiplash. The carolers, with their timeless voices and old-fashioned costumes, seemed worlds away from the raw energy that Priorities brought forward. Joe's fans, a mix of laid-back surfers and starstruck admirers, pressed closer as the guitars hummed and the crowd vibrated with excitement.

That's when I felt a warm hand at my elbow. Paul. I'd seen him lingering on the edge of the square, and now he slipped in beside me, his smile catching in the flickering lights. "Come on," he said, tugging me a little out of the throng. "Before the crowd swallows us whole."

Oscar bounded ahead, tail wagging, eager to follow.

Paul led me toward the sleighs, his charm as disarming as ever, until the driver frowned. "Sorry—no dogs."

Before I could reply, a conspiracy of ravens swooped overhead, their wings slicing the air as they circled the square. The crowd laughed nervously, but Paul's expression darkened, his eyes following their black shapes with unease.

"Bonne Annee," he murmured. "I've gotta take a rain check. Keeping those birds out of the market is my job. And you know as well as I do—they aren't here by accident." He gave me a quick, unexpected peck on the cheek before sprinting toward the commotion, the ravens already scattering in the direction of the Christmas tree.

I touched the spot on my cheek, startled, and muttered, "Sorry about the ravens. Guess I didn't know my theme would be this successful."

Mackenzie and Sylvester, already climbing into the sleigh, looked back at me with amused grins.

I flushed. "Go on, you two. I'll see you later. I'm heading for more hot chocolate."

They settled into the sleigh, laughter mingling with the jingle of harness bells. For a moment, I just watched them—and there it was: our *Christmas in Connecticut* moment, the one Mackenzie and I had dreamed about since forever. Only now, she was the only one living it.

As the crowd roared for Joe and his band, the music pounded louder, filling the square with pulsing energy. I slipped between groups, careful not to draw attention. Mackenzie was too distracted by Sylvester's sleigh ride to notice I'd gone, which was just as well. I had bigger things to deal with tonight.

I took Oscar home first. I couldn't risk having him with me while I snooped around Charlie's house. When I got to my house, Emerson was up, sitting on the couch. "Hey, Annee. You're back early."

"Yeah, I brought Oscar back. I think it was too crowded for him. Mind if he hangs out with you?"

I scratched Oscar behind the ears, murmuring a quick apology.

He whined for a moment, then cozied up on the couch with Emerson. Emerson immediately started petting Oscar. "Of course I don't mind. I think he's the best doodle I've ever met!"

Oscar rolled on his back for belly rubs. It looked like he was already in love with his babysitter.

I waved and was on my way.

The walk to Charlie's house was quiet, the fresh layer of snow muffling my footsteps. But halfway there, I noticed a man coming from the opposite direction. He kept close to the shadows, a dark pea coat buttoned tight, his collar turned up against the cold. His face was unshaven, and he had the sleepless look of someone who hadn't rested in days.

"Late night for a walk," he said as we passed. His tone was polite, almost casual, but his eyes lingered too long, as if he were holding back something sharper.

"I ate too much pie and need to walk it off," I said lightly, hoping my voice didn't sound as strained as I felt.

Something about him tugged at my memory, though I couldn't place from where. In a town as small as Hazelton, that alone was unsettling. For a moment I wondered if he meant to stop, but then he carried on, boots crunching in the snow until the sound faded into silence.

I stayed rooted in place, breath rising in pale clouds, waiting until I was sure he was gone. Only then did I continue toward Charlie's house, my heart thudding harder than before.

There was no police tape, no officers posted outside—just the quiet, dark house of someone who wasn't with us anymore. Who would mind? Was it really so bad to investigate this now-empty home?

I knew it was wrong, but Charlie was dead, Emerson had almost been murdered, and there was something about Alejandro's story that wasn't sitting right with me.

The house, though dark, was still fully decked out in Christmas decorations, thanks to Charlie's habit of getting everything set up on Thanksgiving Day. The lights twinkled on a timer, casting a soft glow over the front yard. A blow-up Santa and his reindeer stood guard at the front door, giving the place an eerie cheerfulness that contrasted to the reality of what had happened to its owner.

I took a deep breath to steel myself, then snuck around the side of the house. The back window was unlocked. Lucky for me. I had a rock ready to do the job if needed. But then I remembered that Charlie was not a fan of modern surveillance or in-home convenience devices with AI brains. He had often mentioned his distrust of modern devices, so I knew there was no security system hooked up. I was pretty sure he thought email was going to end the post office. He was the opposite of Alejandro.

I pushed it open carefully, quietly, and slipped inside. Just as I suspected. There wasn't a sound in protest. The air inside the house was colder than I expected; the kind of cold that sinks into your bones. The place was still and silent—too quiet. I kept my breathing steady and resisted the urge to flip a light switch. Instead, I fumbled in my purse and turned on my cell phone flashlight. The beam cut a narrow path through the darkness. I aimed it low, careful not to let it hit the windows.

The living room looked deceptively calm. Someone had already cleaned it up from the post-funeral gathering. But my pulse quickened as I stepped inside, the silence of the space pressing in around me. I hadn't noticed earlier that Charlie had already hung stockings over the fireplace. A small Christmas tree twinkled in the corner, and a handful of Santa figurines stood proudly on the mantel, watching me like informants.

My palms were damp, and I wiped them on my sweater as I glanced around. This wasn't just a cozy room; it was a crime scene in disguise. I couldn't afford to be sentimental. I needed to search—really search—and ignore how fast my heart was racing.

Thoughts of Charlie's connection to Alejandro, the documents I'd found, and the warnings he never got the chance to share kept rotating in my mind. My gut told me something was still there, something important. Something that might explain how two people had gone into anaphylaxis at my dinner. One had barely made it out alive and the other.... I traced the beam of light from my cell phone over the darkened, empty space before me. I didn't know what I was looking for, but I had to believe I'd recognize it when I found it.

I took a deep breath and headed deeper into the house, flashlight guiding my way, determined to find whatever Charlie had been hiding. I slipped quietly back into the small study where Charlie kept his paperwork. As I approached the desk, I pulled open the drawers slowly, wincing at the occasional creak. Bills, town paperwork, old letters—nothing immediately suspicious.

I was about to give up when I noticed a stack of papers slightly misaligned on the desk. I rifled through them and discovered a thin folder labeled "Market Proposals." Inside were vendor applications and the standard permits for the Christmas market. At the bottom was a list of all the food suppliers, and one name jumped out: Hazelton Farms. That was Felix and Magda's hazelnut farm, which had recently skyrocketed in popularity.

Charlie had pushed for Hazelton Farms to be part of the Christmas market, but for some reason they had originally declined. I remembered the café chatter that I had heard months ago. Something about them being too busy. They didn't think they could participate. I took some photos with my phone and moved to the bedroom. I had the tell-tale heart pounding in my ears and my nerves were getting the better of me. I searched the nightstand, then the closet—still nothing. I exhaled in frustration, realizing I had been holding my breath. Where hadn't I searched? My eyes were drawn to the bed…or more specifically, what might be hidden under it.

Bending down, I felt around the cool, dusty floor, trying not to sneeze. My fingers hesitantly probed, terrified of encountering spiders, cockroaches, or any creature satisfied with living in the dark space under the bed. I was about to quit when my hand touched something solid—a shoebox. I carefully pulled it out, setting it on the bed. The lid was loosely secured by a piece of string, and my fingers hesitated for a moment before pulling off the lid. Inside was a treasure trove of personal items: old photos of Charlie, old train tickets, a few postcards from years ago. But buried underneath these mementos was something far more surprising—a crisp, white envelope addressed to Alejandro.

My breath caught. Had Charlie kept more of Alejadro's mail?

I slipped the letter out of the envelope, my fingers trembling. The official letterhead at the top read *Delano Food Testing Laboratories*. I held my breath as I unfolded it, a sense of dread settling in.

Dear Mr. Alejandro Martinez,

Enclosed are the results of the test conducted on the sample food product containing hazelnuts, as requested. Our analysis has confirmed the presence of a significant contamination of the pathogen Escherichia coli (E. coli). The particular strain found in the product is highly resistant and known to cause severe illness.

We advise that immediate steps be taken to recall any batches of this product and conduct further testing to ensure no further contamination.

Please contact us if you require further assistance.

Regards,

Delano Food Testing Laboratories

Hazelnuts. Around here, that could only mean Hazelton Farms. They were the only ones growing and processing them at any scale, and everyone in town knew it. The letter was addressed to Alejandro, which meant he must have known about a contamination there. But then… why hadn't he told me?

I glanced down at the shoebox, swallowing hard. I reached back inside, rummaging gently, and pulled out a yellow legal notepad. On it was a handwritten list of names—names I recognized immediately. Jasper, Sophia, Paul… Charlie. And Alejandro.

My pulse quickened as I scanned the notepad. The list was titled simply *Hazelton Farms Investors,* with each name written in Charlie's neat handwriting. Underneath it, another document caught my eye—a worn stock certificate with the name *Charles Watson* typed in bold across the top. My stomach twisted.

So this was what Charlie had been caught up in. Not just the contamination, but a web of investors, all with something to lose if word got out about the tainted hazelnuts. I stared down at the stock certificate, my mind racing. If Charlie knew about the contamination, had he tried to blow the whistle? And if he hadn't, why not? Did Alejandro try to expose the contamination— or were others trying to keep it quiet?

Here he was again, caught up in another breakdown of our food system. Had Charlie, or anyone else, influenced him to stay silent? And Paul. How had I missed that he was connected to the farm?

Moving quickly, I went back into the other room and checked the desk. I rifled through the remaining drawers, carefully scanning any papers that seemed relevant, from town records to permits for local events. My hands shook slightly as I reached the bottom drawer and found a slim, leather-bound photo album tucked away behind a stack of old files. Hesitating, I opened it and positioned my phone to scan each page.

The album was filled with snapshots of Hazelton's many celebrations. I scanned images of familiar faces bundled up for winter, children with rosy cheeks sipping hot cocoa, and families laughing as they strolled through fairs

and festivals. Spring parades, summer carnivals, Halloween gatherings—
they were all preserved here, a testament to the town's close-knit spirit.

Then I turned a page, and my heart stopped.

A photo of a bustling European market filled the screen. The image was
distinctly different from Hazelton's familiar scenes, capturing cobblestone
streets, festive stalls adorned with twinkling lights and garlands, and a grand
cathedral rising in the background. I recognized two familiar faces at the
center of the frame: Charlie and a much younger Ilsa. She looked at least fifteen years younger, with her blonde hair spilling over a scarf and ski goggles
pushed up onto her head. She seemed to be laughing at something Charlie
was saying. His arm was slung casually over her shoulder, his face lit with
an easy smile. They looked undeniably close—far closer than Ilsa had ever
let on.

I carefully scanned the photo, feeling a pang of unease. Why had Ilsa hidden this part of her life? Why pretend she wasn't close to Charlie, when this
image suggested otherwise? My mind spun as I took in every detail, hoping
it might lead to more answers.

Flipping through the rest of the album, I saw more scenes of Hazelton, but
Ilsa didn't appear in any of them. I slipped the album back into the drawer,
the photos and documents now secured on my phone, saved as proof of
whatever tangled web Charlie had uncovered—or had been part of.

As I turned to leave, something caught my eye: an old trunk tucked into
the corner, almost hidden in the shadows. I hesitated, then knelt down and
flipped it open. Inside were neat stacks of letters—copies of letters. My
heart raced as I realized what I was looking at. Charlie hadn't been *stealing*
the mail, exactly, but he'd been opening it, copying its contents, and then,
presumably, delivering it as if nothing had happened.

Taking one last, sweeping look around the study, I searched for anything
else I might have missed. The room sat silent and still, its secrets now laid
bare. With my heart pounding, I slipped my phone back into my pocket and
felt the cold of the house settle over me as I made my way to the door.

Chapter 11

C'est du Pain Bénit:
It's Some Blessed Bread (it's a godsend; it's lucky and happening at an opportune moment)

When I got back to the house, Emerson was still on the couch with Oscar. I sat down with them, and Oscar jumped on my lap.

"So what did you guys do while I was gone?"

"Nothing much, just watched TV. I thought you were meeting up with your friend and Sylvester. He called a little while ago to check on me."

"Yeah—I couldn't find them so I came home," I said, trying to cover for my absence. I looked at the scanned images. My copies of the copies. Oscar nudged at me. He was hungry and so was I.

"You hungry, cuz?" I playfully asked Emerson. I was really starting to feel like part of the family clique. Maybe it was an illusion, but it was nice to be familiar with him.

"Yes, *cuz*," he groaned, mocking me.

Okay, so maybe it was too soon to be that familiar with him. But a girl can hope.

I called my best friend. "Hey Mack, I'm home and I'm going to take out the arroz con pollo. Want to come over?"

"Oh boy, do I! We'll be there in five."

I had frozen too large a portion the last time I made it, and I had promised I would invite her over when I finally was ready to defrost it. I wasn't one to thaw and refreeze. Just not my style.

I filled Oscar's bowl with his favorite treat—kibble with a little shredded cheddar cheese on top—then put the rice dish in the oven to reheat. Using the microwave just wasn't my style, either. Since it was going to be a minute before the arroz was ready, I decided to make some tostones. I had a few green plantains left. After peeling the plantains, I sliced them into chunky one-inch rounds. I heated some oil in a frying pan and gave them a quick fry, just a few minutes until they turned a light golden color. Once out of the pan, I let them drain on a paper towel before smashing each one gently with the bottom of a glass. Back into the oil they went for a second fry, this time until they were golden brown and perfectly crispy. I added a sprinkle of sea salt at the end, and they were ready to go.... Just in time for me to hear Mackenzie open the door.

"I'm here! Oh man, it smells so good."

Then I heard other voices too. "It does smell good in here."

Emerson and Sylvester. I had been so immersed in the sense memory of making tostones with my mother and grandmother that I had forgotten about my guests.

Once Mackenzie, Emerson and Sylvester were all in the room, I realized that my leftovers dinner was turning into a lively family gathering. Oscar had already started pacing excitedly at the new arrivals, his tail wagging enthusiastically. The arroz con pollo was still warming in the oven, filling the air with a comforting aroma of garlic and spices. I felt grateful I'd decided to make extra tostones, because I knew they wouldn't last long with this group.

I invited everyone to sit around the kitchen table. I laid out the tostones with a small dish of garlic-lime dipping sauce. The sizzling sound from the oven hinted that the arroz was nearly ready, so I pulled it out and carefully served generous portions onto each plate, topping the golden rice and tender chicken with a sprinkle of fresh cilantro.

Mackenzie dug in immediately, a satisfied sigh escaping her. "Annee, this is amazing, as always. I swear, you could turn this whole bookstore into a restaurant," she said between bites.

Sylvester and Emerson nodded, clearly too absorbed in their food to say much at first. But after a few minutes, Sylvester looked up with a grin, pointing his fork at me. "This arroz takes me back to those summers we spent here with Grandma. I'd forgotten how much I missed her cooking."

Emerson chimed in. His usual edge seemed to have vanished completely as he looked around the table. "Yeah, she made the best meals. I don't think I've tasted anything like it until now. Thanks for doing this, Annee."

I smiled, feeling a warm sense of nostalgia and connection. Dinner carried on with lighthearted stories from our past, laughter over silly arguments, and moments of shared memories that made it feel like we'd never lost touch. I tried not to think about the lies I felt Alejandro had been telling me.

Chapter 12

Être Soupe au Lait:

To Be Milk Soup (to get irritated easily and therefore handled carefully)

The first thing I did the next day was arrange a meeting with Ilsa. I needed to know what she knew, and I wasn't about to wait any longer. Oscar trotted happily beside me, his curly coat bouncing as we made our way down the winding path into town. It was a crisp morning, the kind where every breath felt like a clean slate. But despite the refreshing air, my mind churned with thoughts of Charlie and the strange series of events that had turned my life upside down. I pulled out my phone and scrolled through my contacts until I reached Cora's number.

As it rang, Oscar nudged my leg, sensing my unease. I glanced down, giving him a quick scratch behind the ear to calm us both.

"Hey, Annee," Chief Cora answered, her voice steady but a bit rushed.

"Hi, Cora. I know the case was closed, but my insurance agent is asking for more information about Charlie's passing. They want me to provide additional context…to make sure everything on my end is clear. I really don't think it was an accident," I added carefully.

She hesitated, and I could almost picture her on the other end, weighing her words. "I know you've been speculating about the case. This is a small town, and people talk, Annee. And…I'll tell you this much: the case was re-opened. But I really can't say more than that right now. When I know more, I'll call you."

Relief at this news mingled with a new, nervous energy. "Thanks, Cora. I appreciate you letting me know. I'll wait to hear from you."

We hung up, and I felt Oscar tug gently on the leash, pulling me back to the present. "Let's go, buddy," I murmured, giving him a reassuring pat.

We reached Katie's Café just as the sun started breaking through the morning haze, casting a warm glow over Hazelton's quiet streets. The familiar smell of fresh coffee and pancakes wafted through the air as I pushed open the door, guiding Oscar to our usual spot by the window. He settled in, curling up at my feet as I ordered a coffee, waiting for Ilsa.

As I sipped, I ran through the questions I had for her about the clues and lingering doubts that had kept me up at night. Whatever secrets Hazelton was hiding, I was ready to dig in—and it seemed Cora was, too.

Ilsa arrived but didn't seem to want to be there as she slid into the seat across from me. She fidgeted and looked at her classic Swiss watch. Maybe she wanted to be back at the market managing and controlling the flow. She had appeared excited about the town's swelling numbers and the potential for next year's market.

I drank my usual coffee with cream and one sugar. Whenever I was feeling virtuous, I would forgo the sugar, but never the cream. Ilsa drank tea. She had ordered hot water and pulled out a sachet from her bag. I could smell the peppermint, thyme, lemon balm, and chamomile as it steeped in the hot water. My superpower—a heightened sense of smell to keep me safe from things that could kill me—was at work.

"That smells nice," I said as I took a long, deep breath.

"Oh, you like? Good. I'm thinking of adding teas to my booth." She opened up her bag. "I have the Edelweiss Tea, Fencheltee, and the Früchtetee." She stared at my puzzled face as I was trying to sort out the names and what they were. She continued, "I'm sure even you know Edelweiss. No? Maybe the Fencheltee and Früchtetee. Fennel and Fruit teas. They're very popular." She had a bit of disdain in her voice, as if she wouldn't even bother to try and convince me.

"Nice. I'm sure people will love it. It's just getting to be fireside and tea season. Maybe I should get some for my store. Can you write down the names for me?" I pulled out my pen from my bag and slid a napkin over to her. I thought it might come in handy to have a sample of her handwriting.

She seemed irritated but obliged. "Not just for cold weather. Tea is every day." She scribbled down the names of the tea on the napkin and I quickly put it in my bag.

I lifted my coffee cup and nodded. "I hear ya."

She wrinkled up her nose, pursed her lips together, and finished her tea ritual.

I glanced over to Katie in desperation. I was going to need more coffee for this interaction. I tried to signal her. I wish she hadn't given up the practice of leaving a carafe of coffee on the table for self service. I loved those days, but with the tough economy, she couldn't afford to waste a drop of coffee.

She caught my eye and came over. "You gals look serious over here." She poured slowly into my cup so as not to spill. Ilsa just looked at her.

"Yep." I raised my eyebrow to her, and she gave a little nod and hustled to the next customer.

"So," I started, mentally holding my breath. "You knew Charlie."

"Yes. We all knew him. He's the reason we started the market!"

"No, I mean before that."

Isla was suddenly stiff and sat very tall. Her eyes sharpened, and she looked at me fiercely for a moment, then glanced downward towards her drink. "Ah. Why you ask? What do you mean?"

"Well, we found a note in his desk and this picture." I decided to make it seem like more people were aware of this information. I pulled out the printed old, faded photo of what looked like a young Charlie with a full head of hair and Ilsa. The years had been kind to her, and at first glance, everything would tell you that it was her. I had analyzed this picture over and over. She was so attractive, and she and Charlie were definitely romantically attached, given the way they were embracing and the way Charlie smiled. It was like he had caught the biggest fish ever.

"How do you have this? May I?" She held out her hand.

She looked at the photo longingly, then looked up and said, "Yes, this is me." Then she quickly ripped the photo into several pieces and dropped it in her tea.

My eyes widened in shock. I was holding my breath at this point. She got up just as Katie was delivering our eggs.

"Where is the note?" Ilsa asked. "What did it say?"

Now I was the one being interrogated.

"Uh, it just had your name and number on it," I said, lying about the note. I had been hoping that she was going to reveal some further details, thinking that I already knew.

"Chau. Goodbye."

She walked out. I was stunned. My mind spiraled as I watched her walk away. What had she said? "Chau."

Not really crack interrogation work. So it was her in the photograph—but what next? Should I chase her down?

I grabbed her teacup and tried to retrieve the bits of photo before they became mush. It was too late.

Katie watched Ilsa leave. "Is she coming back?"

I shook my head. "I don't think so."

"Should I box it up?" She grabbed Ilsa's plate.

I nodded. "I guess Oscar gets to try lox today."

Katie laughed. "Fancy!"

I pulled out my phone and tried my best to type in the foreign words Ilsa had snapped at me. Even with my clumsy spelling, the translation app recognized it as Romansh, one of Switzerland's four official languages, though not a common one. It wasn't what they would be speaking in primarily German-speaking Basel, which was where she said she was from. At the Poe party, she'd discussed her Swiss heritage in quite a bit of detail. I'd thought she was just humblebragging about being European and having the expertise of the "real" Christmas markets. But maybe she was trying to cover something else up.

I pulled up my photos on my phone. The woman in the photograph was definitely her, which meant that she had known Charlie for over twenty years. Had they been in contact all along? What were they to each other? Were they merely at "pen pal" status, like I was with my semester-in-Spain friends, or did they have a lasting connection?

Why hadn't Charlie told anyone that they knew each other? My best guess was that he didn't want anyone to think that he was playing favorites. He was that kind of guy. Then again, she was the only one he had put forward for the job, and everyone on the council was just happy to give her the position and cross it off the list. Charlie always knew what he was doing. Everyone trusted him. But who might have been unhappy with his choices?

My phone rang, jolting me out of my thoughts.

"Hello?" I hadn't looked to see who was calling.

"You were right. It wasn't an accident," Chief Cora said. "It was murder."

Chapter 13

> Mettre son Grain de Sel:
> *To Put One's Grain of Salt (to give your opinion)*

A fter leaving Katie's Café with Ilsa's conversation replaying in my mind, I decided I couldn't go straight home. Not yet. Was I a suspect? What would people think now? I made my way to the senior center to visit Mr. Morrison and fill him in on Cora's bombshell and what I had discovered. Since Mr. Morrison had voiced his own doubts about Charlie's death, I figured he was the safest person to compare notes with until I knew more from Alejandro.

When I stepped inside, the scent of burnt coffee lingered in the air, mingling with the faint sound of a television droning from down the hall. I found him where he usually was in the afternoons, settled in his favorite chair by the window. His eyes lit with recognition as soon as he saw me.

"Annee," he said, his eyes creasing with that familiar, quiet welcome. "Didn't expect you today."

I sat down beside him, hesitating before I took a breath and spoke. "Mr. Morrison, I need to tell you something…something I haven't told anyone else. After the funeral, I looked around at Charlie's house and in his study. And…later that night, I went back to look some more."

He raised an eyebrow, a knowing smile tugging at the corner of his mouth. "I figured you were snooping in his business. I saw you slip off toward the back during the gathering."

A flush of embarrassment washed over me. "I… alright, I was snooping," I admitted. "But something didn't feel right. It was like I couldn't leave without trying to understand what was really going on."

He nodded slowly, his expression open. "I get it, Annee. Charlie was one of us—a good friend and a good man. And you've got that instinct in you, that feeling when something's amiss."

I let out a shaky breath, clutching the papers tightly. "I found some things, Mr. Morrison. Documents that link Alejandro to a contamination issue at Hazelton Farms. There's a letter from Delano Labs about a potential problem with hazelnuts, a list of investors—including Charlie—and even a stock certificate with Charlie's name on it."

Mr. Morrison's gaze sharpened, though his tone stayed calm. "So, Charlie was deeper in the Hazelton Farms drama than he let on. And since he used to open other people's mail, there's no telling how much more he knew. What about Alejandro? Did he tell you he was part of that whole scandal?"

I shook my head, feeling the weight of the situation. "No. He never mentioned anything about being tied to Hazelton Farms. He's on the investor list, along with Jasper, Sophia, and Paul. I don't know how much they knew about the contamination or what their involvement was, but they're all associated."

Mr. Morrison leaned back, exhaling slowly. "So, Alejandro kept quiet about it. Maybe he thought he could fix it, or maybe…" His voice trailed off as his gaze narrowed. "You know, even here at the center we have to stay on top of recalls. A contamination issue like E. coli? That can ruin a business overnight. If word got out, it could mean lawsuits, fines, inspections, even closing the kitchen."

I nodded, his words sinking in. "So, they thought hiding it would be better? That no one would find out?"

"It's possible," he said grimly. "Covering it up might have seemed like the only way to protect their investment—keep consumer trust, avoid the lawsuits and penalties, keep the stockholders happy. But if they were wrong..." He let out a slow breath. "If they were wrong, it's not just a bad decision. It's criminal."

I swallowed hard, the implications hitting me all at once. "Charlie—he was part of it. And Alejandro too. But if he was involved, what was he doing? Exposing it? Or helping to keep it quiet?"

His jaw clenched. "That's the real question, isn't it?" He paused, his expression tightening. "And remember, Hazelton Farms isn't just any business. Around here it has a celebrity status – people tour the place, brag about the candies, send gift boxes across the country. If contamination was traced back to them, the fallout wouldn't stop at the farm. It would drag down the whole town's name with it."

He placed a gentle hand on mine. "Annee, it's clear you're carrying a heavy weight. Trust doesn't mean burying the truth to protect someone else's secrets. If this affects you, your safety, or those you care about, you've got to decide how much you're willing to keep hidden."

I looked down, absorbing his words. "So, you think I should tell Mackenzie? About the contamination, the investors, all of it?"

He gave me a small, reassuring smile. "She's your best friend. You know you can trust her. Start with something small, and you'll get a sense of where to go from there. Trust that instinct of yours. You're not alone in this, Annee. We're here to help you carry the burden. I know you're scared, and that's why I also think Cora should know."

I gave him a grateful nod, feeling a bit lighter. "Thank you, Mr. Morrison. I needed someone to remind me of that. Until I reach Alejandro, I don't want to cause more trouble with Cora."

He patted my hand gently, his warmth calming the storm inside me. "Anytime, Annee. Sometimes, just knowing someone else is in your corner makes all the difference."

Chapter 14

Être Mi-Figue, Mi-Raisin:
*To Be Half Fig, Half Grape (to be both good and bad; to be contradictory
in some way)*

I left him, determined to tell Mack what I was up to, but then decided I wanted to search just a little longer to see if I could find any more clues. The cold December air wrapped around me as I made my way toward the Christmas market, which was thriving with vendors and townsfolk, even on this gray, frosty evening. The market was set to run until December 23rd—Christmas Eve Eve. Tonight, the stalls were brightly lit, bustling with activity, and adorned with festive decorations that seemed to capture the magic of the season.

I needed to gather my thoughts and make sense of what Cora had told me. *Murder.* The word echoed in my mind, unsettling and sharp. If Charlie's death was intentional, I couldn't ignore the implications. I'd need to speak with my insurance agent, sort out the liability, and…well, if someone could be held responsible for the tragedy that happened in my home and business, I didn't want it to be me.

I strolled past the small wooden stalls, decked in garlands and twinkling lights. Each vendor was wrapped in scarves and mittens as they greeted customers with wide, cheerful smiles. As I glanced around, a strange absence caught my attention: Ilsa wasn't in her booth. She was usually there, overseeing everything as a figure of quiet authority. Yet her space was empty, a simple "Back Soon" sign hanging where she should have been. It was curious, but I couldn't dwell on it now.

I spotted Karl, the sound technician, sitting alone on a bench just outside his booth, tapping away at his phone. I remembered he'd sat near Emerson at the Poe-themed dinner, and as I approached, he gave me a friendly nod, his blue eyes crinkling slightly against the cold.

"Hi, Karl," I said, sitting next to him. "It's busy here today, isn't it?"

"Very," he replied, slipping his phone into his pocket. "The crowds have been almost nonstop. Anything I could do for you?"

"I was hoping to talk to a few people who might have known Charlie." I watched his face for a reaction. He frowned slightly, but he didn't look surprised. "You sat near him at my dinner, didn't you?"

"I did." He nodded slowly. "Poor guy. I never thought something like this would happen here." He shifted uncomfortably. "You know, he was talking about Magda's hazelnut candies earlier that day, before your dinner. I even tried a few," he admitted, patting his pocket as if remembering he'd stashed one or two there. "He was talking to everyone about them—said they'd be a hit, with them being local and all. Everyone was raving about them."

"Did you share any with the others?" I asked, curious now.

He nodded. "He nodded. "I offered one to Emerson before the dinner started, didn't think much of it. He waved me off, but he didn't say why. I figured he just wasn't in the mood for sweets."

My stomach tightened. "Karl, Emerson has a nut allergy. A serious one. Even a trace could set him off. You can't hand out hazelnut candy without checking."

His eyes widened. "I had no idea. He didn't say."

"That's why my home is strictly nut-free," I said firmly. "I can't risk it. Not for my business, not for myself, and not for my friends." I glanced at his hands, remembering how easy it would be for nut dust to travel. "Sometimes it doesn't even take eating it. Just touching something after holding a nut can be enough."

Karl looked stricken, his coffee halfway to his lips. "I swear, I didn't know. I'm sorry, Annee."

I softened, giving him a small nod. "It's okay. You didn't know. Just be careful next time."

As I moved on, I spotted the carnival family near the Ferris wheel. Skye, Scott, and their father, Steve, were huddled together, adjusting the lights on their ride. Skye noticed me first and waved, her smile wide and welcoming. I decided to approach them, too, since they'd also been at the dinner.

"Hey, Annee," Skye said as I came closer, brushing her gloved hands together to warm them. "Cold night, huh?"

"Definitely," I replied, trying to keep my tone light. "I just wanted to check in and see how you're doing after…everything."

They exchanged glances, their smiles fading slightly. Scott rubbed the back of his neck. "It's rough," he admitted. "We didn't know Charlie well, but we worked with him to get all our permits and insurance in place. He made sure we felt welcome here."

Steve nodded in agreement. "He even brought us those hazelnut candies to your house," he added, grinning. "'Free samples,' he said. Those things are addictive."

I paused, considering the implications. "Did you…shake hands with Emerson or anyone else who was at the dinner?"

Skye shrugged. "Yeah, we probably did when we arrived. I mean, it's polite, right? We all introduced ourselves."

The realization hit me like a stone dropping into water, ripples of dread spreading through my chest. Hazelnut residue could have slipped into the dinner in so many innocent ways—a crumb on a sleeve, a casual handshake, a careless touch on a serving spoon. But would that really have been enough to trigger such a violent reaction?

Unless it wasn't innocent at all.

I quickened my pace through the market, my thoughts racing ahead of me. What if someone had planted hazelnuts at the dinner on purpose, knowing Charlie or Emerson might suffer for it? That wasn't contamination. That was intent. And intent meant murder.

I stopped at the Misto food truck next, where Johnny and Lucca were busy serving up hot bowls of seafood pasta to a line of eager customers. They spotted me and waved, gesturing for me to step around the back of the truck.

"Hey, Annee!" Johnny greeted me with his usual charm. "Enjoying the market?"

"Trying to," I said, returning his smile. "I've been thinking about my dinner a lot—you know, beating myself up over what happened. I keep thinking back to that night. I heard you all were offered some of Magda's hazelnut candies. Were they going around?"

Lucca nodded. "Oh, absolutely. Magda's got a goldmine with those things. They were delicious!"

"Did Charlie give them to you?" I asked, keeping my tone as casual as possible.

Johnny paused, scratching his head. "Yeah...yeah, I think he did. Told us we should try the local treats, said it'd give us a real hometown feel. Why do you ask?"

I forced a small smile, hoping I looked more relaxed than I felt. "Just curious. Thanks, Johnny."

He nodded, then paused, as if something had just struck him. "You know, I might still have one left in the truck, if you're interested. Hold on a sec."

I watched as he strode over to his truck and leaned into the front seat, rustling through a few items. After a moment, he straightened up, holding a small package wrapped in a clear, thick plastic wrapper, the type that seals in freshness.

"Here it is," he said, handing it over. The sample gleamed through the clear wrapper—a neatly packaged hazelnut treat with a glossy, chocolate-coated surface, untouched and secure. The wrapper looked well-made with no tears or weak seams. It had the kind of seal that would make it perfectly safe for handling—even for someone with a severe allergy. Charlie must have known the treat wouldn't pose any risk as long as it stayed sealed.

I nodded, my mind racing. "Thanks, Johnny. "

"Sure thing, Annee," he replied, still giving me a curious look. "If you need anything else, just let me know."

I slipped the sample into my bag, feeling its weight, as if it held the answer to a hundred questions.

As I walked away from the truck, a cold chill swept over me that had nothing to do with the winter air. Hazelnuts had been everywhere that night—handed out, pocketed, passed around with barely a thought. Too easy to explain away as an accident, but I knew from experience how little it could take: a smear of oil, a trace of dust, a crumb in the wrong place. Charlie had been the one to push those candies on everyone, but someone else could have seized the chance and weaponized that treat. With one last glance around, I noticed a few ravens strutting nearby as if they were waiting for me to catch up to what they already knew. My intuition whispered that there was nothing random about these reactions. Was it a crime of opportunity?

I pulled out my phone, knowing I needed to make two calls: one to my insurance agent and one to Cora.

As I rounded the corner toward my house, the familiar sight of my blue Gothic Revival home brought a small sense of comfort. But it was quickly shattered by the sight of two police cruisers parked out front, their red and blue lights flashing, casting eerie shadows across the snow-dusted lawn. My heart sank, and my steps slowed as I took in the scene. Two officers stood on the porch, talking in low voices, their expressions serious.

Oscar, who had come to greet me as he always did, was now sitting at the edge of the lawn, his tail tucked low and his gaze fixed on the officers. Even he seemed uneasy, his usual energy dampened by the heavy atmosphere around the house.

One of the officers spotted me and raised a hand, motioning for me to come closer. As I approached, my stomach twisted. A strange mixture of apprehension and defiance was building inside me. I forced a steadying breath, bracing myself for whatever was to come.

"Good evening, Ms. Steele," the officer said, his voice professional but flat. "We're here with a warrant to search the property."

I blinked, caught off guard. "A warrant? For what?"

Officer Kim glanced down at the paper in his hand before meeting my gaze again. "We're searching for any items or substances that could be linked to the recent incident involving Charles Watson and Emerson Steele. As you may know, there's an investigation underway."

I nodded, trying to keep my expression neutral. "I understand," I said, feeling the weight of his words settle over me. "You're welcome to search, of course. But could someone tell me exactly what you're looking for?"

Officer Kim exchanged a quick look with his partner. "It's just standard procedure, ma'am," he said, his tone clipped. "If you'll stay out here, we'll let you know when we're done."

"Actually, this is my home," I replied, struggling to keep my voice steady. "I think I have a right to stay inside."

His partner, a younger officer with kind eyes, gave me a small nod. "We won't be too long," he assured me. "But it's best if you let us do our job."

They moved past me and into the house, leaving me standing on the porch with Oscar at my side. I rubbed his head absent-mindedly, trying to quell the anxiety building in my chest.

Peering through the window, I could see them moving carefully, systematically, as they checked the front rooms first—the ones lined with antique bookcases and my shelves of cookbooks, mysteries, and classics. Their flashlights skimmed across spines and display tables before they continued into the living room, the kitchen, and then made their way toward the back of the house.

The minutes dragged on, each one stretching as I tried to calm my racing thoughts. I went over everything that had happened in the past few days—the dinner, the Christmas market, the hazelnuts, the strange series of events that had led to this moment. And now, a search warrant from the police. It seemed impossible, yet here I was, watching them comb through my home as if I were hiding something sinister.

I felt my phone buzz in my pocket, and I pulled it out, grateful for the distraction. It was a text from Mackenzie: *Heard about the search from Emerson and Sylvester. Call me later if you need anything. I'll bring more of that mulled wine if you're up for it.*

Her simple message brought a small smile to my lips, but I wondered why my cousins hadn't reached out to me themselves. I typed a quick response, assuring her I'd fill her in once this was over. As I tucked my phone away, the door opened, and the two officers stepped back outside. One of them was holding a small brown box in his hands.

"What's that?" I asked, my stomach lurching at the sight of it. The box looked familiar, but from this distance, I couldn't place it.

"Just a few items from the cottage," Officer Kim replied, his tone unreadable. "We'll need to take them for further analysis."

My mind raced as I tried to recall what could possibly be in that box. Alejandro had moved into the cottage years ago, and his belongings were mostly confined there, save for the occasional gadget he brought over to the main house. I had no idea what they might have found in his space that would warrant this kind of scrutiny.

The officers thanked me for my cooperation and promised to inform me of any updates, but I knew from their tight-lipped expressions that I'd be left in the dark for now. They headed to their cars, sending one last wave in my direction.

I watched them drive away, the tension in my shoulders loosening slightly as their taillights disappeared down the road. Oscar nudged my leg, as if sensing my distress, and I knelt down to hug him, grateful for his unwavering presence.

Stepping back into the house, I took in the small signs of the search—the slight misalignment of the couch cushions, the cabinet door left slightly ajar in the kitchen, the faint smell of cold air from when they'd moved in and out. It was unsettling, feeling like a stranger had been in my home.

And then, the box. The image of it lingered in my mind, nagging at me. What had they found in Alejandro's cottage? Why would the police think it was important enough to take with them?

I grabbed my phone, scrolling through my contacts, until I found Cora's number. She was my best chance at answers. As I hit "call," I glanced out the window. Snow fell in gentle, silent flakes, turning the lawn and garden into a blanket of pure white.

"Cora, it's Annee," I said as she answered. "The police just left. They took some items from the cottage. Do you know what's going on?"

Cora sighed. "Annee, I wish I could tell you more, but we're keeping the investigation tight to the chest for now. I'll give you what I can—there's something we found linked to Charlie, and then Alejandro's name came up. It's complicated."

My pulse quickened, my mind racing as I tried to make sense of her words. "Alejandro? But he wouldn't—"

"We don't know anything for certain," she interrupted gently. "For now, just...try not to worry. And stay out of trouble. I'll be in touch."

She hung up before I could ask anything else, leaving me with more questions than before. I set the phone down, feeling the weight of everything pressing down on me. Oscar sat at my feet, gazing up with his wide, trusting eyes.

"We've got a mystery to solve, Oscar," I whispered, stroking his head. "And I think it's going to be a long winter."

Oscar nudged my hand with his nose, sensing my tension.

"Looks like it's just you and me again, buddy," I murmured, scratching his head as he leaned into my leg for comfort. I was in the clear as far as the police were concerned, but the uncertainty still lingered. What had they taken from Alejandro's cottage?

I began repositioning the couch cushions and shutting cabinet doors. There was something deeply unsettling about knowing they had combed through every inch of my property, as if I were some kind of criminal. Yet I couldn't shake the faintest hint of curiosity. Something inside me needed to understand how this tangled mess had come to my doorstep. Charlie's quiet influence, his choices, and his hidden connections had somehow twisted their way into my life.

As I stepped into the kitchen, Oscar padded along behind me, his quiet presence as steadying as a deep breath. I set the kettle on the stove to boil, deciding chamomile tea might calm my nerves better than cocoa. The soft whistle of the kettle filled the quiet house, giving me a moment to gather my thoughts. Just as the steam began to rise, a faint knock at the door broke the stillness.

A glance at the clock told me it was late. Too late for visitors, especially considering the night's events. I wiped my hands on a dish towel and headed straight for the door. Oscar was already there, his tail wagging with excitement. With a deep breath, I cracked the door open to find Mackenzie on the other side, bundled in her oversized coat, snowflakes clinging to her hair.

"I thought you could use some company," she said, offering a small smile as she held up a thermos. "And maybe a stronger drink than cocoa."

Relieved, I stepped aside to let her in, nodding gratefully as she handed me the thermos. "You have no idea," I said, unscrewing the cap to let the warm, spiced scent of mulled wine waft through the air. We sat together at the kitchen table, drinking the treat. Each sip was soothing and each moment was a reminder that not everything had been lost in the chaos.

"So," Mackenzie began, leaning forward, her voice quiet but intense. "What do you think the police were looking for?"

I bit my lip, glancing out the window toward Alejandro's cottage, its dark silhouette casting long shadows across the yard. "Honestly, I'm not sure. They took something from his place, but I couldn't see what it was. The whole thing just feels...wrong."

Mackenzie studied my face, her brows knitting together. "Alejandro *has* been acting strange lately."

I sighed, looking down at the mulled wine in my hands, feeling the warmth seep through my fingers. "I can't argue with that. He's been distant, and there's this tension I can't shake, but...he's always been so good to me. It's hard to believe he'd get involved in something dangerous. He wouldn't bring anything like that here...would he?"

Mackenzie's expression softened, and she leaned closer. "He was good to you, Annee, and maybe he still is. But people change. Sometimes, they get caught up in things we can't understand."

I held her gaze, feeling a pull between loyalty and the gut feeling I'd been ignoring for days. Finally, I took a deep breath, deciding it was time to come clean about my investigations. "Mack, there's something I need to confess. I've been...looking into things. Snooping, I guess you could say."

Her eyes widened, but she didn't say anything, waiting for me to go on.

"It started at Charlie's funeral," I admitted, glancing down at my hands, unable to look her in the eye. "I...I poked around his study, and I found documents linking Alejandro to another contamination issue, this time at Hazelton Farms. There was a letter from a testing lab confirming that there was *E. coli* in the hazelnuts. Apparently, the memo went out to an entire list of investors. Charlie, Alejandro, even some other people we know.... They all had stakes in the farm."

Mackenzie's face went pale, and her hand flew to her mouth. "Annee, why didn't you tell me?"

"I wanted to, but I didn't know what to make of it. And honestly, I wasn't sure how to bring it up without feeling like I was betraying Alejandro. He was acting so suspiciously—going off at odd hours, avoiding questions. And then...then the whole tree house thing."

I walked to the kitchen counter, where his note was sticking out from beneath a recipe book. I pulled it free and handed it to Mackenzie.

She looked at the note, her eyes scanning Alejandro's neat handwriting. "Why not tell you in person? Why leave a note?"

"I have no idea," I murmured, feeling a strange, sinking feeling in my stomach. "I've been piecing things together on my own, trying to make sense of it all. But now I think I need to see what he's up to for myself."

Mackenzie held the note, her expression hardening. "If Alejandro's hiding something, you need to know."

I gave her a grateful nod, slipping the note back into my pocket. She squeezed my hand. "We'll figure it out. Together."

I felt a weight lift. It was time to face whatever Alejandro had been hiding—even if it meant learning something I wasn't ready to know.

I said, "I think it's time I locate that tree house."

Chapter 15

Les Carottes Sont Cuites:
The Carrots Are Cooked (it's over; there's nothing to be done about it now)

I gripped the steering wheel of my old Karmann Ghia, my heart racing as the coastal road curved ahead of me, the ocean roaring beside the cliffs. The top was down, despite the chill in the air, and the wind whipped through my hair, pulling tangled strands against my face. I was heading north, up the Oregon coast, following nothing more than a hunch and a half-remembered story Alejandro had told me years ago.

The last time I'd seen him at the dinner, he had seemed quiet and distracted, but I thought that was because Emerson was there. I remembered the time Alejandro mentioned a small tree house retreat, nestled away on a working farm not far from Hazelton. It was right after he'd left his corporate job and was trying to write his book. I hadn't thought much of it then, but now, it was all I could think about.

As I neared the farm, the landscape shifted into a holiday wonderland. Twinkling lights lined the gravel driveway, wrapping around the farmhouse and the tree houses beyond, their glow casting a soft warmth in the cold evening air. Wreaths hung on the doors, adorned with red ribbons, and pine garlands framed the windows of the little tree houses. Even the animals on the farm seemed to carry the festive spirit, with bells and bright bows tied to their collars. It was the kind of place where one could forget the world and get lost in the magic of the season—if only the weight of everything else hadn't been pressing so hard on my chest.

As I approached the farmhouse, my eyes landed on Alejandro's car parked off to the side. I pulled in nearby and made my way toward the farthest tree house, the one half-hidden by a thicket of trees. Small, warm lights twinkled around the porch railing, and a miniature Christmas tree, adorned with simple wooden ornaments, stood just outside the door. It felt both festive and secluded, like the perfect hideaway.

The wooden stairs creaked softly as I climbed them, and I knocked on the door, my heart in my throat. After a moment, Alejandro opened the door, his face filled with surprise and something else—relief, maybe? But his eyes were dark with something deeper, something haunted. "Annee, you got my note. I thought you'd get here sooner," he said softly, stepping aside to let me in.

The tree house was warm, a fire crackling in the small hearth. Inside, the Christmas lights gave the space a soft glow. It felt cozy, like a home. But the tension radiating from Alejandro was palpable, and I knew something was terribly wrong.

We sat down by the fire, and for a moment, we didn't say anything. The sound of the wind rustling through the trees and the distant ringing of bells from the farm below filled the silence. I was there to find answers, but I didn't know where to start.

Finally, he broke the quiet. "I saw Charlie's obituary." Alejandro's gaze was distant. "I've been out here at the tree house, avoiding town.... I didn't even pay my respects. I should've been there."

I looked at him, surprised. "I didn't realize you and Charlie knew each other that well."

Alejandro let out a long sigh, his shoulders slumping. "He and I...we weren't best friends, but we had an understanding. We'd talk now and then, usually about town business or whatever project he was working on. Charlie was a good man, and he had this way of knowing when things weren't quite right in our community. That was what worried me."

"What do you mean?" I asked, my pulse quickening. "What would Charlie have noticed?"

Alejandro looked down, rubbing his hands together as if trying to warm himself. "It's...complicated. The company I used to work for, the one I left— let's just say they don't take kindly to loose ends or people who know too much. I have this sinking feeling that Charlie was getting wind of something he shouldn't have known."

I stared at him, stunned. "Do you think...they'd go that far? They'd get rid of Charlie?"

Alejandro looked up, his eyes shadowed with worry. "I can't say for sure, Annee. But that company—they don't like risks. To them, it doesn't matter if you're a mailman or a CEO. One person with the wrong information in the right hands can start an avalanche. And Charlie was exactly the kind of man who would've kept digging if he thought something was off."

My mind raced, piecing together everything he was saying. "Is that why you left the burner phone for me to find? So I could use it to reach you if things went wrong?"

Alejandro nodded, barely lifting his eyes enough to reach mine.

I punched him softly. "That's so cloak and dagger! Couldn't you just tell me?"

Alejandro nodded, his expression softening. "It worked out fine, didn't it? Aren't you here now?"

I nodded, rolling my eyes.

"When you turned it on, it notified me right away. But it also gave you a lot of information that would allow you to find me if you needed to. There's even a map in the phone's notes showing the way here. I...I didn't want to leave you guessing if things went south. I knew something could happen at any time. People have been after me for a while, or at least I thought they might be after me. That line between paranoia and reality seemed to be blurring for me more and more each day."

I took a deep breath, processing his words. "And Monique? She's been giving you advice through all of this?"

"Yeah," he admitted, his voice barely above a whisper. "Monique's been my lifeline. She's neutral, just offering guidance, keeping me steady when everything feels like it's slipping out of control."

"And you think the company might be involved in...in what happened to Charlie?"

He didn't answer right away. He just looked away into the darkening woods. "I don't know, Annee. But if they are...I don't know how far they'd be willing to go next."

A cold shiver ran through me as I watched him, understanding the depth of the fear that had driven him into hiding. "Alejandro," I whispered, barely able to believe it. "What are we dealing with here?"

When he didn't say anything, I took a deep breath, steadying myself. He seemed so worn down, as if the weight of everything was finally catching up to him. But I needed answers.

I kept my voice as even as I could. "I know you were in business with Charlie and the others. With Magda and Felix's farm. Hazelton Farms. Why didn't you tell me?"

His head snapped up, surprise flashing in his eyes. "You know about that?"

I nodded, watching him closely. "Yes. I found out after Charlie passed. I found some information about the venture in his study. But it would've been a lot easier if you'd just told me the truth."

Alejandro opened his mouth as if to respond, but then his gaze fell, and he seemed to reconsider. For a moment, it looked like he was going to explain, but instead, he just ran a hand through his hair, his expression guarded. "Annee, it's...complicated," he finally said, his voice barely above a whisper.

"Complicated?" I echoed, feeling a mix of frustration and worry. "Do you even realize what this looks like? Why would you keep this from me? I thought we trusted each other."

He looked away, his jaw tense. "It wasn't about trust, Annee. I just...I didn't want you involved. Charlie's death doesn't end this. If they silenced him, it only proves what they'll do to anyone who gets too close. And I'm still carrying pieces they'd rather stay buried."

The raw edge in his voice sent a shiver through me. I thought back to the day he'd first arrived at my doorstep, his electric car packed with everything he owned. Back then he'd been my closest foodie friend, vibrant and outspoken, always fighting for fair trade and predicting the next food trend. But the man who showed up that day had looked worn down, hollowed out. His fire had been smothered.

It wasn't until months later that he admitted why. He'd worked for a fast-food parent company that promised change and ethics but delivered something far darker. An outbreak, people dead. And when a powerful agrochemical giant swept in to "absorb the ruins," it didn't just mean buying the company—it meant erasing its ideals, covering up its failures, and burying every voice that might have exposed the truth. Alejandro had tried to blow the whistle, but in the end he broke.

His voice was low when he finally went on. "I've been looking over my shoulder ever since. I knew too much, and companies like that don't forgive. They don't forget. Some days I even wondered if having you near me was selfish, if keeping close to you meant I was painting a target on your back."

I swallowed hard, the pieces clicking into place. "So keeping this secret wasn't just about you," I whispered. "You thought it wasn't even safe to have me near you."

Alejandro raked a hand through his hair, his fingers trembling slightly before he dropped them to his lap. He still wouldn't meet my eyes, and that silence told me more than any answer ever could.

Before he could say anything more, a sharp knock echoed through the tree house. Alejandro and I both froze. My heart leapt into my throat as I stood and walked to the window.

Outside, Chief Cora and two officers were outside the door, their flashlights cutting through the darkness.

"Alejandro," I whispered. "It's Cora."

He paled and stood up abruptly. "No," he muttered, backing away. "They can't—this isn't happening."

I barely had time to react before the door swung open and Chief Cora strode inside, her presence commanding the small space. The two officers positioned themselves just behind her as she looked at Alejandro. Her expression was unreadable, but the weight of her purpose filled the room. "Alejandro Martinez," she said firmly, holding up a piece of paper, "I have a warrant for your arrest in connection with the murder of Charlie Watson."

Her tone was steady, but not without a hint of regret. She glanced at me briefly, her eyes softening for a moment, before turning her attention back to him. "This is serious, Alejandro. I'd suggest cooperating fully."

The room felt impossibly small, the silence stretching taut as the words settled.

Alejandro's eyes widened in shock. "What? No, that's not possible!" His voice cracked, and he took a step back, shaking his head. "I didn't—"

Cora raised a hand. "Charlie was injected with a concentrated hazelnut extract, Alejandro. You knew about his allergy. The syringe was found in your cottage."

Alejandro froze, staring at her in disbelief. "A syringe? No, that's...that's impossible." His voice wavered, and he looked at me, desperation in his eyes. "Annee, I swear, I didn't do this."

I felt the floor drop out from under me. "Cora, wait—this has to be some kind of mistake. Alejandro would never—"

"The evidence was found in his cottage, Annee." She shook her head, her face grim. "And he knew about Charlie's allergy. The syringe contained a large enough dose to trigger a fatal reaction in someone with Charlie's allergy. Whoever prepared it knew exactly what they were doing. We also believe the incident with Emerson, though accidental, served as a cover. It diverted attention from Charlie's death."

Alejandro's face went white. "No, no, I didn't...I would never...." He stammered, his voice breaking as he looked between me and Cora. "This is insane."

"I'm sorry, Alejandro," Cora said, stepping forward. "But we have to take you in. We'll let the courts decide the rest."

The officers moved in, and I felt the room closing in on me. Alejandro raised his hands slowly, his eyes filled with a mix of disbelief and terror. The sound of the handcuffs clicking around his wrists echoed in the small tree house, and I stood there, as if in a trance, silently watching as they led him toward the door.

"I didn't do this, Annee," Alejandro said over his shoulder, his voice barely a whisper. "You have to believe me."

Tears filled my eyes, and I nodded. "I believe you, Alejandro."

I kept my focus on him as the officers closed the cuffs around his wrists. He flinched at the cold snap of metal and looked up, his eyes catching mine with a flicker of fear he couldn't hide.

The Christmas lights twinkled softly around us, a cruel contrast to the scene unfolding.

Cora didn't say it, but from the way the cruisers had rolled in just moments after I arrived, I knew they'd tailed me. She gave my arm a quick squeeze before turning back to her officers.

I tried not to feel helpless as they took him away, but the evidence was stacked against him, and now it was up to me to find the truth before it was too late.

Chapter 16

Avoir la Moutarde Qui Monte au Nez:
To Have Mustard That Goes Up the Nose (to lose your temper)

The early snow had blanketed the town in a soft, quieting layer of white. There hadn't been a real winter like this in years, the kind when you could feel the chill settle deep into your bones. With the cold snap hitting hard, the market had been slowing down. Crowds were thinning, and vendors were already packing up, deciding it wasn't worth braving the icy weather. The town council was doing their best to rally local crafters, food trucks, anyone they could get to fill the empty spaces. But with the streets growing colder each day, even the locals were choosing cozy indoor gatherings over wandering around the market, huddling for warmth.

And then, of course, there was Alejandro.

I couldn't stop replaying everything he had told me, wondering how much he had left out. But one thing was clear: the wrong man was behind bars. Alejandro hadn't killed Charlie, and with him in custody, the police had officially closed the case. Cora had made that clear. She wasn't looking for any more clues, and there would be no more digging around or following up on loose ends. As far as the law was concerned, the matter was resolved.

But I knew the case wasn't over. Maybe the corporation wasn't pulling the strings this time, but I was certain of one thing: it wasn't Alejandro.

I wove through the thinning crowd, my cup of cocoa warm in my hands, when a man stepped into my path. At first I only knew he looked familiar, and then it struck me—he was the man I had passed outside Charlie's house, the one whose eyes had unsettled me even as his words were polite.

It took me a moment to place him. Roy. Charlie's stepbrother. The town librarian. Gone was the weathered pea coat, the sleepless stubble. He was clean-shaven now, his collar pressed, as if he had resumed his rightful place in Hazelton society.

Maybe there was room for him again now that Charlie was gone.

"Miss Bonne Annee," he said, inclining his head in a mock-formal greeting. "I've heard your name whispered everywhere since the dinner. Funny how quickly one becomes the talk of a small town... especially when tragedy is involved."

He let the words hang before adding, "Alejandro and his digital books... a man like that is easy to distrust. But I can understand why he might have wanted Charlie gone."

I forced a brittle smile. "Poe warned us, didn't he? 'Believe nothing you hear, and only one half what you see.'"

Roy's mouth curved in the faintest smirk, but he said nothing, letting the silence stretch until my skin prickled. Before he could speak again, I slipped past him, cocoa sloshing as I hurried into the crowd, pulse racing.

I was so tangled in my thoughts that I nearly walked straight into someone. My cup tipped, half-empty and cooling, and I looked up just in time to see Paul steadying me with a gloved hand.

"Hey, stranger," he murmured, his eyes scanning my face. "You okay?"

I forced a smirk. "Super, comme toujours."

"So maybe not okay... you know you're speaking French, right? Maybe another cup of hot cocoa?"

I sighed, pushing a gloved hand through my hair. "Sorry. Just a lot on my mind."

"Come on," he said gently, gesturing toward the nearby cocoa booth. "Let's warm you up." He put his arm around me, guiding me toward the booth.

"I'm sorry about Alejandro," he said, his voice low. "I haven't wanted to crowd you, but I've been worried."

"Thanks. I'm worried too." I sighed.

We stood in silence for a moment, sipping the steaming cups the vendor handed over, until Paul spoke again, carefully. "So...did you hear what happened with Ilsa?"

I glanced up, surprised. "What do you mean?"

"She's apparently Charlie's cousin," he said, his tone edged with disbelief. "On his European side. His next of kin. He left everything to her—the house and the land. And she's already moving in."

I blinked, trying to process it. "I didn't even know he had family overseas."

"Neither did anyone," Paul said grimly. "That's what makes it strange. The paperwork's all official, but it blindsided everyone. And with Roy back..." He lowered his voice further, as if the snow-dampened streets themselves might overhear. "The way they both turned up at the same time is hard to ignore. I don't like the feel of it either."

I frowned. "Roy and Ilsa?"

Paul nodded once. "People are saying there might have been something between them. Maybe that was part of the rift between him and Charlie.

And if it's true, it makes her inheritance and his sudden return all the more tangled. It wouldn't be the first time Hazelton kept a family scandal quiet."

Now, with Ilsa moving into Charlie's home, I'd lost access to one of the few places where I could have looked for more answers. No more snooping through Charlie's things, no more late-night attempts to piece together clues in his quiet, empty rooms. I had no choice but to let it go, at least for now.

I wrapped my scarf tighter and pulled my coat around me as I wandered silently with Paul through the near-empty market. The world felt muted under the thick blanket of snow, but inside, my mind buzzed with questions I couldn't silence. Alejandro hadn't been completely honest with me, but his fear had been real. If he was right about the corporation being dangerous, about Charlie knowing something he shouldn't have...was Alejandro truly in danger?

Paul could see I wasn't with him, that emotionally I was somewhere else. "Bonne Annee, I've got to get back to the office. Don't stay out here too long."

"I won't. Thank for the fresh cocoa." I looked up at him and he brushed a stray hair away from my face. For a moment, maybe I did believe Christmas was the most romantic time of the year, because even in my mental fog, my heart leapt.

"I'll call you later. Okay?" He smiled.

I nodded, and then he turned and walked away.

As I watched a few vendors load up their trucks, ready to leave before the next snowfall, a surge of determination cut through the haze. Alejandro didn't belong behind bars, and I wasn't about to let my friend take the fall for something he didn't do. If the police thought the case was closed, then it was up to me to pry it back open.

Charlie had brought Ilsa here for the market job, and now she was settled into his house as heir. At the same time, Roy had returned after years away, slipping back into Hazelton life just as if there'd always been a place waiting for him. Maybe there was—now that Charlie was gone. I couldn't ignore how neat it all looked, or how quickly the story shifted from tragedy to inheritance.

There were too many secrets circling Charlie's death, and I wasn't about to stop until I uncovered them.

But first, I had to get through my favorite hosting event of the year.

Chapter 17

Ce n'est pas de la tarte:
It's not pie (It's not easy)

The Sugar Plum Fairy Tea had always been one of my favorite holiday traditions at The Literary Table, and this year, it felt more important than ever. After everything that had happened, I needed something to bring a sense of joy and normalcy back to the bookstore. I needed something to remind me that the holidays still held magic, even in the shadow of all this uncertainty.

As families began arriving, I watched the kids in pastel tutus and tiny tiaras twirling around the room, their faces lit up with excitement. The sitting room of the inn was bathed in soft, warm light, and I had taken extra care with the decorations this year. Candy canes hung from every garland, tucked between the boughs of pine and holly that draped the banisters and mantel.

Twinkling fairy lights danced across the walls, and a towering Christmas tree sparkled in the corner, its branches heavy with ornaments and strands of tinsel. I'd even managed to go against my purist rules and find those rare sugar-plum-flavored candy canes that tasted like a combination of figs and maple syrup, which I tucked into the garland alongside the traditional red and white stripes.

Tchaikovsky's *Nutcracker Suite* played softly in the background, the delicate notes of the "Dance of the Sugar Plum Fairy" filling the room. The music wove its way through the soft murmur of conversation and laughter, creating a serene atmosphere. For a moment, it felt like everything was exactly as it should be—peaceful, festive, and joyful.

I made my way around the room, refilling tea cups with hot chocolate instead of tea for some of the little ones and chatting with the guests. All while I kept one eye on Emerson, who was sitting quietly by the fireplace. He was still recovering from his allergic reaction and though he smiled at me whenever our eyes met, there was something fragile about him now. My heart tightened a little every time I thought about how close we came to losing him. He had agreed to stay on for the rest of the holiday season, while Sylvester had returned to his life in the big city. I took him a plate of all the treats I'd prepared.

To distract myself, I busied my hands with the food table. The candy cane scones, crumbly and delicate with their peppermint crunch, disappeared almost as quickly as I set them down. The sugar plum tarts, filled with spiced plum compote and dusted with powdered sugar, looked like little snowdrifts and vanished just as fast. Children clutched mugs of rich peppermint hot chocolate, each with a candy cane stirring stick, and licked the whipped cream moustaches from their lips before taking a sip. A cluster of chocolate mice, complete with licorice tails and tiny chocolate chip eyes, had been an ode to the Nutcracker's Mouse King, but by now only a few tails remained. For balance, I'd baked cranberry orange tea cakes too, their citrus tang cutting through all the peppermint sweetness.

The atmosphere was so festive that I almost managed to forget about the knot of anxiety that had been twisting in my stomach for days. Almost. But then I saw Magda, one of the owners of Hazelton Farms, sitting at a corner table with a polite smile on her face, sipping tea with a small group of women while other families with children dined nearby. I knew she'd only gotten her ticket earlier that day, a last-minute addition to the guest list. She looked perfectly at ease among the laughter and music, but I couldn't shake the feeling that her presence was more deliberate than casual. For all the warmth in her smile, her eyes seemed to be watching more than they were enjoying. I felt a chill run through me. Hazelton Farms. Ever since I'd found that letter confirming the contamination of their hazelnut products, I hadn't been able to stop thinking about the farm, the food, the investors, and what it all meant. Magda's presence felt too convenient, too calculated.

I glanced at Emerson by the fire. He gave me a slow nod, as if to say, *Go on—ask her.*

By now, I had filled Emerson and Mack in on all my theories of Alejandro's innocence, including the potential contamination. I remembered a conversation I'd had with Emerson earlier, when I'd tried to learn more about his connection with Alejandro outside of Hazelton. He hadn't had much to share. Alejandro had once reached out to him while writing his book, hoping for connections in the publishing world, but Emerson hadn't lifted a finger. Reflecting on that now, I realized Emerson had always struggled to form deeper ties, even with people who needed him. Maybe, though, he was finally starting to change. He was on my team.

Taking a deep breath, I straightened my shoulders and walked over to Magda's table, trying to keep my tone light, even as the nerves fluttered in my stomach.

"Magda," I said, smiling. "I'm so glad you could make it today."

She looked up, her smile warm, but a little too practiced. "Oh, Annee, this is such a lovely event! The children are having the best time, and these sugar plum tarts are delicious."

"Thank you," I replied, forcing my own smile to stay in place. "I'm glad you're enjoying them. It's always such a pleasure to bring everyone together for the holidays."

There was a pause. I could feel my mouth getting dry and my pulse quickening, but I knew I had to ask. "I've been meaning to ask—how's everything going at the hazelnut farm? You must be busy with the Christmas market."

Magda's expression flickered, just for a second, but long enough for me to notice. "Yes, it's been busy," she said, her voice measured. "The market has been great for business."

I nodded slowly, my smile fading. "I've heard there's been some trouble. Something about contamination?"

Magda's hand froze as she reached for her teacup. She set it down slowly, and I could see her knuckles turning white as she gripped the saucer. "Where did you hear that? Alejandro?"

"I came across some…concerning information," I said carefully, keeping my voice low. "A letter from a lab. It seems some of your products were contaminated with *E. coli*. And after what happened to Charlie…and to Emerson…." I trailed off, watching her face.

Magda's gaze darted nervously around the room to see if anyone else was listening. The children's laughter and the soft strains of the *Nutcracker Suite* seemed to wrap around us, insulating our conversation, but the tension between us was thick.

"That's not true," she whispered, shaking her head. "Our farm is inspected. We're careful. We'd never—"

"Charlie had the test results, Magda," I interrupted, my voice sharp and accusatory. "He knew. And now he's dead. Emerson nearly died. What do you think that means?"

She paled, her eyes widening as she finally met my gaze. "It's not what you think," she whispered, her voice trembling. "We didn't know about the contamination until it was too late. Felix—he thought we could fix it before anyone found out."

My heart pounded in my chest as anger surged through me. "People are dead, Magda. You can't just cover it up and hope it goes away."

"We didn't mean for anyone to get hurt," she said, her voice barely audible. "We were just trying to take care of our business."

"Business?" I hissed. "You have to make this right."

Her eyes filled with tears, and for a moment, I almost felt sorry for her. She nodded. "We already have fixed it. It's over. It had nothing to do with Alejandro and Charlie. Cora already talked to us. We did a quiet recall. No need to hurt the brand over this."

"What do you mean it doesn't have to do with Alejandro? He's sitting in jail as I'm trying to raise bail for him. I know he didn't hurt Charlie. And I also know that he knew about the contamination. Charlie's death, Alejandro's arrest... it's all related to your farm, isn't it?"

"I'll talk to Felix," she said, her voice cracking. "We'll figure it out. Maybe we can help with bail. But if Alejandro *did* kill Charlie, he deserves to be there."

I straightened up, my fists clenched as I turned away from her. My heart was still racing, but I knew I had to calm down before I went back to the guests. I caught Emerson's eye from across the room. He was watching me closely, and when I gave him a small shake of my head, he nodded back, a frown of understanding in his eyes. It was comforting to have another ally in this house. My secret wish was that Emerson would stay on forever, and if I ever did fill this house with a spouse and children, maybe he would settle in this town and we could all become one big happy family.

The idea was irrational, I knew that. But the weight of exclusion—of always feeling like I didn't quite belong—made that dream feel almost unbearably appealing. The desperation to create that connection overshadowed the reality that he already had his ticket home.

The children continued to laugh and dance as the *Nutcracker Suite* played in the background, and the Sugar Plum Fairy Tea carried on as though nothing had happened. But for me, the sweetness of the holiday had turned bitter. I wouldn't be able to celebrate the season until Alejandro was free.

Chapter 18

S'Occuper de Ses Oignons:
To Take Care of One's Onions (to mind one's own business)

I decided I needed to see what the other investors knew about this "quiet recall" Magda told me about at the tea. At the top of my list was Sophia. She always had an air of elegance about her, even when surrounded by the musty scent of ancient books and the quiet hum of the community college. She was one of those people who could juggle multiple academic pursuits without ever seeming frazzled. Managing the college extension program at the library, overseeing the historical society, and teaching online courses at prestigious universities had somehow not been enough for her. She had earned multiple PhDs, and her thirst for knowledge only seemed to grow. Every time you thought she had reached the peak of her capabilities, she would find another hill to climb.

But for someone so accomplished, Hazelton seemed like an odd place for her to stay. It was no secret that she was ambitious, and her sights had long been set beyond the confines of this small Oregon town. The few glimpses I'd had into her personal life had come from rumors and snippets of conversation. At the Poe dinner, I remembered Charlie saying she had suggested inviting Emerson, and that meant she had been the reason Emerson was in town. And when I looked through Charlie's papers, I noticed that there had been copies of Sophia's opened letters as well, so I wanted to see what the full picture was.

When I'd asked Emerson about Sophie, he only said that she had reached out about using him as a job reference in New York. She had made the Christmas market sound so intriguing and he had been feeling weirdly nostalgic, so he had decided to check it, and her, out. I just happened to live here too.

My mind kept circling back to what I'd uncovered at Charlie's house. On my second trip through his study, I found a small folder tucked beneath his correspondence, letters between Sophia and Emerson that Charlie had quietly copied. It was just like him, always observing, always recording details others overlooked. This time, though, what he'd kept revealed far more than I expected.

Sophia always had her dark hair swept up, her clothes impeccable, as though she were perpetually preparing to step onto a lecture stage. But in her letters, she dropped the facade. She was candid about her ambitions, angling for a job in New York, desperate to run her own department. Hazelton, with its quaint traditions and close-knit community, wasn't enough for her anymore. She wanted the city, the prestige, the recognition she believed she deserved.

Emerson's response had been blunt, almost cutting. *You're not really qualified for the position, Sophia,* he'd written. But he added that out of friendship, he would "see what he could do." But then he sent her letters back, as if to draw a firm line. That small gesture said more than the words themselves; it was the same pattern I'd seen with Alejandro. When he could have stepped in, he didn't.

Maybe that rejection had stung more than Sophia let on. And with her money tied up in Hazelton Farms, perhaps she saw Charlie as an obstacle too. If he had uncovered the contamination issue, it could have ruined the very investment she was counting on to buy her way out of this town. Two problems, one solution.

I decided to stop by her office at the college to ask a few questions, though I wasn't entirely sure what I expected to learn.

The community college wasn't particularly remarkable—it was a red brick building, unadorned, with faded carpets lining the halls and the scent of freshly printed paper filling the air. It was the kind of place where dreams either blossomed or withered in the face of practicality. Students hustled between classes, balancing books and phones, their faces a mix of youthful optimism and finals fatigue. They were mostly locals, many of whom probably saw Hazelton as a stepping stone, just like Sophia had done.

As I walked through the halls, I couldn't help but notice the dichotomy of the student body. There were the younger students, fresh out of high school. Then there were the older students, the ones who had perhaps taken a break from education or who were now returning to reinvent themselves. Their faces were lined, their stares more focused—like they knew exactly what they wanted and weren't going to waste any more time getting it.

Sophia's office was at the far end of a quiet wing, its door slightly ajar. I knocked lightly, hearing her voice inside. She was speaking with someone, and after I peeked in, I saw her sitting across from another professor. He was tall, maybe in his mid-forties, with silver streaks running through his dark hair and a smile that seemed a little too knowing. Sophia laughed lightly at something he said, and the way she leaned back in her chair, crossing her legs, gave the impression that this was more than just an exchange of academic ideas.

I cleared my throat softly, and Sophia glanced up. For a split second, there was something unreadable in her eyes—surprise, maybe even annoyance—but it quickly vanished. She straightened up, smoothing her blouse, and waved me in.

"Come in, come in. What a nice surprise," she said, her voice as polished as ever. "I was just finishing up here."

The professor stood, offering me a polite nod before turning to Sophia. "I'll see you later?" he asked. His tone was casual, but there was a hint of expectation beneath it.

Sophia's smile was quick, calculated. "Of course."

As he left, I couldn't help but wonder. Was she cultivating yet another connection, keeping her options open since the path with Emerson was closed and the Hazelton Farms investment was possibly in jeopardy? I wouldn't put it past her to use every tie left in this town as a rung on her ladder out.

I took a seat, glancing around her office. It was meticulously organized and her shelves were lined with academic journals, history books, and framed certificates. A large window overlooked the quiet campus courtyard, where students milled about, bundled up against the December chill.

"I wasn't expecting a visit," Sophia said, her smile tight. "What can I do for you?"

I wasn't sure how to approach the topic of the letters without tipping my hand too much, so I started with something else. "I wanted to ask about the Christmas market," I said. "You were the one who invited my cousin to town for it, right?"

Her smile softened, and she nodded. "Yes, your cousin really helped me organize some thoughts about press for the event. Charlie had asked me to write something academic to support Hazelton's aspirations to create something authentic. European Christmas markets are a lovely tradition, aren't they?"

I could tell she was deflecting, trying to steer the conversation away from anything too personal. But I wasn't here for pleasantries. "I've been hearing some things," I said carefully, "about your plans. Specifically, something about a job in New York?"

For a moment, her eyes flickered with surprise, but she quickly regained her composure. "It's not public yet," she said. "But yes, I've been exploring opportunities. Hazelton is a lovely town, but it's not where I see my future."

Her tone was casual, but I could sense there was more beneath the surface. "Emerson's involved, isn't he?" I pressed.

Sophia's gaze sharpened. "What exactly do you know?"

"I know a few things. But let's start with your investment in Hazelton Farms," I said, choosing my words thoughtfully. "What do you know about the recall?"

For a moment, I thought she might shut me down, but then her shoulders sagged slightly, and she sighed. "That's one of the reasons I felt like leaving this town. I sold my shares back to Felix and Magda after the recall."

I was surprised. "You don't have any shares left?"

"No. They offered me a way out, in case things got messy. They didn't want me to rescind my full investment."

I leaned in. "But you're in the middle of it, aren't you? You're part of whatever's going on. How close were you and Charlie, really?"

Sophia met my gaze, her expression unreadable. "I just tried to make the best of my situation. Charlie was a great guy. He's the one that told me about the investment in the first place. I was hoping to make a little more money than what I make on my academic salary." She gave a little shrug. "Hazelton…it's fine for some people. But for me? I need more. I want more. And if Hazelton Farms could help me get that, I wasn't going to turn Charlie down."

There was something almost vulnerable in her admission. For all her intelligence and accomplishments, Sophia was still chasing something— validation, success, or maybe an escape from the small-town life she had outgrown. The ambitious academic who was so often in control now seemed to be at the mercy of forces beyond her control. And as I sat there, I realized that whatever was happening in Hazelton was different than I had imagined. There were secrets everywhere, and I had only begun to scratch the surface.

Chapter 19

Rouler Quelqu'un dans la Farine:
To Roll Someone in Flour
(to trick someone)

T he strains of "Rockin' Around the Christmas Tree" mingled with the laughter and chatter of the partygoers. Mackenzie's Ugly Sweater Country Christmas Party was in full swing, and it seemed like every corner of the large, wood-paneled family room was filled with people celebrating. The Gothic Victorian details of the inn's social club space—the dark beams, ornate fireplace, and massive windows draped in red and gold—were decked out in holiday decor. Twinkling lights wrapped around everything they could be wrapped around, and a massive Christmas tree stood tall in one corner, covered in vintage ornaments.

I took in the scene from the food table, smoothing the front of my ridiculous sweater—a garish, light-up monstrosity with a cartoon Santa riding a reindeer. I had to admit, the vibe was festive, even if I felt a bit distracted. In the center of the table sat my nine-layer dip, a nod to the season. I'd swapped out the traditional ingredients for some holiday flair—layers of refried beans, spiced sour cream with a hint of cinnamon, salsa, guacamole sprinkled with pomegranate seeds for a pop of color, and sharp cheddar topped with a scattering of festive green onions and cilantro. It was a hit, and I watched as Katie's brother Mickey scooped up a hefty portion with a red tortilla chip, grinning from ear to ear.

"Annee, this is amazing," he said, waving a chip in my direction. "I'm going back for thirds!"

I laughed, though my mind was elsewhere. "Glad you like it."

Mackenzie bounced over, her energy infectious. Her ugly sweater—decorated with glittering cowboy boots and Christmas lights—flashed in sync with the Christmas song playing overhead. She pulled me into a quick side hug.

"Come on, Annee! The ugly sweater contest is about to start. You've got to enter. You'll win for sure—look at that thing!" She gestured dramatically at my sweater, and I couldn't help but laugh.

"Maybe next year. I think this one would dim out any competitor," I teased, pointing at the flickering lights in her outfit.

Mackenzie shook her head, her eyes sparkling. "Suit yourself. Wait until you see Katie's sweater—it's got a full-on light-up Nativity scene."

I spotted Katie across the room, and her sweater did indeed have an over-the-top spectacle of glowing stars and shepherds. I shook my head with a grin.

Mackenzie leaned closer. "Oh, and did you hear? Charlie's stepbrother is back in town."

My smile faltered. "Yes, the old librarian. I've seen him."

She nodded eagerly. "Yeah, Roy. that's the one. He's been back since before the Poe dinner. Already stirred things up at town meetings, making a fuss about the Christmas market. Says it's gotten too money-grabbing, not looking after the town's best interests.

"And the Santa fight? He's practically leading it. He can't stand that the committee gave the role to some out-of-towner who went to *Santa school*, instead of picking one of our own. He keeps saying Hazelton doesn't need a professional Santa to tell us how to do Christmas."

A chill ran through me. Now I remembered him clearly. Before he left, I had donated a stack of books to the library where he worked, and he had fussed over cataloging every last one. Polite, meticulous, but with an edge to him, as if he were always judging people by their book choices. I could only imagine what he thought of me and my donations—maybe that I owned far too many Jane Austens.

"How's he handling Charlie's death?" I asked quietly.

Mackenzie shrugged, lowering her voice. "I don't think they were close. But I guess they were family, and that has to mean something."

"Funny," I murmured. "If that's true, you'd think he would've shown up at the funeral."

I tried to stay in the moment, but my thoughts kept wandering back to Alejandro, sitting alone in jail. It didn't seem right that we'd be out here tonight, celebrating and gossiping, while he was locked up for something he didn't do.

Marc and Mickey were setting up a dance floor at the far end of the room, their ugly sweaters almost as wild as Mackenzie's. Then Joe's band kicked on some music with "Santa Looked a Lot Like Daddy" in the lyrical refrain. Couples started to gather in the open space to dance, and the party's energy shifted up a notch. Music and laughter filled the air.

I glanced down at Oscar, who sat patiently by my feet, his Christmas bow-tie slightly askew. He looked up at me with those big eyes, as if sensing my internal debate. But I still hadn't questioned Paul. I whispered to my furry confidant, "*Quoi faire, chéri*, what should I do?"

Just then, my phone buzzed in my pocket. I fished it out, and Cora's name flashed on the screen. I moved to a quieter corner, pressing it to my ear. "Hey, Cora, what's up?"

Her voice was heavy, more serious than I expected. "Annee, I need to talk to you about something. It's about Charlie."

I froze. "Charlie? I'm listening."

"The autopsy results just came back," Chief Cora said, her voice sounding grim. "The coroner found something in his system—ricin. It's a naturally occurring poison from castor beans. It's incredibly toxic and was mixed into the hazelnut extract. The symptoms it causes will typically mimic a severe allergic reaction."

Alejandro's case was getting worse by the second. His background in food science and manufacturing made him an easy suspect. If someone had wanted to frame him, his expertise as a food specialist would make it seem plausible that he had access to and knowledge of these substances.

I felt the blood drain from my face. "Ricin?"

"Yeah. I know you've been asking questions around town. And since evidence was found on your property, that's the only reason I'm giving you a heads up," she said bluntly. "I'm saying you might need to lawyer up. The murder happened on your property, and while you're not being accused of anything, your house, your land—they're right at the heart of all this. Evidence was found there. You might also want to check in with your insurance agent again. It might make sense to close up shop during this investigation."

I clutched the phone tighter. I couldn't even connect with the party's joyful hum right now now.

"I know this is hard to hear, but I thought you should know."

"I…I have to go," I said abruptly, my voice tight. "Thanks for telling me, Cora."

I ended the call and stood there for a moment, trying to gather myself. The music and laughter around me felt so far away, like I was watching the party from another world. Something was seriously wrong, and I couldn't just stand there, pretending everything was okay.

I glanced down at Oscar, who wagged his tail, as if urging me to make a move. I couldn't ignore this any longer. Alejandro might be in danger—or worse. I needed to see him.

"Sorry, Oscar," I whispered, feeling a twinge of guilt. "You're staying here this time." His ears perked up as if he understood, but his eyes stayed glued to me. He clearly was not thrilled.

Standing, I spotted Mackenzie across the room and called her over. She approached me with a curious look. "What's up?"

"I have to head out," I said, nodding toward the door. "Can you keep an eye on Oscar for me? He's not too happy about being left behind."

Mackenzie smiled and reached down to scratch behind Oscar's ears. "Don't worry—he'll enjoy the party. I'll make sure he gets plenty of attention."

"Thanks," I said, giving Oscar one last pat before heading toward the door. The stars twinkled overhead as I stepped outside, my breath puffing in the crisp air.

I hoped it wasn't too late for a visit at the jail.

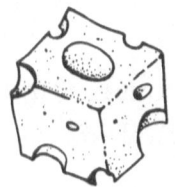

Chapter 20

En Faire Tout un Fromage:

To Make a Whole Cheese About It (to make a big fuss over nothing)

I took a steadying breath and stepped through the doors of the jail, still wrapped in my ridiculous ugly Christmas sweater. I knew I looked more suited for a holiday party than a late-night visit to a jail, but I pushed that small truth aside. I was determined to find a way to help Alejandro, even if that was just bringing him a friendly face and some holiday cheer.

I was led to a small room where Alejandro was already seated. He looked haggard, his eyes dimmer than usual, and when he looked up at me, I saw the faintest flicker of relief.

"Annee," Alejandro began in a low voice, "I know you're not here just to check in. I'm guessing you've heard some of what's going on?"

I nodded, settling into the chair across from him. "Cora told me. They found ricin in the syringe, blended with hazelnut extract. She said things aren't looking good for you."

He gave a slow, weary nod, his gaze fixed on the table. "I never wanted you pulled this far in. But now... I don't know who else I can trust."

I leaned forward. "Then tell me everything. No holding back."

Alejandro rubbed a hand over his face. "All right. You still have the burner phone?"

I pulled it from my bag, the weight of it heavier than it should have been. His eyes darkened when he saw it.

"Annee, I need you to listen carefully. Weeks ago, I planted two motion-triggered recorders on Felix and Magda's farm. I know it was illegal. That's why I didn't tell you—I didn't want you dragged into this. I thought I could manage it on my own."

The air between us seemed to thicken. "So you have recordings?"

He shook his head. "I didn't set up remote access. Too risky. If anyone traced the feed, it would've led straight back to me. The files are only stored on the devices themselves. Which means if the police ever find them..." His voice trailed off.

Understanding jolted through me. "They'd have proof you trespassed."

"Yes." His voice was barely above a whisper. "That's why I need you. The maps and instructions are hidden in Monique's chat on the phone." He hesitated, then added, "I stashed a kayak near their property. It's the only way to get in without being seen."

I tightened my grip on the phone. "So you don't want me to spy. You want me to get rid of the evidence."

His gaze lifted to mine, raw and unguarded. "Exactly. Annee, if they find those devices, I'm finished. You're the only one I can trust to keep me safe."

Before I could answer, the door opened. Cora stood in the frame, her expression grave. She beckoned me into the hall.

As we walked together, she lowered her voice. "You were right to keep digging, but you need to be careful. Working with ricin takes real expertise, and I'm not convinced your friend isn't hiding something. Don't let loyalty blind you."

I forced a tight smile. "I hear you."

But inside, my resolve only hardened. Alejandro didn't belong behind bars, and I wasn't about to let my friend's life be destroyed by Hazelton Farms or anyone else. Whatever it took, I would protect him.

I gripped the phone tighter, my pulse racing. "Thank you, Cora. For everything."

She gave me a quick nod. "Don't do anything reckless, and don't go making things harder for yourself. You don't want to be implicated in any way."

"I won't." I forced a tight smile, though my pulse betrayed me, beating hard in my throat.

The burner phone weighed heavily in my pocket as I walked toward the exit, Cora's words still ringing in my ears. Reckless or not, I knew what I had to do. If I wanted to save Alejandro, there was only one choice. I had to reach those devices before anyone else did.

Chapter 21

Ramener sa Fraise:
To Bring One's Strawberry (be in someone's business)

Kayaking in December along the Oregon coast wasn't something I'd usually sign up for, but there I was, pulling my kayak silently along the shoreline. Alejandro knew I couldn't afford to be seen on the road, since Felix and Magda's hazelnut processing plant was just inland. I was following the GPS coordinates I found on Alejandro's phone, hoping they'd lead me quickly to the recording devices.

I'd kayaked before, mostly in calm lakes during the summer when the air is warm and the water reflects the sky like glass. But this? Kayaking in early December off the Oregon coast was a whole different beast. The wind bit at my face, and each time I dipped my paddle into the water, the chill seeped through my gloves. The gray waves slapped against the sides of the kayak, splashing icy saltwater over my boots. The cold was a constant, prickling presence. My fingers had already gone numb, and my breath came out in cloudy puffs that quickly vanished into the mist.

Still, I pushed forward, paddling hard but keeping my eyes alert. The road wasn't far, just up the hill past the dunes, and if Felix or Magda were around, I didn't want them to see me. Adrenaline and anxiety kept my heart pumping strong, so I was warmer than I should have been. I felt flushed as I pulled my paddle the water, stroke after stroke.

The coastline here was rugged, lined with jagged rocks that jutted into the sea like ancient, broken teeth. Thick, windswept pines clung to the cliffs, their branches bent and twisted by years of harsh weather. And the fog—it was everywhere, wrapping the shoreline in a damp, ghostly veil that made it hard to see more than a few yards ahead. Even the birds seemed subdued, their cries muted as they circled above the waves. A few ravens broke away, their dark forms gliding toward the horizon, as if pointing the way and guiding me toward my destination.

I put down the paddle and glanced at my phone. The screen showed the location of the devices I was trying to find. Alejandro had equipped them with a tracking system similar to that of an Air Tag. I'd just need to be close enough, and my phone would reveal their locations.

I was close. The coordinates led inland, but I had to time my landing perfectly. There was a small cove ahead, shielded by the cliffs, where I could slip onto the beach without being seen. I glanced toward the processing plant, its low buildings barely visible through the trees, and spotted movement. Someone was walking along the edge of the property. My pulse quickened. I knew that walk and that blond hair.

Ilsa. She was there, too.

The wind shifted slightly, bringing with it the earthy smell of damp foliage and wood smoke from somewhere in the distance. I pulled the kayak up onto the shore, hiding it among the rocks and driftwood before crouching low, keeping my eyes on Ilsa as she moved along the perimeter of the plant. Why was she there? And why was she so comfortable on Felix and Magda's property?

I took a deep breath, the cold air burning my lungs as I fumbled with my phone. On the "Find My Device" app, the location pinged again, just inside the processing plant. I waited, watching as Ilsa disappeared around the corner of one of the buildings. Then I made my way up the slope toward the plant, keeping close to the trees for cover. My body moved on instinct, fear and adrenaline making my steps quick but silent.

Felix and Magda's hazelnut farm didn't run a full crew on the weekends, and that was why I chose today to sneak in. During the week, it was a bustling operation. Trucks came in and out, picking up shipments of their hazelnut products and delivering them all over the Pacific Northwest. There were always truckers stopping in at Katie's Café, fueling up on a good meal before hitting the road again. But on a Sunday in December, the place was quiet— just the hum of machinery and the occasional clang of metal from someone checking equipment.

I knew from casual conversations in town that Felix and Magda followed a strict routine. Felix, the early riser, started his day before dawn, checking the hazelnuts in the silos and making sure the humidity levels were perfect. He moved through the warehouse, inspecting every corner with sharp eyes. Magda, on the other hand, handled the paperwork and business contacts. On weekends, she preferred to walk the plant, keeping an eye on the few employees working odd shifts. They ran this place like clockwork, knowing every inch of the property.

I slipped around the back of the plant, staying low. The factory hummed softly. The machines that usually roared with activity on weekdays were silent now, waiting for Monday morning to resume their work. Felix had probably checked the silos already, so I was anticipating a basically empty site.

The Christmas decorations scattered around the property felt out of place, like someone tried to bring a little holiday cheer to this otherwise cold and sterile place. A half-deflated inflatable Santa slouched near the entrance, his jolly face sagging. Strands of mismatched lights were haphazardly wrapped around wooden posts, blinking irregularly, giving the whole scene an eerie vibe. A tired plastic snowman stood by the office door, his smile cracked and his scarf faded, but someone had draped him in fresh tinsel, a weak attempt at festivity. Even the factory windows were decorated with cheap, peeling adhesive snowflakes.

Just outside the main entrance, a small, scraggly Christmas tree was set up, its branches sparsely adorned with chipped ornaments and a lopsided angel topper. The wind rustled its meager decorations, making the glass baubles clink together softly. Next to the tree was a wire reindeer, wrapped in white lights that flickered intermittently, like it was struggling to stay lit in the misty coastal air.

I glanced toward the silos, thinking about the unfinished message on Alejandro's phone—*they're hiding it in the silos.* Whatever "it" was, it was there among the hazelnuts. My stomach tightened. I checked my bag for my EpiPen, just in case. One wrong move around all those hazelnuts, and I could end up in serious trouble.

I ducked behind a stack of crates near the back of the plant, peering through the window. My eyes were drawn to the small processing line visible through the cracked window. Even on a quiet weekend, the machinery was still at work, churning out the hazelnut candies that made Felix and Magda's farm famous.

The candies rolled off the line, carefully wrapped in holiday-themed packaging—bright red foil with tiny gold stars, a perfect nod to the season. The finished chocolates were then packed into boxes with festive ribbons, ready to be shipped off as Christmas gifts.

The door to the plant stood slightly ajar, just wide enough for me to slip inside. The factory was dim, and instead of the roar of machinery I'd expected, only a faint, distant hum echoed from somewhere deeper in the building. The unnatural quiet set my nerves on edge.

I took a deep breath, bracing myself, and moved quietly down the hallway, glancing at Alejandro's burner phone. The screen displayed two small red dots: one marking the location of a device there in the plant, and the other in the office nearby.

The signal on the phone grew stronger as I moved past a row of crates, and I spotted the device, nestled near the base of a storage rack. It was a small, discreet motion-activated recorder, its black casing blending into the shadows. Alejandro had made sure it was well hidden. I reached down and quickly pocketed it, feeling a rush of relief. *One down.*

As I turned to head toward the office, I heard faint footsteps echoing from down the hall. My heart skipped, and I ducked behind a nearby stack of boxes, waiting. The footsteps slowed, then stopped. I held my breath, my pulse blaring in my ears.

After a few tense moments, the footsteps resumed, fading away. I exhaled and pressed forward, following Alejandro's map. The office door was closed, and as I pushed it open, the phone's signal grew stronger. The device was somewhere inside, but I'd need to be fast.

The office was sparse, but organized, with stacks of files and a few cabinets. I scanned the room, watching the phone's indicator carefully. The red dot hovered in one corner, leading me to the edge of a filing cabinet. *Got it!* I reached down.

Just then, I heard the faint sound of voices outside. I froze, my hand inches from the device. The voices grew louder—Ilsa, speaking with someone, her tone serious. I couldn't risk making a sound. Slowly I crouched, edging myself against the cabinet, out of sight.

Ilsa's voice grew louder as she entered the office next door. Her words were muffled by the walls, but her presence was unmistakable. I had to remind myself to breathe while my hand hovered over the device. And I forced myself to wait—to listen—praying they wouldn't come in.

After what felt like an eternity, Ilsa's voice faded again, her footsteps retreating down the hall. I recognized another voice with her. She was walking with Magda. I let out a shaky breath, my hand finally closing over the device. I stuffed it into my pocket, resisting the urge to check the burner phone again. Better to switch it off now and move quickly, before anyone noticed I'd been there at all. Outside, the cold night air felt like freedom, and I took a deep, calming breath. I had both devices, but Ilsa's presence lingered in my mind—an unsettling reminder that this wasn't over yet.

I slid the kayak into the water, the icy waves splashing against my hands as I climbed in and pushed off from the shore. My whole body was tense and my senses were on high alert as I paddled away from the farm and from everything I'd just seen. The fog was thick, curling around me, muffling every sound except the faint splash of my paddle slicing through the water.

My breath came in quick puffs, visible in the cold night air as I dug the paddle deeper, pushing myself farther from the shore. Relief mingled with fear, I had the devices, tucked safely away. Whatever they contained, at least they hadn't fallen into the wrong hands. I looked up, glancing back over my shoulder just as the silhouette of a figure emerged on the dock. My stomach dropped as I recognized him. It was Felix, scanning the water, his eyes squinting through the mist as he searched the shoreline.

"Annee?" he called out, his voice cutting through the silence like a knife. "Is that you?"

I forced myself to stay low, tightening my grip on the paddle. I pushed forward, pretending not to hear him, each stroke propelling me farther into the darkness. The water was freezing. It seeped through my clothes and numbed my hands, but I paddled harder, my arms aching as I tried to keep my movements steady and quiet.

I didn't look back again. The fog swallowed everything behind me, including Felix's voice. Only when the farm was nothing but a small, dark outline against the mist did I finally allow myself to breathe, slowing my strokes, letting the weight of what I'd just done settle over me.

I'd escaped, but the truth felt heavier now than ever, resting in my pocket— dangerous, elusive, and almost within reach.

Chapter 22

Aller se Faire Cuire un Œuf:
To Go and Cook Oneself an Egg (to go somewhere to be left alone)

The next morning it was still too early to visit Alejandro, and I didn't know how to listen to the recordings on the devices. He hadn't filled me in on that part. I wasn't sure what my next move was, so I made a batch of gluten-free lemon blueberry muffins, and then bundled up and made my way with Oscar over to Jasper's house.

It was a chilly, crisp day, the fields dusted in white. Jasper's greenhouses glowed faintly against the snowy landscape, a small oasis of green in the dead of winter. It was how he kept his garden thriving, even now. His house sat on the outskirts of Hazelton, where the land opened up into wide fields and dense woods. You'd think a fire chief might live closer to town, but Jasper liked his space and privacy.

Even so, he had never been removed from the community. He was the sort of man who brought baskets of tomatoes to the firehouse in the summer, herbs and greens to the inn's kitchen in the fall, and shared seeds with anyone who asked. That steady generosity, paired with his reliability on duty, was part of what made him such a trusted figure in Hazelton.

As I approached, I could see the towering figures of snowman scarecrows dotting the landscape, their coal eyes staring blankly out at the horizon. They had been up since the fall harvest, Jasper's defense against the flocks of ravens that had grown bolder after the Poe dinner brought so many into town. Now, instead of taking them down, he'd redressed the figures in old winter coats and scarves, some of them even wearing hats. They were eerie and oversized, his own quirky version of holiday decorations. Jasper had no love for the birds, particularly ravens, and even less so after they started loitering around his property, scavenging for food.

Jasper was bent over in his greenhouse, hands dirty from the soil as he adjusted the temperature on the climate controls. He looked up when he saw me approaching, wiping his hands on a rag before walking out to greet me. His tall, broad frame moved easily despite the cold, and he smiled warmly as I neared, though there was always something a little weary behind his eyes.

"Well, well, if it isn't the queen of the literary event," he said, his voice gravelly but kind.

I laughed, the sound more awkward than I intended. "Not quite, but thanks for the vote of confidence." I glanced around at the snowmen. "Still fighting off the birds, I see?"

He chuckled, nodding toward the scarecrows. "Yep. They don't like the look of these fellas. Keeps them off my garden and out of my hair. Can't say I miss their cawing, either."

I stood next to him, looking over his shoulder into the greenhouse. The plants inside were lush and green—vibrant despite the season. Jasper had always had a gift for gardening. He grew everything from heirloom tomatoes to winter greens and root vegetables, all tucked away in the safety of the temperature-controlled greenhouse. I admired his setup. It reminded me of how people like him were the backbone of Hazelton, quietly nurturing the town in ways that didn't always make the headlines, but mattered deeply to those who lived here.

"You've really outdone yourself," I said, peeking inside at a row of leafy greens. "I'm guessing the firehouse is well-stocked."

He grinned. "I try. The boys love it. There's something about pulling a meal together from things you've grown or caught yourself, you know? It just tastes better. Come see what we have growing back here."

He led me toward the back of the greenhouse, where a small, shallow pond glistened under the soft glow of overhead lights. It was part of a clever aquaponics system, with the water carefully maintained to stay room temperature, even in the winter. The pond held the last few trout of the season, their silvery bodies darting lazily through the clear water. "And when I'm not gardening, I'm fishing," he added with a wink, his pride evident in the way he gestured to the setup.

I nodded, knowing he took pride in bringing fresh catches to the firehouse for communal meals. Jasper's specialty was Oregon trout, though he was known to go out for salmon and even steelhead when the weather was warmer. He'd clean and fillet the fish, then prepare it with his signature recipe—a blend of fresh herbs from his garden, lemon, and a touch of olive oil, cooked over an open flame. The firefighters loved it, and it had earned him more than a few blue ribbons at local cooking contests.

"You ever get tired of it?" I asked, half-joking. "Living off the land, catching your own food?"

Jasper smiled. He bent down and picked a few heads of cabbage, placing them in a basket. "Nah. It's in my blood. There's something honest about it. You plant the seed, tend the soil, and eventually, you get what you've worked for. Same with fishing—there aren't any shortcuts."

He glanced over at me as he handed me a head of cabbage. "It's like anything in life, really. Things grow best when you give them the right environment. And when something starts to go wrong, well, you notice."

The way he said it made me pause. I wasn't sure if he was talking about gardening or something else. His words hung in the air, and I wondered if he knew what I'd come here to ask.

"About Charlie…" I began cautiously, watching his face for a reaction. "You were close with him, weren't you?"

Jasper straightened up, setting his basket of vegetables down. "Yeah. Best friends since grade school. Why?"

I hesitated, unsure how much I should push. "I've been thinking a lot about him lately. About what happened."

Jasper's face remained neutral, but his eyes darkened a little, like he knew where I was headed. "It's a damn shame, what happened to Charlie," he said quietly. "But what can you do? Sometimes things go wrong, no matter how well you tend them."

I bit my lip. This was Jasper's way—never quite giving a direct answer, but always speaking in metaphors. It was part of what made him so good at what he did. He could calm people down in a crisis, make them feel like everything was going to be okay, even when it wasn't.

"I heard rumors," I continued carefully, "that Charlie had some…habits that weren't exactly aboveboard."

Jasper didn't react immediately, but I saw his grip tighten on the edge of the greenhouse door. "People talk," he said slowly. "They always do."

"Did you ever know anything about Charlie's, um, interest in other people's mail?" I asked, feeling a little bold. "It's come up more than once in town gossip, and I wondered if you ever noticed anything strange."

Jasper's eyes met mine, and for a moment, I thought he was going to answer me directly. But then he gave me a small, wry smile and shook his head. "Charlie was a good man," he said firmly. "He took care of this town in ways people didn't always appreciate. But we all have our secrets. That's the thing about small towns like Hazelton—we're fragile. Everyone's playing a part, keeping the gears turning, but once you pull a major piece out, the whole thing could come crashing down."

He bent down again, plucking a few more vegetables from the garden and placing them in the basket. "My advice? Let Chief Cora and her team do their job. They know what they're doing."

There was so much more I wanted to ask, so many things I didn't understand. But Jasper had drawn his line, and I respected that.

"Thanks, Jasper," I said softly. "I just don't want things to get worse."

Jasper gave me a long, measured look before handing me the basket. "I know. But sometimes you've got to trust that things will grow back, even after they've been trampled on."

He walked me through the greenhouse, his large frame brushing past rows of leafy greens thriving in the carefully controlled environment.

"This is where I keep the good stuff." He let out a little chuckle.

The longer I stood among the rows, the more I noticed the air wrapping around me, humid and earthy, so different from the crisp chill outside.

Toward the back, a small shelving unit held neatly lined jars of preserved goods, their amber and ruby hues catching the soft glow of the greenhouse lights.

He stopped and grabbed a jar from the shelf, holding it up with a small smile. "Here," he said, handing it to me. "Pickled peppers from last summer's harvest. Good on just about anything."

I took the jar, its glass cool against my hand. "Thank you," I said, glancing at the shelf filled with the fruits of his labor. "You've really got this whole setup figured out."

He shrugged, the hint of pride in his expression belying his casual tone. "It keeps us going through the winter. Nothing like a little summer in a jar when the world outside is gray."

I smiled, taking the jar from him. "I'll put it to good use."

"Take care, Annee," he said, giving me a gentle pat on the shoulder before turning back toward his greenhouse. "And don't forget to water the seeds in your life. With a little trust and patience, they'll grow when the time's right." I knew he was speaking metaphorically, but was he talking about the clues to Charlie's murderer, or Paul?

I watched him walk away, his figure fading into the misty morning, and felt a mixture of gratitude and frustration. Jasper knew more than he was letting on—I was sure of it—but in his own way, he had given me an answer. The town was fragile, and everyone was connected. Charlie's death, Emerson's allergic reaction, Alejandro's trouble—it was all part of something larger, something I didn't fully understand yet.

As I made my way back toward town with Oscar trotting beside me, I couldn't help but feel a chill that had nothing to do with the cold. Hazelton was changing, and whether I liked it or not, I was caught in the middle of it all.

Chapter 23

Être Bonne Poire: To Be a Good Pear
(to be gullible or easily swayed by others; to be a pushover)

I decided to stop by and pick up some hot chocolate for Cora on my way to the jail. I hoped she might be open to letting me have some extra time with Alejandro. The Christmas market buzzed around me, full of warmth and holiday cheer, but then I saw someone moving toward me, whose determined step made me feel like there was ice sliding across my skin. She moved through the crowd with her usual grace, her sharp eyes catching mine with unsettling precision. She was wrapped in her deep green coat, her fair hair pulled back neatly.

Maybe on a usual day, an encounter with Ilsa wouldn't have scared me so much. But now, knowing what I did—that she had likely seen me at the

Hazelton Farm yesterday, and that she and Charlie were related, which she had hidden from everyone—her presence felt menacing.

"Annee," she said, her voice soft, but as chilly as the December air. "Good to see you out here. I wasn't sure you'd have the nerve after…everything." She tilted her head, her eyes narrowing just slightly as she studied me, as if searching for cracks.

I swallowed, fighting to keep my expression calm. "It's a public market, Ilsa," I replied. "And I have a right to be here, especially when people I care about are in trouble."

She gave a faint, humorless smile. "Care about? Yes, that's what I assumed you'd say. Poor Alejandro, don't you think? Such a shame your friend turned out to be a murderer." She stepped closer, her voice dropping to a low, almost intimate murmur. "But then, people have their suspicions, don't they? How convenient that you were so quick with your EpiPen that night. Quite the savior."

I could feel my face getting hot, her words agitating me. "I was prepared because I needed to be, Ilsa. I didn't expect anything to happen. It was a coincidence."

Her expression didn't waver, but I caught the faintest glint in her eyes, something cold and calculating. "Coincidence. Yes, that's one way to explain it. But it's interesting, isn't it? How you were the first one to respond to Emerson's episode… and how it almost looked as if you knew exactly what to do. As if you'd seen it coming." She leaned in a little closer, her breath curling like frost in the cold air. "Tell me, Annee, do you always carry a syringe around?"

The question hit me like a slap, and I forced myself not to flinch. "You know as well as anyone that I have allergies, and I'm prepared for them. That's all it was."

Her eyes drifted to my bag, and she lifted a delicate eyebrow. "Really? And tell me, Annee, are you…up to date on your prescription? I'd imagine someone with your condition would be careful about things like that. You wouldn't want to be caught off guard, after all."

I felt the blood drain from my face. I hadn't refilled my prescription, hadn't even thought to check the expiration date. The realization settled over me, a chilling awareness that I'd been carrying an outdated EpiPen, that I was more vulnerable than I'd even known. And somehow, Ilsa knew—or was she just guessing I hadn't replaced the one I had used at the house to save Emerson?

"Why are you bringing this up, Ilsa?" I asked, my voice barely more than a whisper.

She leaned even closer, her voice dropping to an almost conspiratorial whisper. "Oh, just thinking of you, Annee. It would be such a tragedy if something happened to you, especially after all this unfortunate attention around Alejandro. And with your allergies, well…." She gave a cold, tight smile. "Let's just say a little exposure to the wrong ingredient could be disastrous, couldn't it? A slice of the wrong pie, a sample of hazelnut candy—anything could be dangerous in the wrong hands. Maybe you should think about refilling that prescription soon…for your own safety. And you might also want to stay away from places that have an abundance of your allergen, like the Hazelton Farm."

Her words washed over me like a freezing wind, every syllable layered with a threat. Felix had seen me and he must have told her. My hand instinctively tightened around the strap of my bag, where my outdated EpiPen rested. Ilsa's gaze flickered down to my hand, a faint smile curving her lips as she straightened, looking away casually, as if we'd been discussing nothing more than the weather.

"You might think me cold, Annee," she continued in a low, measured tone, "but I did care for my cousin Charlie. We kept our connection quiet, out of respect for others who wanted to run the market. He gave me the job, and you know how people talk. I guess he thought you were trustworthy." Her eyes snapped back to mine, and I caught the flash of something dark in her gaze, something that felt dangerously close to anger. "So I hope, for both our sakes, that you stay out of this. Let the police handle it. After all, isn't that what Charlie would want?"

I stood watching as she turned and melted back into the crowd, her green coat blending seamlessly with the festive shoppers, her pale hair a faint glimmer in the distance. I stared after her, watching her disappear, each word she'd said pulsing through me, leaving an unsettling rhythm in its wake. The thought crashed over me, cold and relentless: Ilsa knew everything that Charlie had known.

And if I wasn't careful, would she use it against me and suggest that I was involved in Charlie's murder?

Chapter 24

Compter Pour des Prunes:
To Count for Plums (to be worthless or unimportant)

I entered the police station, clutching the hot chocolate I'd picked up for Cora, hoping a small gesture might ease some of the tension. The place was quiet. Only the distant hum of conversation and the shuffle of paperwork broke the silence. I spotted Cora at her desk, looking more tired than usual, her brow furrowed in concentration.

"Hey," I said, offering the cup. "Thought you might like this."

Cora looked up, her expression softening just a bit as she took the cocoa. "Thanks, Annee. Appreciate it." She took a sip, seeming to relax for a moment before she glanced back up. "Here to see Alejandro, aren't you?"

I nodded, trying to keep my tone casual. "If it's all right. Just want to check in on him."

Cora sighed, giving me a long look before she nodded. "Five minutes, and I'll be right outside the door."

I followed the officer down the hallway to the small, bare room where Alejandro sat, looking tired but alert. His eyes lit up a little when he saw me. "Annee," he said, leaning forward. "Glad you made it."

I took a seat across from him, keeping my voice low. "I managed to retrieve the devices, but I need to know how to access the recordings."

Alejandro nodded, glancing at the door before meeting my eyes again. "The instructions to unlock the recordings are on the burner phone. Go to the folder labeled 'M' and look for a file named 'Memory.' The password and access instructions are all there."

I nodded, storing the details in my mind, but I couldn't shake the nagging feeling that this visit was being closely monitored. "Alejandro… they're listening, aren't they?"

He gave a resigned shrug. "I'd say there's a good chance, yeah. But you needed to know."

Before I could ask more, the door opened. Cora stepped in, her expression sharp, and fixed her gaze on me. "Alright, Annee. Time's up."

She held out her hand, palm up, and I knew there was no way around it. I reluctantly took out the burner phone and handed it over, feeling a pang of regret.

Cora pocketed the phone, her gaze hardening. "And those recording devices you retrieved? Those are evidence now. You shouldn't have touched them in the first place."

I opened my mouth to argue, but Cora's voice took on a sharper edge. "Listen, Annee, you've been meddling enough. Keep it up, and you'll find yourself in a cell right next to Alejandro's."

My heart sank, a mix of frustration and defeat settling over me. All I could do was nod. "Understood," I muttered, not bothering to hide my disappointment.

Cora softened slightly, her tone almost grateful as she took the devices. "Thanks for bringing these in. This might actually help us move things forward. Now, go home, get some rest, and stay out of this."

I glanced at Alejandro as he was led back to his cell. There was a look of apology in his eyes. I gave him a small, sad smile, but it was all I could manage. There was nothing more I could do here.

As I left the station and stepped into the cold air, feeling defeated, my phone buzzed in my pocket. I pulled it out, surprised to see a message from Paul.

I'd reached out earlier, needing to talk, since he was one of the last investors in the farm. But I was nervous about what I might learn.

Now, his message glowed on the screen:

I've got something special planned for you. Let's talk soon.

I stared down at Paul's message, my heart doing an odd little flip. *Something special planned for you.* I couldn't help but feel a thrill of curiosity mixed with a pang of nerves.

My fingers hovered over the call button, and before I could overthink it, I pressed it, holding my breath as the line rang.

"Bonne Annee!" Paul's warm voice came through. "Hey, I wasn't expecting to hear from you so soon."

I felt myself smile, my nerves loosening just a bit. "Yeah, I...well, I saw your message, and I'm intrigued. Something special?"

There was a slight pause, a hint of amusement in his tone when he responded. "I've been thinking it's time we went on a proper date, you know? Not just a quick coffee or a chance run-in. How about dinner tonight? You can bring Oscar."

The words hit me like a spark, my pulse quickening. I'd known Paul for years, but we'd always been somewhere in between friends and something more. We always skirted the edge but never quite crossed it.

"A real date?" I repeated, my voice coming out a little breathier than I'd intended.

"Yeah. Just you and me and Oscar, no interruptions."

I could feel the warmth rising to my cheeks. "I'd love that."

"Good." His voice softened. "I'll pick you up at four—we need to get an early start. Sound good?"

"Perfect," I said, barely containing the smile that spread across my face.

"Oh, and Bonne Annee?" he added with a playful edge in his tone. "I promise we'll talk about Charlie and anything you want to know. And I'm taking you to the lighthouse."

I laughed softly, the nervous excitement settling into something warmer. "Deal. See you tonight."

As I hung up, I felt a mixture of relief, excitement, and maybe even a touch of hope. Tonight wasn't just about answers anymore. It was about the possibility of something more—something I'd been waiting to feel for a long time.

Chapter 25

took a final glance in the mirror, adjusting the collar of my snug wool coat over the thick sweater underneath. I'd paired it with my favorite plaid holiday scarf and soft gloves. As the doorbell rang, I pulled on a knit hat and hurried to answer.

When I opened the door, Paul stood there, looking so handsome in a dark jacket and a similar plaid scarf. He flashed a smile, his eyes twinkling as he looked me over. "You're looking beautiful and well-prepared for a chilly evening."

I laughed, patting the layers. "I figured I'd need to dress warm if we're spending time at the lighthouse in December."

Paul's grin widened as he held up a bag filled with garlands, fairy lights, and small ornaments. "Exactly. I thought we'd have a little dinner there, but I might have signed you up for decorating duty too—if you're up for it." This was one of Hazelton's community traditions. Anyone could sign up to decorate the lighthouse for the holidays. It was an inclusive opportunity which had led to a Diwali makeover in October.

"Decorating the lighthouse? Absolutely!" I replied, grinning. "Oscar and I are ready for anything."

At the sound of his name, Oscar trotted over, already bundled in his new winter sweater. Paul gave him a good scratch, then held the door open for both of us.

Once in the car, with Oscar cozied up in the back seat, I leaned back, feeling the excitement settle over me. I was trying to take mental pictures. Tonight was my first real date with Paul.

I wanted to remember every moment—the twinkling lights, the quiet beauty of the lighthouse, and this long-awaited moment with him.

Why was I being so naïve? I still didn't know what I might find out. Did he know about the contamination? Was he part of the cover-up? I needed to temper my romantic hopes until I knew more. Charlie had been murdered, and I still didn't know by whom.

The crunch of snow beneath our boots was soft and steady as we made our way toward the lighthouse at the edge of Hazelton's coast. Oscar trotted happily beside me, his black and white fur a striking contrast to the dusting of white powder that coated the ground. The salty air from the ocean mixed with the faint scent of pine from the garlands Paul carried over his shoulder. There was something enchanting about decorating a lighthouse in the midst of winter, with the waves crashing in the background and the cold, bracing air reminding me of the promise of a new season.

Paul walked beside me, his strong figure silhouetted by the setting sun's golden glow across the snow-covered landscape. His presence always brought a sense of comfort, grounding me in a way that felt both new and familiar. Today, we weren't just decorating any building—we were adding life to one of Hazelton's oldest landmarks. And I knew Paul cared for it deeply, as part of his role with the Parks and Rec department.

I kicked a little snow in his direction. "It's a little colder than I thought it would be."

"Bonne Annee, I thought you were used to the cold," Paul said, turning towards me with a grin. I smiled at the use of my true name, the one my mother had chosen for me—a name that felt distant now, like a relic of the past.

"I still can't believe you call me that," I teased, brushing a strand of hair out of my face. "You're one of the only people who ever uses it."

"I like it," he said, adjusting the garlands in his arms. "It suits you. It means new things and new beginnings. And I think you're in for some new beginnings yourself."

The words struck me. New beginnings. It was a beautiful thought, though tinged with a bit of sadness. Christmas always made me think of my mother and grandmother, who were both gone now. My mother, missing and presumed dead, left a hole in my heart that hadn't healed. My grandmother, who had been my anchor after my mother's disappearance, was also gone. Every Christmas I longed for the closeness I once had with my family. I had missed my cousins deeply, the warmth of those bustling holiday gatherings, and now with Alejandro's recent arrest, I was worried that without clearing Alejandro's name, I would lose another loved one.

But I pushed those thoughts aside as we reached the lighthouse.

"We should start with the wreath on the door," Paul suggested, pulling a large wreath from the cart we had wheeled over. The lighthouse was small but sturdy, standing proud against the winds of the Oregon coast. The stone structure was simple, its whitewashed walls weathered by years of guiding ships to safety.

Paul handed me the wreath, and we worked together to hang it on the old wooden door. The cold made my fingers tingle, but the satisfaction of seeing the wreath in place—a simple but beautiful touch—warmed me.

"Perfect," I said, stepping back to admire our work.

Paul smiled at me, his breath visible in the chilly air. "Let's do the lights next."

The snow glittered around us as we strung twinkling lights along the small fence that bordered the lighthouse. The sun was dipping lower on the horizon, casting pink and purple hues across the sky, and soon the only light would come from the twinkle lights we had carefully wrapped around the fence and doorway.

I paused to look out at the ocean, the waves lapping against the shore, rhythmic and constant. The sound was soothing, and for a moment, I closed my eyes and let it wash over me.

"You okay?" Paul asked gently.

I opened my eyes to find him watching me, concern etched on his face.

"Yeah," I said softly, "just...thinking about my mom. Christmas was always her favorite time of year." I hesitated before continuing, "She's been gone for so long, and now my grandmother is too. I guess I just miss that sense of family, you know?"

Paul stepped closer, his arm brushing against mine. "I know it's not the same, but you're not alone, Annee. You've got people who care about you— my family, for one."

I smiled at him. His family had always been warm and welcoming. His mother, a lover of literature like me, had attended several of my Literary Table events. She was everything a matriarch should be—strong, kind, and always ready with a fresh pie. And then there was Paul, the only unmarried sibling in his family, now an uncle to a growing brood of nieces and nephews. His family always went to church together on Christmas Eve, something I admired from a distance, even though I hadn't set foot in a church since my childhood.

"Thank you," I said, meaning it more than he probably knew.

We finished the decorations, wrapping the lighthouse in lights, garlands, and even a few vintage ornaments inside, giving the cozy interior a festive glow. Once the work was done, Paul set out a blanket on the snowy ground. The air was crisp, but there was no wind, and the cold wasn't biting. It was the kind of winter evening that invited you to sit outside and enjoy the beauty of the world while wrapped in a blanket. Paul started a little bonfire.

He had also packed a picnic basket, and I'd brought one as well. His was filled with thermoses of gluten-free pasta topped with grilled chicken and olives. He'd also tucked in a small gift—a box of candy canes, knowing how much I loved them. But when I opened it, I realized these weren't just any candy canes—they were "ugly sweater" flavors. Instead of peppermint, they came in mac and cheese, pickle, hot dog, ketchup, and, most shockingly, sour cream and onion.

I tried to hide my horror as I looked up at Paul, who was grinning with genuine excitement. "Try one!" he urged. "I bet you'll love the mac and cheese. I almost got the bacon flavor, but I figured, as a candy cane fan, you might've already tried it."

Taking a deep breath, I unwrapped the mac and cheese candy cane and hesitantly took a bite. As a novelty, it wasn't terrible, but it certainly wasn't Christmas. I forced a smile. "Oh, wow! It really does taste like mac and cheese. Thank you for remembering I love candy canes." And I meant it—he had remembered, and he had tried, and that counted for something.

We settled by the fire, with me cozied up next to him, determined to appreciate the thought behind the bizarre candy canes as he shared stories from the Christmas market. "The most popular booth today was the West African Gullah fusion spot," he said, still animated. "I thought it would be the German booth with the bratwurst and mulled wine, but there was no contest."

"Oh really?" I replied, popping another bite of the macaroni-flavored cane into my mouth, grimacing a bit. "That's surprising. Any market drama?"

"You bet. There was a fight at the booth selling nesting doll Santas." He chuckled. "And the hazelnut booth? Completely unmanned all day."

My interest piqued at that. "Really? Why weren't they there?"

He shrugged. "No one knows. I saw Magda and Felix around town, but I'm not sure why they ditched the Christmas market. Not sure what could have been more important than showing up to their own booth."

I nodded, filing that curious detail away. The strange candy cane flavor lingered on my tongue, but I relaxed beside Paul, thankful for the cozy evening, odd treats and all.

I opened up my picnic basket. "I made something special," I said, a little nervous. "Mini Bûche de Noël—two versions, one with peppermint cream, and the other with hot chocolate cream."

Paul's eyes lit up as he took in the sight of the small yule logs, each one carefully decorated—one with tiny candy cane pieces and the other with a light dusting of cocoa powder. I poured us both steaming mugs of hot chocolate from a thermos, and we settled on the blanket, watching the last rays of sunlight disappear over the horizon.

"This is amazing," he said after taking a bite of the peppermint one. "I didn't think you could outdo yourself, but this…wow."

I laughed, feeling a warmth spread through me that had nothing to do with the hot chocolate. "I wanted it to be special."

"It is." He looked out at the water, his face bathed in the soft glow of the lights we had hung. "Everything about this night is special, Bonne Annee."

I smiled. His glowing endorsement warmed me up inside.

For a moment, we sat in silence, the only sound the gentle rhythm of the ocean. The lighthouse stood tall behind us, its light just beginning to glow in the encroaching twilight. I rested my head on Paul's shoulder, feeling the weight of everything lift, even if just for a little while.

He wrapped his arm around me, pulling me closer. "Bonne Annee," he whispered again, "new things are coming. I can feel it."

And under the magical Christmas lights, I believed him.

Oscar settled himself between us on the blanket, his eyes glued to the slice of cake on Paul's plate. Every time I shifted, Oscar nudged his nose closer, his tail wagging slowly as he tried his best to look innocent. Then finally, he inched his nose just close enough to try and sneak a nibble.

I laughed, gently pushing him back before he got his taste. "Oscar, this is people cake! You already had your treat," I said, but he ignored me, attempting to cozy himself right between Paul and me, determined to be the center of attention.

Paul chuckled, scratching Oscar behind the ears. "Persistent little guy, isn't he?"

"Oh, you have no idea. He's got a way of charming his way into just about anything." I leaned back against Paul, savoring the warmth of his arm around me and the coziness of the evening.

But as much as I wanted to relax, there were questions I needed to ask. So I took a breath, looking up at Paul, and said, "So…about Hazelton Farms. You're one of its investors, right?"

He nodded slowly, his gaze fixed on me and his expression blank. "Yes. Why do you ask?"

I hesitated, my voice softer. "Did you know about the contamination?"

He shook his head, his tone turning defensive. "No, I didn't. I would never have supported anything like that, Bonne Annee. I believed in the farm, and I trusted that they were doing things right."

I let his words hang in the air for a moment, then said, "I spoke with Sophia recently. After she found out about the contamination, she decided to sell her shares. She was given the chance to get out." I studied his face. "Did they make the same offer to you?"

His expression hardened. "I wasn't offered any way out. And honestly, Bonne Annee, I don't appreciate the implication here." His voice was strange, like there was a note of hurt creeping in. "I trust Magda, Felix, Jasper…and especially Charlie. The only Hazelton Farms investor who's proven to be untrustworthy is Alejandro."

I swallowed, surprised by his reaction. "Paul, I'm just trying to understand what's really going on. Why would Alejandro—"

"You need to ask yourself why your friend would have wanted to kill Charlie." His gaze was steady, unwavering. "That's the real question."

We sat together in silence for a long while before, wordlessly, we began packing up the picnic. Paul's hands paused over the basket, and he looked over at me, his expression softening.

"I'm sorry, Bonne Annee," he murmured. "You didn't grow up here like I did. Charlie…he was like family to me. It's been hard to wrap my head around everything that's happened."

I nodded, feeling the weight of his words. "I understand," I replied gently, reaching out to give his hand a reassuring squeeze.

We packed up the rest of our picnic in silence. Even Oscar seemed to sense the change, settling quietly in the back seat on the drive back. The warmth between Paul and me was gone.

As we sat together in the car, I felt a pang of regret for bringing up Charlie and the investigation. On the car ride home, I tried to recapture the easy feeling we'd once shared, but I could see the tension in Paul's face as he kept his eyes fixed on the road.

Finally, I turned to him, my voice sincere. "Paul, I'm sorry for upsetting you. I thought Charlie was special too. I just know this isn't something Alejandro could have done." I took a breath, gathering the courage to add, "Can we put this behind us? I'd love for you to come with me tomorrow to deliver my annual town gifts."

He looked at me, his expression softening, and I could see the glimmer of the warmth that had drawn me to him in the first place. After a pause, he shook his head slightly. "I'm sorry too, Annee. I shouldn't have snapped. I know you're only trying to do what's right."

Without another word, he stepped out of the car, came around to my side, and opened my door. Oscar hopped out eagerly, and Paul reached out to take my hand, guiding me gently from the seat.

Then he leaned in, brushing his lips against mine in a tender kiss. "I'll meet you in the morning," he said softly. "Just text me when you get there."

I smiled, trying to suppress the excited tingling feeling that made its way through my entire body. "I will."

With a final look, he turned and headed back to his car. Oscar and I watched him go, a sense of calm settling over me as I thought about the day ahead. I felt like the sixteen-year-old version of me. I didn't know if I should write in my diary first or call Mack. After all, I'd just had my *first kiss with Paul.*

Chapter 26

Couper la Poire en Deux:
To Cut the Pear in Two (to split the difference; to compromise)

The next morning, the wind cut through Hazelton as Paul, Oscar, and I made our way through the streets with the snow crunching under our boots. Despite the cold, the town bustled with holiday shoppers moving between the small, locally owned businesses that dotted the town. People shuffled along the sidewalks, bundled in thick coats and scarves, their gloved hands gripping paper bags filled with Christmas gifts. Wisps of warm breath rose in the frosty air, and the hum of friendly chatter gave Hazelton that unmistakable sense of home—where everyone's traditions and laughter intertwined.

But beneath the glow of twinkling lights and familiar faces, the tension weighed on me, pulling me away from the holiday warmth. The comfort of the season felt out of reach, replaced by a lingering unease that seemed to seep into the cold, settling into my bones.

Charlie was dead, Alejandro was under suspicion, and now there was news that the Christmas market was hanging on by a thread. It hadn't brought in as much revenue as they thought it would, and with Charlie gone, they didn't think it was worth doing again.

Paul, walking beside me, offered me a sidelong glance. "You're awfully quiet today."

I shook my head, forcing a small smile. "Just thinking."

"You've been doing a lot of that lately." He chuckled softly, giving Oscar's leash a gentle tug as the dog paused to sniff at a snowbank. Oscar, dressed again in his new little red sweater, was blissfully unaware of the tension. He trotted happily between us, his tail wagging as snowflakes landed on his fur.

"I've been trying to piece everything together," I said, sighing as we passed under the towering pine tree in the town square, its branches covered in twinkling lights. "It's just…a lot. Everything's gone sideways. I feel like I'm missing something big."

Paul nodded thoughtfully, his breath puffing out in small clouds. "Well, that's why we're out here, right? Asking questions? I thought about it and if you really trust Alejandro, then I'm going to have your back on this."

I was feeling lucky that he trusted me more than he distrusted Alejandro. It helped to have him by my side. Paul had always been level-headed—a grounding force—especially when things started to spiral. But there was a complication: his family's long-standing friendship with Magda and Felix. Alejandro had suggested that Magda might be involved in Charlie's death, and while Paul was willing to help investigate most leads, I knew digging into Magda's life made him uncomfortable. That meant I'd likely have to do some of this on my own.

Just then, a sharp voice carried across the square.

"Hazelton deserves answers!"

I turned to see Roy standing near the fountain, bundled in a dark wool coat with a clipboard clutched in his hand. A small knot of townsfolk huddled around him, their breath misting in the frigid air as he pressed them for signatures.

"Charlie's gone, and we're supposed to believe everything's fine?" he was saying, his tone clipped, urgent. "The market's coffers don't add up. Funds vanished. No accountability. And now Ilsa—his so-called heir—is sitting pretty in that house. Convenient, isn't it?"

Someone murmured assent and leaned in to sign. Another hesitated, glancing around before scribbling their name.

Paul muttered under his breath, "Of course he's stirring things up." His hand tightened slightly on Oscar's leash.

I felt a prickle of unease. Roy's face was calm, almost polished now, but the fire in his voice was sharp enough to splinter the air. He caught my eye across the crowd, and for a heartbeat too long, his gaze held mine. Then he offered the faintest curve of a smile, as if he'd been waiting for me to see him there.

I drew in a slow breath, unsettled. I knew I didn't like Roy, but I wasn't sure that meant I didn't trust him. Sometimes the two weren't the same thing.

I looked down at the box in my arms—the annual Bûche de Noël I delivered to the local businesses each year as a thank you for their support. It was my tradition, and this year it was giving me a convenient excuse to ask some questions. There were people I needed to talk to—those who knew Charlie, Magda, Felix, and Ilsa. People I hadn't initially suspected, but who were beginning to raise red flags in my mind. This holiday treat would hopefully loosen a few tongues.

Our first stop was Hazelton's Cozy Coffee, the new coffee shop that had recently opened near the market. It wasn't a direct competitor to Katie's Café—this place was more of a grab-and-go spot, a quick stop for busy commuters or visitors, rather than a place to sit and linger over coffee. The sleek modern design stood out among the older, quaint buildings of Hazelton, and its bright neon sign was a stark contrast to the subtle charm of the town's typical storefronts.

As soon as we stepped inside, the rich smell of coffee beans and freshly brewed espresso enveloped us. The warmth was a welcome change from the bitter cold outside. The shop was busy but efficient, with customers grabbing their orders and heading back out into the snowy streets.

I approached the counter, placing the Bûche de Noël on the counter. The barista, a young woman with a friendly smile, eyed the cake with appreciation.

"Well, this is a surprise!" she said, wiping her hands on her apron. "What's the occasion?"

"Just my way of saying thanks for being part of the community," I replied, smiling. "I've been making these treats for years. It's a little tradition of mine."

"Well, we appreciate it! You sure know how to brighten up a cold day."

As she took the cake, I leaned in slightly. "You've been here for a while now, right? How has business been with the market?"

The barista—Jenna, according to her name tag—shrugged as she set the cake aside. "It's been good. Lots of foot traffic, but I've heard rumors about next year. People are saying the market might not happen again."

I nodded. "Yeah, I've heard that too. It's tough without Charlie around. Were you close with him?"

Jenna thought for a moment, her expression softening. "Not really close, but he was in here a lot before everything happened. It always seemed like he had a lot on his plate."

"And Magda? Felix?" I asked, trying to sound casual.

"Magda's been in a few times," Jenna said, frowning slightly. "She and Charlie didn't seem to get along all that well. I saw them talking once, and it didn't look friendly."

I leaned in, intrigued. "You saw them argue?"

"Yeah," she said, nodding. "It wasn't a big scene, but I could tell something was off. She didn't look happy."

I thanked Jenna for her time, and Paul and I headed back outside, my mind already racing with this new piece of information. Another argument between Magda and Charlie. Was this a personal conflict, or was there something more going on?

Next, we made our way to the Hazelton Senior Center, where the familiar faces of the elderly residents greeted us warmly. The main room radiated festive cheer. A tall Christmas tree sparkled with handmade ornaments, while nearby tables held a menorah and kinara, each surrounded by thoughtful touches honoring Hanukkah, Kwanzaa, and other winter holidays. The staff bustled around, offering cups of hot cocoa and holiday cookies to the residents.

Cynthia, one of the senior center's coordinators, came over to greet me. Her face lit up when she saw the Bûche de Noël in my arms.

"Annee! You're an angel," she said, giving me a hug. "We always look forward to your cake this time of year."

I smiled, setting the cake down on the nearby table. "I'm happy to spread a little holiday joy."

Cynthia glanced over at Paul, who was helping Oscar out of his little sweater, shaking snow from his fur. "And you've brought company! What a treat."

We chatted for a few minutes before I gently steered the conversation toward Charlie. "I've been thinking a lot about him lately," I said softly. "It's hard to believe he's gone. Did you know him well?"

Cynthia sighed, nodding. "Charlie was a good man. He came by here every now and then to see if we needed anything. He seemed to have a lot on his plate right before his death. I heard things weren't going so smoothly at the market. He and Magda...well, they didn't get along."

I raised an eyebrow, feigning surprise. "Really? What happened?"

Cynthia lowered her voice, as if sharing a secret. "I don't know the details, but I saw them arguing just before the market opened. Magda looked furious, and Charlie...well, he seemed like he was trying to calm her down. I didn't think much of it at the time, but with everything that's happened...."

As she trailed off, I nodded slowly. "It makes you wonder."

As we left the senior center, the snow began falling in earnest, thick flakes swirling around us as the wind picked up. The streets had quieted down, with fewer people braving the cold now that the sky was darkening. Paul was unusually quiet as we walked, and I wondered if the conversations about Magda were starting to get to him.

We were heading toward my last stop for the day, Hazelton's Bakery, when I felt a snowball hit the back of my coat. I whirled around, catching Paul's sheepish grin just as he bent down to scoop up more snow.

"Oh, you are not starting this," I warned, narrowing my eyes.

"I already have," he replied with a mischievous glint in his eye.

Before I could react, another snowball came sailing toward me. I ducked, narrowly avoiding it, and reached down to grab my own handful of snow. Oscar barked happily, darting back and forth between us as we launched snowballs at each other, the air filled with laughter and the soft thud of snow hitting coats.

For a few minutes, it was just fun and games—no mystery, no stress. Just me, Paul, and Oscar in the middle of a snow-covered street, having a good old-fashioned snowball fight. I couldn't remember the last time I'd laughed so hard.

Eventually, breathless and covered in snow, we called a truce. Paul shook the snow from his hair, his face flushed and bright with laughter. "Okay, okay, you win."

I grinned, brushing snow off my coat. "I always do."

We reached the bakery just as Mackenzie was stepping out, holding a paper bag filled with pastries. She waved when she saw us. "Annee! You're just in time," she said, giving me a quick hug. "I was inside and heard some interesting things about Felix and Magda. People are starting to talk."

Paul stiffened beside me, and I could feel the tension radiating from him as Mackenzie continued. "I heard Felix has been involved in some shady business deals. People are starting to question if he's really as upstanding as he seems."

Paul's jaw clenched, and with a brief, "Bye, see you later," he turned and walked away, heading down the street.

I watched him go, my heart sinking. I'd known this would be hard for him, but it didn't make it any easier to watch.

Mackenzie frowned, confused. "What's with him? Trouble in paradise?"

I sighed, shaking my head. "His family is close with Magda and Felix. This whole investigation is…complicated for him."

Mackenzie winced. "I didn't mean to upset him. I was just passing on what I heard."

"I know," I said, glancing down the street where Paul had disappeared. "I'll talk to him later."

We walked back to my house, theorizing and gossiping about everything we had each heard in town. I was enjoying our little story creations about who was in town for the holidays and what people were saying about the murder. We didn't even notice the cold pressing in around us as the snow continued to fall.

When we finally reached my house, I unlocked the door, letting Oscar dart inside. The warmth of the house was a welcome relief.

Mackenzie plopped down on the couch, kicking off her boots and sighing. "So, what now? What's the next move?"

I sat down beside her, running a hand through my hair. "I'm not sure. Everyone keeps mentioning Magda, but I can't shake the feeling that there's something we're missing. And then there's Ilsa…."

Mackenzie quizzed. "Ilsa? What about her?"

"I've been hearing things," I said slowly. "People saw her fighting with Charlie before the market started. She was in town a few days before Thanksgiving, and someone even saw her coming out of his house early one morning."

Mackenzie's eyes widened. "Sounds suspicious."

Emerson came in the room with a hot apple cider. "Ilsa was Charlie's cousin. Totally not suspicious."

He had a point. Was it suspicious that Emerson was staying with me for the holidays? Nope. Just a little bit wonderful, I mused to myself.

"I don't know," I said, frowning. "She doesn't strike me as someone who would hurt him. But then again, she threatened me the other day."

Mackenzie and Emerson exchanged a look, their concern palpable.

"She threatened you?" Mackenzie asked, her voice rising slightly as she set her mug down. "What did she say?"

I hesitated, the memory of Ilsa's sharp tone and piercing gaze replaying in my mind. "It wasn't a direct threat," I said carefully. "But the way she said things wasn't friendly. She made a comment about my EpiPen and how she wasn't sure I'd have the nerve to show up at the market after...everything. And the way she looked at me—it wasn't friendly."

Emerson frowned as he leaned against the counter, crossing his arms. "Ilsa's not exactly warm and fuzzy, but that doesn't sound like nothing. She's either trying to scare you off or let you know she's watching."

Mackenzie nodded, her brow furrowed. "And why would she care enough to do either? She's tied to Charlie, but what's her stake in all of this? Unless..." Her voice trailed off, the unspoken suspicion hanging in the air.

"I don't know," I admitted, wrapping my hands around my warm cup of cider. "Maybe she's just protective of his reputation, or maybe it's guilt. But she's involved somehow. People saw her with Charlie before the market, and if she was staying in his house, she might know more than she's letting on."

Emerson tilted his head thoughtfully. "I wouldn't dismiss the possibility that she's just shaken up over Charlie's death. Grief makes people act strange."

"Maybe," I said, but doubt crept into my voice. "But then why threaten me? Why try to make me back off? If it's just grief, what does she have to hide?"

Mackenzie sighed, running a hand through her hair. "Whatever her reasons, you need to be careful. If Ilsa's really trying to intimidate you, it might mean you're onto something."

"I'm being careful," I assured her. "But I can't stop digging. If she knows something, I need to figure out what it is."

Emerson glanced at me, his expression softening. "Just don't push too hard. We need to keep you in one piece."

I gave a small smile, grateful for their concern, but feeling the weight of Ilsa's words more heavily than ever.

"Any word from Chief Cora on the recordings?" Emerson asked.

"Nothing! She's not keeping me in the loop at all. But Mack did hear some trash talk about Felix. So maybe there's a leak at the police station." I looked closer at Emerson's apple cider. "Want a cinnamon stick?"

He nodded yes.

"Mack, I think I'm going to have some more cider. Want some? Cinnamon stick, too?"

"I'll grab some hot chocolate. It sounds like there are a lot of secrets in this town. You just have to figure out which one led to Charlie's death."

I sighed as I left for the kitchen. "Easier said than done."

I returned with the beverages as the snow continued to fall outside. I couldn't help but feel like we were running out of time. The market would be over soon, and with it, the opportunity to uncover the mystery, if any of the vendors had been part of the crime.

My phone rang. When I glanced at it, Paul's name appeared on the screen.

I pointed to my phone and mouthed to the duo on the couch. *Paul.*

"Hi, Paul."

"Bonne Annee," Paul said. His voice was steady, a little tight. "Felix and Magda just told Jasper and me that they're selling Hazelton Farms."

"Selling it?" I asked. "To who? And why now?"

"They didn't say much." He sounded tired. "Just that they needed a fresh start. Jasper's not happy, and honestly, neither am I. It doesn't sit right."

"Didn't they have to run it by you?" I asked.

He sighed. "I guess not. With Sophia selling her shares and Charlie gone, they hold the majority stake now."

"Sorry, Paul," I said quietly. "When you find out who they sell it to, please let me know."

"Will do," he replied.

I hung up and turned to Mack and Emerson, who had been listening closely.

"Isn't Alejandro an investor?" Mack asked, her brow furrowing.

"Yeah!" Emerson said. "They've got to keep him in the loop, don't they?"

"I'll have to ask him tomorrow," I said, worrying my bottom lip between my teeth. The snow was still coming down hard outside, in thick flakes.

Mack lifted her mug with a steady hand, and Emerson followed, raising his as well. They both looked at me, warmth and certainty in their eyes.

"To tomorrow," Mack said firmly, "and to us proving what we all knew all along—that your instincts are right. Alejandro is innocent."

I smiled, lifting my own mug to meet theirs. The clink of ceramic felt like a promise. Oscar threw his head back and let out high pitched yowl, as if casting his own vote in agreement. We all burst into laughter, the sound echoing warmly through the room.

Chapter 27

Être dans les Choux:
To be in the cabbages (To be in a bad spot)

Katie's Café was packed, a cheerful buzz filling the room as Christmas music played softly in the background. Katie had gone all out this year, embracing what she called "Super Christmas." In her mind, this meant the café was pure Christmas chaos—colored lights zigzagged overhead, plastic Santas and reindeer crowded the shelves, and a life-size Clark Griswold cutout grinned from the corner. Mini Christmas trees topped every table, sparkling with tiny ornaments and tinsel.

Even the menu joined in. Mackenzie ordered a "Clark's Eggnog Latte," Emerson chose "Cousin Eddie's Pancakes" with extra whipped cream, and I went with "Sparky's Peppermint Mocha."

Oscar lay at my feet, his nose twitching as he took in the scents of cinnamon and peppermint. Katie, who was always up on the latest town news, gossiped as she delivered our food.

"So, did you hear?" Mackenzie leaned in as Katie shared her town scoop. "Felix and Magda are selling Hazelton Farms."

"Everyone's talking about it," I said, taking a sip of my peppermint mocha. "People can't believe they'd sell now. They appeared to be doing so well with it, but they might have their reasons."

Emerson leaned in, lowering his voice. "Do we know who's buying it?"

"All I heard is that it's some big corporation," Katie replied. "It's all moving fast. They're supposed to be out by the end of the year. It's a quick transition."

Katie moved on to other tables, leaving us to study the menu. I scanned the new, quirky items, enjoying that she'd named most of them after characters from *Christmas Vacation* in her Griswold-style holiday tribute.

Mackenzie leaned in, her voice low. "I think this is the break you've been waiting for, Annee. It has to be them. They probably had something to do with Charlie's murder, and now they're bailing before things get too messy."

I glanced up from the menu "Maybe. It's a big leap…but I can't shake the feeling that they're running from something, or that they know more than they're letting on. But I can't imagine both of them being in on murder. Maybe one of them…." My eyes fell back to the menu, and I tried to focus, needing a moment to ground myself.

When Katie returned, I pointed to an item that caught my eye. "I'll also take the Cousin Eddie's Gluten-Free Flapjacks, please," I said with a half-smile, appreciating the absurdity of the name amid the tense conversation.

Katie nodded, giving me a wink. "Coming right up."

I settled back in my seat, glancing over at Mack and Emerson. This investigation was coming to a head, and somehow, in the cozy chaos of Katie's Café, I felt happy.

After breakfast, we made our way to the jail, each of us lost in thought. Emerson, Mackenzie, and I moved quietly, Oscar padding close by. When we reached the small, cold room, Alejandro was waiting, his eyes sharper than I'd seen them, but with an edge of something else in them—something like fear.

I sat across from him, watching his face closely. "Did you hear? Magda and Felix sold Hazelton Farms."

He raised his brows, the shock barely flickering before his expression darkened. "It already sold?" he asked, but he didn't seem that surprised.

"Some big corporation bought it," I said, keeping my voice low. "They're taking on all the liability. It doesn't make sense."

His jaw tightened, and he looked past me, his gaze distant but intense, as if the pieces were clicking together too fast. "They're taking on the liabilities?" he repeated, a hint of panic creeping into his voice. "That's no coincidence. If it's them...if it's who I think it is...they're doing exactly what they did before." He swallowed hard, his hands clenched on the table. "I've seen this happen. They'll do anything for control. They don't care about risk—only power."

Emerson leaned in. "Why Hazelton Farms?"

Alejandro's eyes flashed with anger. "If Evergreen bought them out, it's not because they care about hazelnuts. They'll buy up any operation with a reputation they can exploit. Hazelnuts are profitable, sure, but that's not the point. A farm in trouble is perfect for Evergreen. They can bury the contamination, sweep the bad press under the rug, and spin it into some story about sustainability. Meanwhile, the smaller investors see no way out but to cash in before the whole thing collapses."

He broke off, his jaw tightening. "I've seen it before. They promise change, promise reform, but it's always the same. They strip everything bare and walk away richer, while everyone else is left to choke on the fallout."

I could feel the weight of his words, the chill that seemed to creep into the room. "Alejandro, have you heard anything about those recordings on Hazelton Farms? What do you think is in them?"

He shook his head, his voice low. "I don't know. But I was pretty sure Felix and Magda had an offer on the table to sell the farm, even before the *E. coli* scare. It makes me wonder...."

Before I could press further, Cora stepped into the room, her gaze sweeping over us and her face set. "Time's up," she said, her tone threatening. I noticed that her hair had started to gray again. I wondered if she was regretting her choice to dye, since she probably didn't have the time to keep it up.

I met her eyes, steady. "Cora, did you find anything on those recordings?"

She crossed her arms. "Annee, if there's anything worth knowing, you'll hear about it in due time. Right now, stay clear." Then she ushered us out.

As we walked through the hallway, Mackenzie whispered. "She's hiding something, isn't she? I don't think she thinks Alejandro is guilty."

I nodded, feeling the cold sting of air as we stepped outside.

Emerson looked at me, his expression tight and grim. "This is bigger than we thought," he said.

I took a deep breath, steadying myself. "I know. But we're getting closer. One way or another, we've got to get Alejandro out of there."

"How much are we short for the bail?" Mack asked.

"A lot," I responded.

"Well, why don't we try to raise it? How about opening a pop-up at the Christmas market?" Emerson suggested. "You could make some of that delicious food of yours, just like you did the other night."

I thought it was a great idea, but I was also stunned. Emerson liked my food. He liked me. I was having my moment. "Yes! Let's do it! We can put a donation sign out too. Maybe we can get him out by tomorrow, if our sales are high enough."

Chapter 28

> Mettre du Beurre dans les Épinards:
> *To Put Some Butter in the Spinach (to earn a little extra money)*

The cold bit at my cheeks as Mackenzie and I hustled around the pop-up booth, adjusting the last of the Christmas decorations and setting up our food station. The booth had been left vacant by a vendor who'd had to pack up early for the season. We had draped it in evergreen garlands, holly, and twinkling white lights across the top. In one corner stood a small Christmas tree I had adorned with tiny Puerto Rican flags and tartan ribbons—in a tribute to my heritage and a heartfelt effort to raise funds for Alejandro's bail.

My grandmother was Puerto Rican, and every Christmas, she made sure the house was filled with the smells of pernil—roasted pork shoulder—and pasteles, a labor-intensive dish made of green bananas and pork wrapped in banana leaves. I could almost hear her voice as I sliced the plantains for the demo, humming one of her favorite holiday songs. But alongside her influence was the mark of my French-Scots grandfather, who always insisted on including his favorite French Christmas dishes every year. I had grown up balancing coquito and Bûche de Noël on the same table, the flavors blending in my childhood memories.

"This looks amazing," Mackenzie said, adjusting one of the garlands as she stood back to admire our work. She was bundled in a red coat with a matching knit hat, her breath fogging in the cold air. "Do you think we're ready?"

"I think so," I said, stepping back to take it all in. We had a wide selection of food spread out—slices of Bûche de Noël dusted with powdered sugar, plates of crispy tostones, cups of coquito, and a large slow-cooker filled with caldo gallego, a warm Galician soup my grandfather swore kept the cold at bay. The cooking demo would start soon, but people were already starting to gather, curious about the blend of cultures and flavors.

Oscar was sitting by the booth, wearing a small red and white scarf that I'd made for him last Christmas. His tail thumped against the ground, and every time someone stopped by, he gave them his most charming, soulful-eyed look, drawing them in. He pulled the crowds in as much as the food.

Joe's band had set up nearby, their instruments tuned and ready. At Mackenzie's request, they were playing a mix of Christmas classics, and the air was filled with the twang of a guitar playing "Silent Night." The sound added to the festive atmosphere, and I could see people gravitating toward our booth, the music, and the warmth of the food and drink we offered.

Mackenzie grinned at me, her eyes sparkling with excitement. "Look at all the people, Annee! We might actually raise enough for Alejandro's bail."

I nodded, feeling a mixture of relief and pride. The booth was already a success, and the donations were coming in quickly. People were drawn not only by the food, but also by the story. Hazelton might be small, but it had heart even if they weren't sure who was guilty. People wanted to help.

A couple approached the booth, shivering slightly as they looked over the offerings. "What's this drink?" the woman asked, pointing to the cups.

"It's coquito," I said with a smile, ladling a cup. "A Puerto Rican Christmas drink. It's like eggnog, but with coconut milk, spices, and rum. Warms you right up."

They each took a cup, their faces lighting up as the tropical flavor hit their tongues. "This is delicious," the man said, pulling out his wallet and slipping a few bills into the donation jar. "Good luck with your cause."

Mackenzie gave me a look of satisfaction, then turned to serve another group who'd been drawn in by Oscar's charm. "This little guy should get a cut of the profits," she said, rubbing his ears as he wagged his tail, enjoying the attention. "You're our secret weapon, aren't you?"

Just then, I heard the crunch of boots on snow behind me, and I turned to see Paul approaching. He looked handsome, as always, bundled in a navy jacket and scarf that ironically matched Oscar's. Although Paul's was a not-so-subtle candy cane motif.

"This is quite the setup," he said, glancing at the decorations and the line of people. "Looks like you're doing really well." A hesitant smile tugged at his lips.

"We are," I said, smiling. I felt a flutter in my chest at the sight of him. "We've raised a lot already. I'm hoping we can hit the goal by tonight."

He stepped closer, his hands in his pockets, and for a moment, the rest of the world seemed to fade away. His eyes met mine, and I could feel the warmth between us, the way it always felt when he was around. "You're really doing everything you can for him," he said softly. His tone carried an edge I couldn't quite place.

I nodded. "He's my friend. He didn't do it, Paul."

Paul's smile faltered, and he glanced away, his gaze landing on Joe's band for a moment before he looked back at me. "I know you believe that," he said, his voice low. "But I'm not so sure. I've always wondered...."

"Wondered what?" I asked, my heart sinking a little, though I already knew where this was going.

"If there's more to it," he admitted, his eyes searching mine. "Between you and Alejandro. You're doing all this for him, and I can't help but think...were you ever interested in him?"

I blinked, taken aback. "Alejandro? No, Paul, it's not like that. He's my friend, and he's in trouble. That's all."

Paul nodded slowly, but I could see the doubt lingering in his eyes. "I'm just worried," he said quietly, reaching for my hand. "I don't want you to get hurt, Bonne Annee."

I squeezed his hand, feeling the warmth of his touch, but also the tension beneath it. "I'm not the one who's going to get hurt, Paul," I said softly. "Alejandro is. And I can't just stand by and let that happen."

Before Paul could respond, a small crowd had gathered in front of the booth for the cooking demo. Mackenzie shot me a look, and I knew it was time to push aside the personal stuff and focus on what we were here to do.

"Looks like you've got a crowd," Paul said, stepping back with a small smile. "I'll leave you to it."

I nodded, watching him walk away, his figure fading into the fray. There was a knot in my chest, a part of me wishing he could just trust me. He had said he had my back, but it seemed like jealousy was taking over. For now, I had to focus on raising the money and clearing Alejandro's name. The romantic moment, however brief, had to be set aside.

"All right, everyone!" Mackenzie called, clapping her hands. "Gather around for Annee's famous tostones and pernil demo!"

I took a deep breath, rolling up my sleeves and letting the energy of the crowd pull me back into the moment. Oscar bounced happily, as if sensing the excitement. The Christmas lights twinkled overhead, and as Joe's band played "Feliz Navidad" in the background, I threw myself into the demo, showing everyone how to press and fry the plantains to crispy perfection.

The warmth of the food, the laughter of the crowd, and the sense of purpose filled me. We were making a difference. I just hoped it would be enough.

Chapter 29

Avoir la Banane:

To Have the Banana (to be in a good mood, to have a big smile)

Alejandro stepped out of the holding area, looking thinner and more worn than I'd seen him in a long time. His steps were deliberate, and his eyes immediately found mine across the waiting area of the police station. I wanted to say something comforting, but the exhaustion in his face kept me quiet for a moment.

"Annee," he said softly when he reached me.

"You're out!" I said, managing a small smile. "Finally."

Before he could respond, the sharp click of boots echoed behind him. Cora, clipboard in hand, approached with her usual commanding presence. "Hold on," she said, her tone making it clear that he wasn't leaving just yet.

Alejandro sighed and turned to face her. "What now? Am I free or not?"

"You are," she replied firmly. "But I've got some things to say, and you're going to listen." She glanced between the two of us before locking her sharp gaze on him. "First off, you should've been out sooner. You chose not to consult with an attorney, refused legal advice, and made things harder for yourself than they needed to be."

Alejandro crossed his arms, the muscles in his jaw tightening. "I don't trust attorneys. I know what I did and what I didn't do."

Cora raised an eyebrow. "That might sound noble in your head, but out here? It's just reckless. You've got court dates coming up, and you need someone who knows the system. Stop being stubborn and get a lawyer. I think everyone deserves due process—even the guilty ones."

Alejandro's eyes darted to me, as if looking for backup, but I held his gaze steady. "She's right," I said firmly. "You can't handle this alone."

He sighed, rubbing the back of his neck. "Fine. I'll look into it."

Cora's face was relaxed, but her tone remained authoritative. "Good. Because while you're out on bail, you'll be under surveillance. No funny business, no leaving town without notice, and no stunts that make the judge regret setting bail."

"I've already told you," Alejandro replied, his voice sharper now. "I'm going straight to Annee's. That's it."

"Fine," Cora said, but she didn't move. Her gaze lingered on him, assessing. "Anything else you want to get off your chest?"

Alejandro hesitated, then stepped closer, lowering his voice. "Yeah, actually. You're too focused on me. What about the recordings? What about Hazelton Farms and Charlie's connection to it? If you spent half the time looking into the sale of Felix and Magda's business as you've spent questioning me, you might actually find something worth your attention."

Cora's brow furrowed. "The sale of their business?"

"Yes," he said, his tone insistent. "Something about it doesn't add up. The timing, the buyer—none of it makes sense. If you dig into the details, you'll see what I mean. With Charlie and me out of the picture, there was nothing to stop the sale. You're looking in the wrong direction."

Cora tilted her head, her expression skeptical, but intrigued. "You have evidence? Or is this just a hunch?"

"Call it an educated guess," Alejandro replied. "I don't have proof, but I've been around the food world long enough to know something's off. Start with their inspection paperwork, their buyer, and their contracts. Something stinks over there—I can almost guarantee it."

Cora studied him for a long moment, then glanced at me. "I'll look into it. But don't think for a second that this gets you off the hook, Alejandro. You're still a person of interest, and you've still got a lot to answer for."

He nodded, his face unreadable. "I'm not asking for a free pass. Just…keep your eyes open, Cora. That's all I'm saying."

Cora straightened, her clipboard tucked firmly under her arm. "Get yourself an attorney," she repeated.

Alejandro gave a small, tired nod. "Understood."

As we turned to leave, Cora's voice followed us. "And Annee?"

I paused, glancing back at her.

"Just curious what you know about Charlie's cousin, Ilsa?"

"Nothing really," I said. "She seems good at what she does. She doesn't like me, that's for sure."

"I know," Cora responded. "She made a complaint about you. Thinks we should look into you as well."

My stomach tightened, but I kept my face neutral. "Is that so?" I managed.

"Mm-hmm," Cora said, nonchalantly flipping her clipboard shut. "Just thought you'd want to know."

Outside, Alejandro let out a low sigh, his shoulders sagging as we walked to the car. "She doesn't trust me," he muttered.

"She doesn't seem to trust anyone," I replied, trying to keep my voice steady, though my mind was racing.

When I stepped out of the police station, I was still lost in thought. Ilsa really had it in for me. Maybe she didn't like that I was supporting the person she thought had killed her cousin.

Chapter 30

Avoir un Cœur d'Artichaut:

To Have an Artichoke Heart (to be a hopeless romantic)

O utside the police station, I was greeted by an unexpected sight: a horse-drawn sleigh parked just beyond the curb. The sleigh was a perfect, gleaming red, its edges dusted with fresh snow that sparkled under the streetlights. A chestnut horse with a flowing mane stood patiently in its harness, steam curling from its nostrils into the cold night air. For a moment, I just stared, the surreal beauty of the scene momentarily overwhelming me.

And then I saw Paul.

He sat perched on the driver's bench, his grin as wide as the starry sky above. "Surprise!" he called. His voice was rich with delight and the faint jingling of the sleigh bells added to the magic.

I blinked, trying to process what I was seeing. "What…how?" I stammered, utterly caught off guard.

Paul hopped down from the sleigh, his boots crunching on the snow as he strode toward me. His eyes sparkled with boyish excitement, and there was a warmth in his expression that made the cold night feel less biting. "I promised you a *Christmas in Connecticut* sleigh ride, didn't I?" he said, stopping in front of me. "I figured after everything you've been through, tonight might be the perfect time to make good on that promise."

Before I could respond, a familiar voice broke through my astonishment. "Well, well, if it isn't the knight with the sleigh," Alejandro said, his tone teasing but kind. I turned to see him standing with Emerson and Mackenzie, who had just arrived to celebrate his homecoming. Judging by their knowing smiles, it was clear the three of them had been in on Paul's surprise all along.

Paul looked at Alejandro and extended a hand, his smile not wavering. "Glad to see you out, man," he said warmly.

Alejandro shook his hand, then shot me a mock-serious look. "Don't keep her out too late," he said with a half-smile.

I hesitated, glancing between Alejandro and the sleigh, my emotions tangled. Alejandro caught my eye and gave me a slight nod, his expression calm and encouraging. "Seriously, go. You deserve it."

Emerson raised an eyebrow but said nothing, while Mackenzie gave me an enthusiastic thumbs-up behind Alejandro's back.

I took a deep breath and turned to Paul, who was waiting patiently, the reins of the horse in his gloved hand. "All right," I said, my voice trembling with a mix of nerves and excitement. "Let's go."

Paul's grin widened, and he extended a hand to help me up onto the sleigh. As I settled onto the bench, the world seemed to quiet, the jingling of the bells and the breathing of the horses were the only sounds I heard.

"Comfortable?" he asked, as he climbed back up beside me and took the reins.

I nodded, a small smile creeping across my face. "More than comfortable."

With a gentle cluck of his tongue and a light tug on the reins, the horse began to move, pulling us forward through the snowy streets of Hazelton. A special snowy-shouldered path had been left along the main road to accommodate the market sleigh rides, allowing the sleigh to glide effortlessly over the packed snow. The faint jingling of the bells on the horse's harness filled the crisp winter air. The town was aglow with twinkling Christmas lights, and every lamppost and storefront was adorned with garlands, wreaths, and ribbons. Snowflakes floated lazily down from the sky, adding to the magic of the moment.

For a while, neither of us spoke. We simply rode through the town, watching families and couples pass by, all bundled up in scarves and hats, laughing and chatting as they enjoyed the festive atmosphere. Hazelton's Christmas charm was in full swing—the glow of Christmas trees inside homes, the smell of pine and hot cocoa from nearby stands, and the occasional strains of carolers singing in the distance.

"I didn't know how to make things right," Paul said softly, breaking the silence. He kept his eyes on the road ahead, his voice gentle. "I know we've been at odds lately, and I didn't want that. I want to be there for you, Bonne Annee, and I don't want our differences of opinion to get in the way."

I let out a breath as his words sunk in. "I've felt the same way. I'm just…everything with Alejandro has been complicated. I know you don't see things the way I do, but I need you to trust me."

Paul's brow furrowed as he nodded. "I do trust you. I don't know Alejandro the way you do. I wasn't there all those years, when you were going to culinary school, and I guess I've always wondered if there was more between you two. You have so many inside jokes, and with him living on your property, I was never sure."

Paul's words caught me off guard. I thought we were past this. I turned to face him, weirdly delighted. He has been wondering. He has been worried. He wants me and doesn't want Alejandro in his way! "Paul, Alejandro is my friend. He's been through a lot, and I care about him, but it's never been romantic. Not even close."

Paul glanced over at me, the tension in his face easing just a little. "I needed to hear that."

I reached for his hand, squeezing it gently. "I'm here with you, aren't I?"

A smile tugged at the corners of his mouth, and he gave my hand a soft squeeze in return. "Yeah, you are."

The sleigh continued to glide through the snow-covered streets, and we passed by the town square, where families were ice skating and kids were building snowmen near the park's Christmas tree.

"I wanted to tell you something," Paul said, his voice thoughtful as we circled the square.

"What's that?" I asked, watching the lights flicker against the snow-covered trees.

As Paul guided the sleigh through the snowy streets, his usual carefree expression had been replaced by a seriousness that sent a ripple of unease through me. I clutched the blanket around me, waiting for him to speak.

"It's about Ilsa," he said, glancing at me briefly before turning his eyes back to the snowy path ahead. "I've been looking into some things, and...I think you need to know what I found out." Paul shifted, clearly uncomfortable. "When Charlie passed, she inherited everything, including his shares in Hazelton Farms."

My mouth fell open. "I thought the shares went back to the farm for some reason."

Paul nodded grimly. "That's not the half of it. Turns out, Ilsa wasn't just sitting back, collecting her inheritance. She was part of the decision to sell Hazelton Farms. She even found the buyer."

I frowned, the pieces of the story clicking into place, but not making any sense. "The buyer? The company that took over recently?"

"Yeah," Paul confirmed. "She pitched it to Felix and Magda, saying the company specializes in buying out struggling food businesses. She made it sound like it was the best option to protect everyone's investments. 'That's what Charlie would've wanted,' she said."

I shook my head, trying to wrap my mind around the information. "But why wouldn't you or Alejandro tell me about your shares in Hazelton Farms? I feel like I'm the only one who didn't know."

Paul sighed heavily. "Because we couldn't. Charlie made us sign confidentiality agreements when he brought us into the deal. Felix and Magda needed help to expand their production—the hazelnut candies, remember? They wanted to try to get shelf space in bigger stores. Charlie brought in Alejandro for his experience, and the rest of us because we had some money to invest."

"That still doesn't explain Ilsa," I pressed. "Why would she push so hard to sell? And how did she even get involved in the first place?"

"That's where it gets weird," Paul admitted. "I'd never even heard of Ilsa before this year's Christmas market. She wasn't on anyone's radar. And when I found out she was Charlie's cousin, I couldn't believe it. They didn't act like family—more like…" He hesitated, then gave a wry chuckle. "More like kissing cousins, if you know what I mean."

The implication made my stomach turn. "Paul, are you serious? You think there was something going on between them?"

He shrugged, his expression troubled. "I don't know. I just know that whatever relationship they had, it wasn't exactly normal. And now, she's benefitting from all of it—his death, the sale of Hazelton Farms, everything."

The sleigh bells jingled softly as the horse plodded forward, but the festive sound did little to ease the growing knot in my stomach. "This whole thing feels wrong," I murmured. "Charlie didn't strike me as the type to just hand everything over. And Ilsa…she shows up out of nowhere and suddenly has all this influence? It doesn't add up."

Paul nodded, his jaw tight. "That's why I'm telling you what I know. I've got a bad feeling about her, Bonne Annee. And you're the one who might be able to figure out if she's up to no good."

I sat back, the warmth of the sleigh suddenly feeling stifling despite the icy air. Charlie's death, Ilsa's sudden inheritance, and the sale of Hazelton Farms—none of it made sense. And the more Paul revealed, the more I realized that this wasn't just a string of coincidences. Something deeper, and more dangerous, was at play.

"Every time I think I'm getting closer to the truth, another layer gets pulled back, and everything changes."

"You'll figure it out," Paul said, his voice full of quiet confidence.

I looked over at him, feeling a surge of gratitude. "Thanks for believing in me."

He smiled, his eyes soft. "Always."

As we turned down a quiet street, Paul spoke again, his tone lighter this time. "You know, all of this drama has made me think a lot about family. Especially around the holidays."

I smiled, curious. "What do you mean?"

"Well, my family has a lot of traditions around Christmas," Paul said, glancing over at me. "We're Italian, you know, and the holidays are a big deal. Every year, we go to Catholic Mass on Christmas Eve, and then afterward, we gather for the Feast of the Seven Fishes."

My eyes widened. "The Feast of the Seven Fishes? I've heard of it, but I've never actually experienced it."

Paul laughed, the sound warm and inviting. "Oh, you'd love it. My mom spends days preparing—there's calamari, shrimp, mussels, clams, cod, lobster…the works. It's a feast, all right. And after we've eaten more seafood than you'd think was humanly possible, we sit around the fire, drink home-made wine, and tell stories. It's one of my favorite parts of the year."

I could picture it clearly: Paul's family gathered around a table piled high with food, the warmth of the fire and the laughter of loved ones filling the room. It made my heart ache just a little, thinking about how different Christmas had been for me lately. "That sounds wonderful," I said softly.

"It is," Paul replied, his voice equally soft. "And I'd really like you to be there this year. You've known Molly and Marc for years, so it won't be all new faces. My family would love to have you."

I looked up at him, my heart fluttering at the invitation. "You want me to spend Christmas Eve with your family?"

"Yeah," he said, turning to face me fully. "I want you there, Bonne Annee. I want you to meet the rest of my family, to celebrate the holidays with me."

His words hung in the air, warm and full of meaning. I hadn't realized how much I needed to feel like I was part of something, especially with everything else in my life feeling so uncertain. And Paul…Paul had a way of making things feel steady, even when the world around us felt like it was falling apart.

I smiled, my heart full. "I'd love to."

Paul's face lit up with a grin, and for the rest of the ride, the weight of the world seemed to lift, even if just for a little while. The magic of Christmas in Hazelton swirled around us as the sleigh glided through the snow, the town aglow with holiday cheer.

In that moment, under the twinkling lights and falling snow, I felt something I hadn't in a long time—excitement.

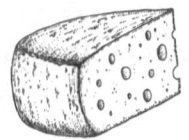

Chapter 31

Ça N'a Rien à Voir Avec la Choucroute:
That Has Nothing to Do With Sauerkraut (that's completely irrelevant)

The cozy warmth of Katie's Café was a welcome escape from the biting cold outside. I slid into a booth across from Katie, letting out a long sigh.

Katie, always intuitive, gave me a knowing look while sipping her tea. "All right," she said with a smile, "what's on your mind, Annee?"

I hesitated for a moment, biting my lip. "Paul invited me to spend Christmas Eve with his family."

Katie's eyes lit up, her smile widening. "Oh my goodness, that's wonderful! He's serious about you, Annee."

I could feel the heat rising in my cheeks, not from excitement, but from a mix of anxiety and uncertainty. "Yeah, it's a big step, but…I don't know if I should have accepted."

Katie's smile softened, and she leaned forward, concern in her eyes. "Why not?"

I sighed, rubbing the back of my neck. "His family is so close-knit. They have all these traditions, like going to church together and eating the feast of the seven fishes. They're really…*happy*. And I don't know if I fit into something like that."

Katie raised an eyebrow. "You don't think you fit into a happy, loving family?"

"It's not that," I said, shaking my head. "It's just…my family has never been like that. I'm not used to it. I've got all this baggage, and they seem so perfect. What if I can't mesh with that?"

Katie sipped her tea, her brow furrowed in thought. "No family is perfect, Annee. But that doesn't mean you won't find a place in his."

Before I could respond, the door to the café chimed softly as it opened. Katie glanced up, spotting Mackenzie and Emerson stepping inside. "Well, look who's here," she said with a smile, setting her teacup aside. "Let me grab a fresh pot — they'll want some coffee." She slipped from the booth and headed toward the counter. Mackenzie immediately spotted me and waved enthusiastically, her face lighting up. Emerson followed her gaze, giving me a quick nod. He looked healthier than he had when I saw him last, his color back and his posture more relaxed.

Mackenzie headed straight to my table, shrugging off her coat as she reached me. "Hey, Annee! Perfect timing. Mind if we crash your party?"

Before I could respond, Emerson slid into the booth across from me, his expression calm but warm. "Looks like we already did," he said, smirking.

I blinked, momentarily caught off guard by their energy. "Uh, sure. Go ahead."

Mackenzie plopped down beside Emerson, her grin contagious. "Katie's outdone herself this year, hasn't she? This place looks like something straight out of a Christmas card."

Emerson glanced around, his eyes softening as he took in the café. "Yeah, it's festive," he said with a hint of approval.

"So what's the topic of conversation?" Mackenzie asked, leaning forward with her elbows on the table. "Or do we just dive into my latest drama?"

I raised an eyebrow. "What latest drama?"

She rolled her eyes dramatically. "Oh, you know. Apparently Joe decided to leave town for a New Year's Eve gig instead of staying to figure things out like an adult. Classic."

Emerson chuckled. "Sounds like it's for the best."

"Right?" Mackenzie said, nudging him with her elbow. "Anyway, who needs Joe when your cousin Sylvester's coming back for Christmas? It's like the universe knew I needed better company."

I brightened at the mention of Sylvester, a smile spreading across my face. "Sylvester's coming back?"

Emerson nodded. "Yeah, he changed his plans last minute. He'll be here in a few days."

Mackenzie clapped her hands together, beaming. "This Christmas just keeps getting better! First snow, then sleigh rides and Alejandro being set free—what's next? Caroling?"

I shook my head, smiling despite the knot in my stomach. Mackenzie's enthusiasm was infectious, and Emerson looked surprisingly at ease. For now, I let myself enjoy their company, and happy thoughts of Sylvester's return lingered in the back of my mind. Maybe I did have happy family potential. I hesitated, unsure if I should bring up everything going on with Paul. Something made me hold back.

Katie returned with a fresh pot of coffee and poured them each a cup. "Enjoy," she said with a smile before retreating to the counter.

Then Emerson blurted out the weirdest thing. "You ever think about going to the Congo? You know, to find your mom?"

The question hit me like a wave. I stared at him, my heart suddenly racing. "The Congo? No, I...I've never really thought about it."

"Why not?" Emerson asked. "You've got the means. Maybe you could find her."

I swallowed hard, caught off guard. "I don't know. I guess it never seemed like something I could do."

Emerson raised an eyebrow. "You think she might be out there though, right? Don't you want to at least try to know what happened?"

I blinked, the thought swirling around in my mind. I'd spent years wondering about my mother, but the idea of actually going to the Congo to find her...it had always felt like an impossible dream. But now, sitting here with my cousin, it didn't seem so far-fetched.

"I never thought I could," I admitted, my voice quieter than I intended. "I mean, I've always been curious, but...actually going there? It seemed like something out of reach."

Mack shrugged. "Maybe it's not. Maybe it's something you should think about."

I stared down at my hands, the idea taking root in my mind. I had spent so long thinking that my mother was a distant, unreachable part of my past, but maybe she wasn't as far away as I thought.

Katie returned with a plate of waffles, setting them in front of us with a smile. "Gluten free and on the house," she said with a wink. "You all look like you could use a little comfort food."

We each took a waffle, and as we dug in, the conversation slowly began to flow more easily. Emerson and I reminisced about our childhoods and visiting our grandmother's inn during the holidays. Emerson reminded me of the time we'd all gotten lost in the woods, and our grandmother had to send a search party after us. We laughed about how scared we'd been, but how, in the end, she just made us hot chocolate and didn't even scold us.

Emerson leaned back in his seat, smiling. "We had some good times back then."

"Yeah," I agreed. "We did."

Emerson glanced over at me, his expression thoughtful. "You know, our families may not be close, but we've always had each other."

I nodded, feeling a lump form in my throat. "You're right."

"We should stick together more," Emerson added, his voice soft. "I know things have been distant between us, but…it doesn't have to stay that way."

I looked between them, suddenly realizing that maybe I wasn't as alone as I thought. "I'd like that," I said, my voice barely above a whisper.

For the first time in years, I felt a connection to my cousin. Maybe things between us weren't perfect, but they didn't have to be. We had history, shared memories, and maybe—just maybe—there was room to build something stronger.

As we finished our waffles, the conversation turned back to lighter topics, but the idea of finding my mother stayed with me, lingering in the back of my mind. I hadn't considered it before, but now…it felt like something worth thinking about.

Maybe it was time to stop running from my past and start seeking answers.

And maybe, just maybe, I didn't have to do it alone.

Chapter 32

Tomber Dans les Pommes:
To Fall in the Apples (to faint)

"Can you help me do some digging on Ilsa?" I asked Alejandro, leaning against the counter as he sat at his desk, his laptop open in front of him. The faint glow of the screen illuminated his face, and he glanced up, his expression sharpening.

"Ilsa?" he repeated, his brow furrowing. "You think she's hiding something?"

"I'm not sure," I admitted. "But she's tied to everything lately—Charlie's estate, the Christmas market, the sale of Hazelton Farms. It feels wrong. She's Charlie's cousin, but they weren't close. And yet, she's suddenly in the middle of everything."

Alejandro nodded, already reaching for his phone. "I know someone who might be able to help—a private investigator I worked with during my whistleblower days. She's good at finding things that are technically public, but somehow buried."

I tilted my head. "An investigator? You never mentioned that."

"It's not something I usually bring up," he said, his expression darkening. "But this one, Callie, is someone I trust. She knows how to dig into records without crossing any lines. Let me give her a call."

Alejandro stepped into the next room, and I heard the low murmur of his voice. When he returned a few minutes later, he looked more focused. "She's on it. If there's anything to find, she'll find it."

We decided to head back to my place. It felt safer, and truthfully, I needed the comfort of my own kitchen to steady myself.

Alejandro followed me into the house with Oscar padding at our heels. The warmth of the kitchen wrapped around us as I turned on the lights, the soft glow spilling across the counters. For a moment, neither of us said anything. I busied myself, straightening a dish towel that didn't need straightening while Alejandro leaned against the doorway, watching me.

"I didn't mean to scare you when I left, Annee," he said finally, his voice low.

I froze, the towel in my hands. "I know you didn't," I replied, not meeting his eyes. "But when you disappeared, even for a little while... it brought back old ghosts. My mom left years ago without a word. That kind of loss—it never really goes away."

Alejandro stepped closer, his hand resting lightly on my shoulder. "I'm sorry. I didn't think—"

"You couldn't have known," I interrupted, finally turning to face him. "But it's why I don't let people in too easily. Losing someone like that— it changes you."

He nodded, his expression unreadable. "I get it. I miss my family, too. It's hard being here, knowing I can't just show up at my parents' place and have my mom feed me like I'm still a kid."

I smiled faintly. "So, what did your mom make when you needed comfort?"

His eyes lit up slightly. "Tamales. We'd spend all day making them—me, my mom, my sisters. It was messy and loud, but it always felt like home."

"Tamales, huh?" I said, tilting my head. "I've got masa and everything else we'd need."

Alejandro raised an eyebrow. "Are you offering to make tamales with me?"

"I'm saying you'll owe me for letting you use my kitchen," I teased. "But yeah, let's do it."

The kitchen filled with the smell of warm masa as we set up an assembly line at the counter. Alejandro mixed the masa, his hands methodical as he added broth, lard, and a pinch of salt. I soaked the corn husks, spreading them out on a clean towel as he tested the dough's consistency.

"You want it to float in water," he explained, dropping a tiny piece of masa into a cup. When it bobbed to the surface, he nodded with satisfaction. "Perfect."

"Should I be taking notes?" I teased, spreading masa onto a husk with a spatula. It wasn't as easy as it looked—Alejandro's hands made quick, even strokes, while mine were clumsy by comparison.

"You'll get the hang of it," he said, smirking. "Just don't overfill it, or it'll be a mess when we fold."

We worked in a rhythm, spreading masa, adding filling—spiced pork, green chili, and cheese—then folding and tying each tamale with strips of husk. Alejandro told stories about his family as we worked, his voice softening when he spoke about his mother's laughter and the chaos of their kitchen.

"Sounds like a good time," I said, smiling as I placed a neatly folded tamale into the steamer basket.

"It was," he said, his voice quieter now. "I didn't appreciate it enough when I had it."

We loaded the tamales into the steamer, covering them with a damp towel before setting the pot on the stove. As they cooked, the warm, earthy aroma filled the kitchen, mixing with the faint scent of coffee I'd brewed earlier. Alejandro leaned back against the counter, watching the steam rise.

"Thanks for doing this," he said. "It helps."

I nodded. "It helps me too."

The tamales were done after an hour, their aroma rich and comforting as we unwrapped the first ones. The masa was soft and perfectly cooked, the filling warm and savory. Alejandro took a bite and closed his eyes, exhaling like he'd been holding his breath all day.

"Just like home," he said, his voice almost wistful.

I smiled, taking a bite of my own. The tamale melted on my tongue, its flavors wrapping around me like a hug. For a few moments, we ate in companionable silence, the weight of earlier conversations easing slightly.

Then Alejandro's phone buzzed on the counter, breaking the quiet. He glanced at the screen, his expression tightening. "It's from Callie," he said, picking up the phone. "She found something. She sent over a report."

My stomach knotted. "What did she find?"

Alejandro opened the email and started scrolling through the attached document, his jaw tightening as he read. "You were right," he said grimly. "Ilsa's not just in trouble—she's deep in it. And it's worse than we thought."

He clicked on a highlighted section and leaned in closer. "She filed for personal bankruptcy last year. Her financial situation has been bad for a while. But that's not the big news."

"What is?" I asked, moving to his side.

Alejandro clicked on a screenshot embedded in the report. "Look at this," he said, turning the screen toward me.

I leaned over his shoulder, my stomach twisting as I read. "Ilsa works for Evergreen Holdings?"

"Not just that," Alejandro said, his tone dark. "She was hired six weeks ago. That was well before the Christmas market set-up."

"Charlie knew about my history with them. If Ilsa learned that through him—or found something in his papers—then she would have understood exactly how to use it. She wouldn't have needed a recommendation. Just the right knowledge, twisted the right way. That would have been enough to make her valuable to Evergreen."

My anger flared. "So she knew what she was doing. She got close to Charlie, used what he told her, and sold out Hazelton Farms to save herself."

Alejandro scrolled further, his brow furrowing. "Callie also found documents suggesting Evergreen was already vetting the Hazelton Farms sale weeks before the Christmas market even started."

My chest tightened. "So she was working with them before Charlie passed? That means that everything that happened with Charlie was premeditated."

Alejandro ran a hand through his hair, leaning back. "She didn't just manipulate Charlie—she was giving Evergreen cover. Owning Hazelton Farms gives them a way to polish their reputation. If people are eating nuts and produce stamped with Hazelton's name, no one's asking questions about Evergreen. It looks wholesome, local, safe—when really, it lets them bury anything they don't want seen. Charlie may have figured that out, and that could be why he became a problem."

I swallowed hard, my throat dry. "Do you think Evergreen killed Charlie? Do you think Ilsa was involved in his death?"

Alejandro hesitated, his hands resting on the edge of the table. "I don't know," he said carefully. "But if Evergreen is involved, it's not just about Hazelton Farms. I wouldn't be surprised if they wanted to buy out the entire town. That's their usual M.O."

I nodded slowly, the weight of it all pressing down on me. "We need to figure out exactly what Isla is planning."

Alejandro gave me a steady look. "Callie's still digging. She'll send more information as she finds it. But we need to stay ahead of Ilsa—whatever she's hiding, it's big."

The room felt like it was spinning. "So, she not only manipulated Charlie—she handed over Hazelton Farms to a company with a history of…questionable practices?"

Alejandro's jaw tightened, his eyes fixed on the screen. "Not just questionable, Annee. When I worked for them, I wrote reports on food supply vulnerabilities—how pathogens like *E. coli* or salmonella could be introduced into the chain. My work was supposed to be preventative, but I found out later that my research was being used for something much darker."

"Darker how?" I asked, barely able to whisper.

Alejandro's hands trembled slightly as he spoke. "Six months after I left, their biggest competitor suffered a deadly *E. coli* outbreak. People died, and their company was ruined. The strain that caused it? It wasn't naturally occurring. It was one that I helped create in the lab. We wanted to see if we could eradicate it. It was the same strain from my research."

I stared at him, horrified. "You think they're doing something similar here? With Hazelton Farms?"

"I don't know," he admitted. "But I can't ignore the connection. If Ilsa is working with them, she might have set this whole thing in motion. And if they're involved, things could get even more dangerous."

My chest tightened as I processed his words. Ilsa wasn't just manipulating Charlie—she was playing a much bigger game. "But do you think they killed Charlie? Do you think *she* killed Charlie? We need to stop her from getting away with this!" I said firmly. "Before it's too late."

Alejandro nodded. "Agreed. But we need to be careful."

I paced the room, my thoughts swirling. "I'm thinking of canceling my last event," I said abruptly.

Alejandro looked up, frowning. "Why? You've been planning that for weeks."

I sighed. "Because I can't focus on anything with all of these thoughts swirling around."

Alejandro leaned back in his chair, crossing his arms. "You think she did it?"

"I don't know," I admitted, stopping to face him. "But I can't ignore the feeling that she's hiding something. And that recording device the police have? I bet it has her on it."

Alejandro tilted his head, studying me. "If that's the case, you're better off hosting the event."

I blinked. "How do you figure that?"

"Because it gives you an opportunity," Alejandro said, sitting up straighter. "If you cancel, you're just sitting here, waiting for Cora to hand you crumbs. But if you go ahead with the event, you have control. You can use it to reveal what Isla's really like."

"You mean, like, set her up?" I asked, my pulse quickening.

"Not exactly," he said. "But people show their true colors under pressure. If you create the right situation, you might get her to slip up. Maybe she'll say or do something that connects her to Charlie's death—or at least to whatever scheme she's running."

As I considered his words, the idea took root in my mind. "That's risky."

"Everything about this situation is risky," Alejandro pointed out. "But you're smart, Annee. You can handle it."

I let out a slow breath, the wheels in my head turning. "Alright," I said finally. "I'll go ahead with the event. But if this idea backfires…"

"It won't," Alejandro interrupted, his voice steady. "Just make sure you're ready. And don't let her see you coming."

I nodded, a mix of fear and determination swirling inside me. "Okay."

Alejandro gave me a rare, encouraging smile. "Good. Now, let's figure out how to make this work."

Chapter 33

Manger les pissenlits par la racine:
To eat dandelions by the root (to be dead)

stood in the center of the dining room, taking a deep breath as I surveyed the scene. The soft glow of candlelight danced off the shimmering ornaments, casting the room in a warm golden hue. From the garlands adorned with miniature Eiffel Towers to the Parisian Christmas village centerpiece, every detail exuded elegance and care. It was "Last Christmas in Paris" come to life, but the beauty of the evening felt like a fragile mask, hiding the tension thrumming beneath the surface.

The room was full of warmth and laughter as guests sipped wine and marveled over the Bûche de Noël I had painstakingly prepared. The menu would be a triumph: the pâté en croûte, rich and flaky; the boeuf bourguignon, hearty and comforting; and the gratin dauphinois, crisp and creamy.

The party had just begun to hum, the cocktail portion where glasses clinked and laughter floated effortlessly through the air. Guests drifted from the garland-draped mantel to the glittering Parisian village centerpiece, nibbling at hors d'oeuvres while a game of *Who Am I?* wound its way through the room.

To break the ice, Mackenzie had suggested the game. Each guest had a card pinned to their back with the name of a famous French figure. Everyone else could see who you were, but you had to guess based on the clues they gave. Once you guessed correctly, you earned the card and got a new one pinned on, the goal being to collect as many as possible before the evening ended.

Mackenzie had even pinned a card on Cora, who played along with a rare, amused smile. Her card read Joan of Arc, and more than one guest joked that it suited her far too well.

The laughter had started light and playful. Paul discovered he was Napoleon after someone teased, "He was short, but had big ambitions." Emerson groaned when he realized he was Voltaire, piecing it together after Mackenzie said, "He wrote a lot and complained even more."

Guests mingled, moving from group to group, dropping hints here, tossing barbs there. Cards changed hands, guesses landed with bursts of laughter, and for a little while the evening glowed with warmth.

Magda and Felix arrived together, wrapped in matching berets and scarves patterned with tiny Eiffel Towers. They looked like they'd stepped straight off a tourist bus, but they wore the getup with small-town pride, nodding at compliments as though it were the height of chic. I'd even invited Roy, hoping to get a better handle on him than just our uneasy encounters in the street. He slipped in late, bundled in a dark wool coat, and someone quickly pinned a card to him. A ripple of laughter went around when the name was revealed: Robespierre.

Mackenzie offered him the first clue, a wry smile tugging at her lips. "He fought for the people, but he wasn't afraid of blood on his hands." The group chuckled a little too nervously, and Roy raised an eyebrow, as if the words amused him more than they should. He didn't answer right away, just gave a small, knowing smile before moving on to mingle with another group.

The rhythm of guesses and clues carried the party along until it was Ilsa's turn. She sat near the fireplace in a red dress that shimmered in the candlelight, commanding her small circle of admirers with polished charm. When I approached, she turned, her smile warm and gracious.

"Annee," she said, her voice smooth. "This is extraordinary. The food, the decorations, it feels almost like home. I've missed Europe, missed Paris especially. And these pastries…." She gestured toward the table with its towers of macarons and sugared tarts, "…they nearly brought tears to my eyes. Thank you for inviting me."

I smiled tightly. "I'm glad you came. I thought you might be curious."

Ilsa swirled the wine in her glass. She leaned back in her chair, her lips curving in that polished, practiced smile.

"So, who am I, Annee? Give me a clue."

Her card read *Marie Antoinette*, and I couldn't resist sharpening the clues.

"She was someone who lived in luxury while others starved," I said, my tone sweetened just enough to keep the edge veiled.

A few chuckles broke out, but Ilsa's smile thinned.

"She believed her position made her untouchable," I added, meeting her gaze directly.

Ilsa swirled the wine in her glass, her smile tightening into something colder. "Some figures are remembered unfairly. Painted as villains when they were simply doing what was necessary."

My card was *Madame Curie*. Emerson offered me a kind one: "She was brilliant—a scientist ahead of her time."

But Ilsa leaned in, very close to me, brushing against me gently as she spoke, with her eyes glinting intensely. "She couldn't stop herself from digging too deep. Curiosity killed her in the end. A woman who thought she knew everything… until it destroyed her."

The jab landed, the room going still.

I lifted my chin, keeping my voice calm. "At least she left the world something that saved lives. Not everyone can say the same." I paused just long enough to let the weight of my words settle before adding, softly but firmly, "Instead of taking lives—or a life, for that matter."

Ilsa's grip tightened on her glass. For a moment I thought she might snap the stem in two. The mask of poise she wore so well wavered, just enough for the first crack to show.

I set my own glass of wine on the side table, freeing my hands as I leaned in, ready to push her further.

Before I could, Sophia swept into the circle near Emerson with the professor in tow. "Where do we get our cards for this game?" she asked brightly, gesturing toward the clusters of laughing guests.

I turned slightly, forcing a smile. "Mackenzie's by the mantel, she's handing them out," I said, pointing her in the right direction.

When I turned back, I lifted my glass and took another sip, my focus narrowing again on Ilsa.

Then, as if on cue, a sudden tightness gripped my throat. My vision blurred, and my chest felt like it was caving in. I stumbled back, clutching at the edge of the table. I collapsed to the floor, clawing at my throat, my mind racing. An allergic reaction! How? Everything I'd served was safe.

"Annee!" Alejandro's voice rang out as he rushed toward me.

Alejandro pushed forward through the group, shouldering past Ilsa in his rush to reach me. The movement jolted her, her handbag slipping against her chair with a muffled clink. He dropped to his knees beside me, panic flashing across his face. "EpiPen!" he barked.

It wasn't a wild request. Ever since Emerson's near miss, I'd set up a safety station near the buffet with two EpiPens and a defibrillator, just in case. Mackenzie darted to it and shoved one into Alejandro's hand.

The sharp sting followed a second later, and slowly the constriction eased, air trickling back into my lungs in ragged gulps.

As the room swam back into focus, I caught movement on the floor. A slim object had rolled free from the direction of Ilsa's chair, spinning once before stopping near the hearth.

A syringe.

Gasps rippled through the room. All eyes turned to Ilsa, whose hand hovered, frozen, at the half-open flap of her handbag.

Before anyone else could speak, Cora stepped forward from the edge of the crowd. She'd been standing quietly, observing, but now her voice cut through the chaos like a blade. "Ilsa Gaines, don't move."

Ilsa's wineglass slipped from her fingers and shattered on the floor. "What? You think I did this?"

Cora's hand rested on her hip, steady and sure. "That syringe says maybe. You need to come with me." Her voice dropped into something calm and practiced. "You have the right to remain silent. Anything you say can and will be used against you in a court of law. You have the right to an attorney. If you can't afford one, one will be provided for you."

Ilsa's face drained of color. "This is insane! I didn't kill Charlie, and I didn't do this either. I was just trying to clean up his mess!"

"Then you can explain it at the station," Cora said firmly. "But right now, you're done here."

Just then, Roy stepped forward from the crowd, his voice smooth. "She's diabetic. That syringe could be insulin. You're rushing to judgment."

Cora's gaze snapped to him, sharp as a blade. "Funny how you know so much about her, Roy. More than anyone else here. Care to explain that?"

Roy's smile was thin, unreadable. "Hazelton's a small town. People talk."

For a moment, the air in the room seemed to freeze, every guest holding their breath. The elegance of the evening had shattered, leaving only suspicion hanging heavy in the air.

Alejandro steadied me into a chair, his hand warm against my shoulder. "You're safe now. The EMTs are on their way."

Ilsa's protests faded into the snowy night as she was escorted out. The room remained eerily silent, the tension thick enough to cut with a knife.

Paul knelt beside me again, his hand steady on my shoulder. "Are you okay?" he asked softly, his voice filled with concern.

I nodded weakly, still trying to process everything. "I'm fine," I whispered, though my mind was racing. Ilsa's words lingered, haunting me. If she wasn't the one who killed Charlie, then who had?

I saw Mackenzie and Emerson hovering nearby.

The room spun slightly, but I steadied myself. Paul moved closer, but Emerson moved quickly by me and sat down next to me. He held my hand as I tried to speak.

The EMTs arrived and I continued to process what was happening.

"She's going to be okay. We don't have to take her in. Just keep an eye on her tonight," they determined.

How did Ilsa know I was onto her? How could she have tried a repeat performance here in my house at another one of my parties? But maybe it was all over. Ilsa was in custody, and Alejandro was home. Maybe I could just let it go.

Mackenzie helped me to my room. Paul stood off in the distance, in the crowd of onlooking guests, never getting close enough to say goodbye.

Mackenzie laid down next to me on the bed. "I won't forgive Alejandro for encouraging you. He was scared while he was in jail. And he left his job and hid here because he feared Evergreen. He was being so selfish, just trying to save his own skin and putting you at risk."

"Thanks, Mack. Thanks for making sure I invited Cora and for being my best friend."

And then I dozed off.

Chapter 34

Être Haut Comme Trois Pommes:
To Be Tall Like Three Apples (to be of short stature)

Christmas Eve had always been a night filled with nostalgia for me, but this year, I felt different. I felt like I was stepping into my evening with the ghost of Christmas future. I drove alone through the quiet streets of Hazelton, the snow lightly falling around me, dusting the pine trees and rooftops with a fresh layer of white. While I was excited to see Paul, I couldn't shake the nerves fluttering in my chest. It wasn't just that I'd be meeting his parents again in a more intimate setting, but that I was stepping into their family's long-standing celebration—one filled with history, tradition, and meaning.

When I pulled up to the house, I was greeted by the warm glow of Christmas lights twinkling from the porch. The home was large, older, and undeniably elegant—a classic Oregon house with dark cedar shingles, a wraparound porch, and tall windows framed by wooden shutters. The house was nestled among towering fir trees, and the scent of pine mingled with the crisp winter air. A large, beautifully lit Nativity scene was displayed on the lawn, the figures of Mary, Joseph, and the baby Jesus illuminated softly under the glow of white Christmas lights. There was a wreath on the door made of fresh greenery, adorned with red velvet ribbons and a simple golden cross in the center.

I paused for a moment, taking in the sight. It felt warm and welcoming, but also a little overwhelming, since I was about to step into Paul's world in a more personal way. I had brought a dish with me, as I always did, especially since my multiple food allergies made it difficult to rely on what others might prepare. Tonight, I'd made bacalao, a traditional salt cod dish with Mediterranean roots that I had adapted slightly to reflect my Puerto Rican heritage. I was happy to contribute to their feast of the seven fishes while still ensuring there was something on the table I could eat. I always pre-ate before attending events, just in case, but tonight I had a good feeling about the dinner.

My recent reaction had me double—and triple—checking all my food. I'd lost a few pounds out of fear of my last allergy scare. It wasn't a good feeling to imagine how my body might betray me. I was still trying to force myself out of the emotional place and negative relationship with food I had experienced after culinary school. I felt ashamed of my weakness. I wouldn't eat out with friends because I didn't want to seem difficult. I didn't want to eat at friends' houses who had made special dishes just to disappoint them as they learned they didn't really understand my multiple food allergies and I wouldn't be able to taste their food—not even a bite. By opening The Literary Table and hosting my own events, I'd healed myself of that burden, but now I felt like I had slipped back into that old world of terror—food as the enemy, my body its accomplice.

I adjusted my dress, taking a deep breath. I had opted for something festive but not too flashy: a deep emerald-green velvet dress that hugged my waist and flared out slightly at the knees. It was simple yet elegant, with a square neckline and delicate lace detailing at the sleeves. I had paired it with black tights and ankle boots, knowing the weather called for practicality more than anything. My hair was loosely curled, and I wore a touch of red lipstick—just enough to feel dressed up for the occasion without overdoing it.

As I walked up the steps, the door opened, and there was Paul, waiting for me with a smile that immediately set me at ease.

"You made it," he said, stepping out onto the porch and closing the door behind him. His breath misted in the cold air as he leaned in to greet me, his arms wrapping around me in a warm, familiar hug. His cologne smelled like cedar and fresh cloves, and I could feel the tension from the drive melting away.

"I did," I replied, smiling up at him. "I wasn't going to miss this."

Paul looked as handsome as ever in a dark gray suit, but he had ditched the tie, making him look just a bit more relaxed. His hair, still damp from what must have been a recent shower, was tousled in that effortlessly charming way he could pull off. His blue eyes sparkled in the dim light, and he reached for the dish I was holding.

"You didn't have to bring anything," he said, though he looked impressed. "But I'm glad you did."

"I always bring something," I said with a laugh. "You know me."

He grinned. "Come on, everyone's inside. My mom's been fussing over the buffet for hours."

I followed him inside, where the warmth of the house enveloped me. The entryway was grand, with polished hardwood floors and a sweeping staircase that curved up to the second floor. The interior was as elegant as the exterior, with high ceilings, crown molding, and large windows that let in the soft glow of the Christmas lights from outside. A tall Christmas tree stood in the living room, decorated with delicate glass ornaments, strings of pearls, and shimmering tinsel. The room smelled like cinnamon and citrus, the scent of the season lingering in every corner.

I could hear the hum of conversation coming from the dining room, where the feast of the seven fishes was well underway. The house was filled with the sound of Christmas music—soft carols playing in the background—and the atmosphere was cozy, even though the gathering was clearly formal.

Paul led me through the entryway and into the dining room, where a long table stretched out, covered in platters of food. The feast of the seven fishes was an Italian-American tradition, and I could see the care and attention that had gone into every dish. There were bowls of calamari, delicately fried and served with lemon wedges, and platters of baked clams topped with bread-crumbs and herbs. A large tray of linguine with white clam sauce sat at the center of the table, its aroma filling the room with the scent of garlic and olive oil. Shrimp scampi glistened under the soft light, and nearby, a beautiful whole branzino was plated with roasted vegetables, its skin crisp and golden.

I noticed a few dishes I wasn't familiar with—likely family recipes passed down through generations. There was a large salad of octopus and potatoes, dressed simply with olive oil and parsley, and a dish of bacalao, which was likely different from the one I had brought, but it was equally inviting. On the table was truly a feast, overflowing with the bounty of the sea.

Paul's parents were in the dining room, greeting guests and making sure everything was just right. His mother, a petite woman with silver hair and a warm smile, welcomed me with open arms. "Annee, so glad you could join us," she said, pulling me into a quick hug. "You've brought something, I see?"

I held up the dish of bacalao with a smile. "I hope it's okay that I brought something. It's a little blend of Italian and Puerto Rican tradition."

"Oh, how wonderful!" she exclaimed, clearly delighted. "I'll add it to the table. Thank you."

Paul's father, a tall man with a firm handshake and an easygoing demeanor, greeted me next. "Nice to see you again, Annee," he said. "Paul's told us all about your holiday events."

I smiled politely, feeling a little embarrassed, but grateful for Paul's kindness. "It's nice to be here. Your home is beautiful."

Before I could take in more of the scene, my eyes fell on someone I hadn't expected to see—Magda, standing near the buffet table with a glass of wine in hand, chatting with a couple of the guests. My stomach tightened for a moment, unsure of what to make of her presence. Magda and Felix had been close with Charlie before his death, and it was hard to separate my suspicions from the reality of seeing her here, so comfortable in Paul's parents' home.

Paul must have noticed my surprise. "Oh, I didn't mention that Magda and Felix were invited, did I?" he said, leaning in to speak quietly. "You know they're old family friends. My parents invite them every year."

I nodded, feeling slightly off-balance, but I tried to compose myself. "Yes, I forgot that you all are close."

Magda glanced in our direction, and for a brief moment, our eyes met. She smiled politely, raising her glass slightly in greeting, but there was something guarded in her expression. I gave her a small nod in return, unsure of what to say.

"Come on," Paul said gently, placing a hand on my lower back. "Let's get something to eat."

We made our way to the buffet, and I was struck again by the sheer abundance of food. Paul tried to fill a plate for both of us, making sure to add a little of everything, including a generous helping of the bacalao I had brought. I had to stop him. I picked a separate plate and found a crudité platter and added some carrots and celery to my plate to complement the dish that I brought. I wasn't ready to eat other people's food yet. We found a spot at the edge of the dining room, where we could sit and eat without being too caught up in the conversation.

As we ate, Paul leaned in, his voice low. "I know seeing Magda and Felix here might be a little strange, especially with everything that's been going on."

I nodded, taking a bite of carrot. "Yeah, it is. But it's fine. I just wasn't expecting it."

Paul gave me a reassuring smile. "If it makes you uncomfortable, we don't have to stay long."

I appreciated his thoughtfulness, but I didn't want to make a scene. "It's okay," I said softly. "I'll be fine."

As the evening went on, I found myself relaxing into the imagined familiarity of the celebration, as if I had always been invited to the party. The sound of laughter filled the room, and the clink of silverware against plates created a soft rhythm in the background. People moved around, refilling their glasses and chatting with one another, while the fire in the living room crackled softly, casting a warm glow over the scene.

Paul's hand rested lightly on mine as we talked quietly, and I couldn't help but feel a deep sense of contentment. Despite the uncertainties swirling around me—the unresolved questions about Charlie's death and Ilsa's guilt—I felt safe here with Paul, in this beautiful house filled with tradition and love.

"Hey, I was really worried about you the other night. I wanted to help, but it looked like you had a lot of people in your corner. I'm not sure why you didn't tell me what you were planning. You knew I had suspicions about Ilsa, too."

I was surprised to hear what felt like a scolding from him. "I'm sorry. I had just a vague plan about confronting her. But as you know, things didn't go quite as I planned."

He brushed a strand of hair away from my face. "Well, it's over now. Maybe this town can get back to a bit of normalcy."

I nodded, but I wasn't so sure. Everyone was talking about this corporation—it had been given an identity with a mask, like a soulless entity that might be responsible for all of this harm for the sake of profit. Yet what was it, really? It was people. People with names, families, and choices they were making to determine the fate of the people in this dwindling town. Would they keep the farm open? Would people lose their jobs?

As the night wore on and the guests began to disperse, Paul leaned over and whispered, "Thank you for coming. It means a lot to me."

I smiled, my heart warming at his words. "I'm glad I did."

We stood by the fire for a few moments longer, the house quieting around us. Whatever lay ahead, I knew I wouldn't be facing it alone.

Chapter 35

Mettre de l'eau dans son vin:
To put water in your wine (to make a compromise)

As the night wore on, the sounds of laughter and conversation softened, replaced by the gentle hum of Christmas carols playing softly in the background. People began gathering their coats and scarves, preparing for the next part of the evening. Paul leaned in close to me as I finished the last sip of wine from my glass.

"Ready for the walk to the church?" he asked, his voice low and gentle, the glow of the fire dancing in his eyes.

I smiled, though I hesitated. Midnight Mass had always been a tradition in Hazelton, and while I hadn't attended in years, I knew it was an integral part of the evening for Paul's family. The guests were already gathering near the door, each of them bundling up against the cold. Outside, the snow continued to fall softly, and I could hear people preparing lanterns and candles for the short walk to the church, their quiet voices filled with reverence and anticipation.

Paul must have noticed my hesitation, because he reached for my hand, giving it a gentle squeeze. "You don't have to come if you're not up for it," he said softly. "It's a nice tradition, but no pressure."

I looked around the room, seeing the guests—Magda and Felix among them—gathering by the door with lanterns in hand, their faces glowing with the spirit of the holiday. There was something serene about the scene, about the way the night was unfolding in quiet reverence. And yet, I felt a pull to go home, to step away from the people and tradition of this gathering and return to my own space, where I could sort through the emotions swirling within me.

"I think I'll head home. It's been a lovely evening, but I need some time to myself."

Paul looked at me for a moment, his eyes filled with understanding. "Of course," he said, gently releasing my hand. "I'll walk you to your car."

Together, we made our way through the crowded hallway, the other guests offering us warm goodbyes and Merry Christmases as we passed. The air outside was crisp and clean, and the snow crunched under our feet as we stepped onto the porch. The lanterns were already lit, their soft glow casting long, flickering shadows across the snowy ground.

Paul and I walked in silence for a few steps, the sound of the guests' quiet laughter and the beginning of Christmas caroling filling the air as they prepared for the walk to the church.

I glanced at him, a soft smile playing on my lips. "Thank you, Paul," I said quietly. "For your friendship, and for tonight. It's been...exactly what I needed."

He smiled back, his expression warm and understanding. "Same here, Bonne Annee. Nights like this remind me what really matters."

I glanced back at the house one last time, taking in the warm glow of the Christmas lights twinkling in the windows, the soft hum of the carolers' voices rising as they gathered on the porch. The Nativity scene on the lawn, bathed in soft white light, seemed almost otherworldly. The figures of Mary and Joseph watched over the peaceful night.

When we reached my car, Paul stopped, his breath visible in the cold air. He turned to me, his eyes soft but full of something deeper and unsaid.

He stepped closer, his hand finding mine once more. "I'll see you tomorrow?"

I nodded, feeling the flutter of something between us that made my heart race. "Tomorrow," I echoed.

Paul leaned down, pressing a gentle kiss to my cheek, his touch lingering just a moment longer than usual. It was tender, sweet, and it sent a warm rush through me, despite the cold night air. When he pulled back, his smile was soft but filled with promise.

"Drive safe," he said, stepping back and watching as I climbed into the car.

As I started the engine, Paul lingered on the porch, his silhouette framed by the glow of the lanterns and the snowfall around him. The sight of him standing there, surrounded by the warmth of the night and the tradition of the holiday, filled me with a strange sense of longing and contentment all at once.

I waved, and he returned the gesture, his breath visible in the cold as he stood there, watching me go. The road ahead was quiet, the snow continuing to fall softly as I made my way home. The town seemed almost asleep, the Christmas lights twinkling from the windows of the houses lining the streets, the warmth of the season evident in every glowing light and every snow-covered wreath.

But as peaceful as the drive was, my mind was buzzing. I kept thinking about Magda—about seeing her at Paul's house and realizing just how close she was to his family. The connection between her and Charlie, the tension around the hazelnut farm…all those thoughts swirled in my mind, but none of them seemed to click into place.

When I finally arrived home, the house was quiet and dark, except for the string of lights I had left on, casting a warm glow over the porch. I parked my car and stepped out, the snow falling lightly around me. Oscar trotted over to me, his black-and-white fur slightly tousled and his tail wagging furiously with excitement.

"Hey, buddy," I whispered, kneeling to greet him before unlocking the door. He nuzzled into me, his warm, sloppy kisses a welcome distraction from the noise in my head.

Inside, I slipped off my coat and boots. Oscar bounded ahead, circling the couch before curling up with a contented sigh, his tail thumping against the cushions. I sat down beside him, sinking into the softness of the pillows, and let out a deep breath. My mind raced over the events of the evening, from the warmth of Paul's kiss still lingering on my cheek to the sight of Magda mingling with Paul's family.

As I sat there, staring into the flickering lights of the Christmas tree, I felt the weight of everything settle over me. There was so much to untangle, so many questions still unanswered, but for now, I let the warmth of the moment soothe me.

Tomorrow, I would see Paul again. Tomorrow, I would try to figure out where all of this was headed. But tonight, the quiet peace of Christmas Eve was laced with a restless energy that I couldn't shake. I glanced at the clock—11:15 p.m. Everyone in the house and in town was either asleep, playing Santa stashing presents under the tree, or at Midnight Mass.

Sylvester, who had returned, was snoring softly in the guest room. Emerson had retreated to bed early. Alejandro, I assumed, was asleep in the guest house, leaving the house steeped in silence. I used my phone to check Alejandro's location—we were back to our old routines.

My thoughts drifted to Hazelton Farms. Felix and Magda had been a strange, quiet presence at my dinner party, and their connection to both the Christmas market and Charlie's untimely death nagged at me.

Oscar stirred at my feet, lifting his head to look at me. His eyes were alert, sensing my unease.

I reached down and scratched behind his ears. "I know, buddy," I whispered. "But I can't just sit here."

I stood, grabbing my coat from the back of the chair. Oscar's tail thumped against the floor.

"No, not this time," I said, kneeling down to rub his head. "You stay here and guard the house."

Oscar let out a small whine but stayed put as I made my way out the back door. I needed to confirm Alejandro was really where his phone said he was. Tonight was a "trust, but verify" moment. It became clear that the only person who I really knew wasn't the murderer was me.

I peeked through the cottage window. Alejandro was sleeping with that orange cat! Mystery solved. Now to trust my instincts...

The snow was falling lightly now, dusting the ground in a thin white blanket. The night was cold and crisp, and as I started my car, the headlights cut through the darkness, illuminating the winding road ahead.

The drive to Hazelton Farms was eerily quiet. The roads were empty, save for a few stray tracks left by earlier travelers. The glow of Christmas lights twinkled faintly from the houses I passed, but they only deepened the unease in my chest.

As I approached the outskirts of the farm, the tall rows of hazelnut trees loomed like silent sentinels in the moonlight. The farm's sprawling barn stood at the end of the long drive. I parked the car and turned off the engine, letting the stillness of the night seep in around me. My breath fogged the air as I stepped out, crunching across the snow-covered ground toward the building.

I guess we lived in the kind of town where people trusted each other's intentions. Even with a murderer in our midst, the building had been left unlocked. The mentality seemed to be, *If you have nothing to hide or nothing to protect, why lock a door?*

I slipped inside, making my way back to the offices where I had snooped around before, searching for the recording device. This time, I pushed further, my curiosity and determination driving me forward. I ventured to their home on the property, crossing the line from snooping into outright breaking and entering.

The house was still, the air heavy with secrets untold. As I scanned the room, my eyes landed on a shelf filled with books on various agricultural practices, everything from beekeeping to advanced irrigation techniques. One book stood out: *Castor Oil Production and Uses.* Its spine was cracked, and several pages were dog-eared, as if it had been referenced often. I pulled it off the shelf, flipping through to find sections marked with notes in the margins. *Ricin,* I remembered, *was a dangerous byproduct of castor oil production.*

As I moved deeper inside, something else caught my eye: a tackle box sitting on a small table near the back door. It seemed innocent enough, just the sort of thing anyone might have for fishing. But something about its placement felt off. I hesitated, then opened it.

Inside, instead of fishing gear, I found syringes neatly arranged alongside small vials, gloves, and scraps of paper covered in handwriting. My stomach turned as the implications sank in.

I took out my phone and snapped pictures of everything—the pages of the book, the contents of the tackle box, every suspicious detail I could find. Questions swirled in my mind. Why hadn't Magda destroyed these things? Did she think no one would look closely? Or was she so arrogant that she believed she'd never be caught?

With each image I captured, the pieces of the puzzle came into sharper focus, but the picture they formed was far more terrifying than I wanted to admit.

It wasn't long before I realized that I was acting like an amateur sleuth in the middle of the night, especially after a few glasses of wine. Meaning, I hadn't exactly thought things through. What was I going to do now? I could call Cora, but I was trespassing, and none of this evidence would likely hold up in court. Would it even count as evidence if I'd found it this way? I wondered if the same issue applied to those recordings on Alejandro's devices. Everything I was uncovering felt precarious, like it might crumble under legal scrutiny.

But I couldn't stop searching. Something about this house—tonight—felt like it was holding answers I wasn't ready to leave behind. I glanced toward the staircase, its shadowy ascent both inviting and foreboding. Before I could talk myself out of it, I took a steadying breath and began to climb, my footsteps soft against the worn wooden steps.

Upstairs, it looked like someone was packing for a trip. An open suitcase sat on the bed, half-filled with neatly folded clothes, and a toiletry bag rested on the nightstand. I paused, taking it all in, noticing the French-themed scarves sitting atop the folded clothes, my mind racing. Why would they be leaving now?

Then, another thought struck me like a jolt. Felix had known that I was at the hazelnut farm the night of the kayaking incident. How? My breath caught as the pieces started to click into place. Maybe the reason everything was left unlocked wasn't about trust or overconfidence. Maybe Felix and Magda had security—real security, the kind that didn't need locks to do its job.

They had to have surveillance of some kind—cameras, recordings, something watching, something listening. The idea sent a chill down my spine, and I began scanning the room more carefully, my eyes searching for anything out of place that might confirm my suspicion.

The truth hit me hard when I heard the sound of a door opening downstairs. My heart stopped. Felix and Magda had entered the house. They knew I was here.

My mind raced. They must have been notified when I entered the first building. The unlocked doors had been bait, part of a system to track intruders. I hadn't even considered it. They must have left Midnight Mass and headed straight here when the alert went off.

I froze, still clutching my phone. The pictures of the syringes and castor oil book were saved to it, but useless in this moment. Felix and Magda were coming upstairs—I could hear their footsteps, deliberate and steady. I was still in the room, trapped, with no time left to think.

Chapter 36

Tourner au vinaigre:
To turn to vinegar (a situation turning sour)

The air felt heavy, suffocating, as Felix and Magda stood in the doorway, blocking any hope of escape. My heart pounded as I slipped my hand into my coat pocket, feeling for my phone. My fingers brushed the familiar edge, and I pressed the side button, unlocking it by feel.

"Magda, Felix," I said, forcing calm into my voice despite the rising panic in my chest. "I didn't expect you back so soon."

Magda's smile was sharp, like a knife's edge. "Well, Annee, we didn't expect visitors on Christmas Eve, either. But here you are. Trespassing."

Felix shifted beside her, his face pale, his hands twitching nervously at his sides. He wasn't like Magda. Her confidence radiated in the way she stood, like a predator savoring its prey. Felix looked like he wanted to be anywhere but here.

"I was just leaving," I said, my voice steady as I carefully tapped my phone, dialing Paul's number. The soft hum of the ringing was muffled by my pocket, and I prayed he was awake, that he would pick up—or at least, hear what was about to unfold.

Magda took a step forward, her eyes gleaming. "Oh no, you're not going anywhere. Not after you've been snooping where you don't belong."

Felix looked at her, his voice shaky. "Magda, maybe we should just—"

"Quiet, Felix," she snapped, her tone icy. "Annee needs to understand why she shouldn't have stuck her nose in our business."

I shifted my weight, glancing toward the window, calculating. "What business is that, Magda?" I asked, stalling. "The hazelnut farm? Or something else?"

Magda laughed, low and cold. "Oh, you think you're clever, don't you? Digging through my home, taking pictures. Did you think we wouldn't notice?" Her eyes narrowed. "Charlie thought he was clever too, reading everyone's mail."

The breath caught in my throat. "Charlie?"

"Yes, Charlie," she hissed, her voice dripping with venom. "He found out what Felix and I were planning. He thought he could stop us. But I couldn't let that happen."

My stomach churned as the pieces clicked into place. "You killed him."

Magda smirked. "I had no choice. He was going to ruin everything. Do you have any idea what this land is worth to the developers? Millions, Annee. Millions."

Felix flinched at her words, his hands trembling. "Magda, she knows too much now. We should—"

"Shut up, Felix!" Magda snapped, her patience unraveling. She turned her attention back to me. "And you...you've been a thorn in my side since that ridiculous dinner party."

My chest tightened as I remembered the chaos of that night. "You mean Emerson's allergic reaction. And Charlie's death." I staggered back a step, my heart racing. "Just the other night... you tried to kill me."

Magda didn't respond, but Felix stepped forward, his voice cracking as he spoke. "The other night, it wasn't supposed to go that far. We knew you suspected Ilsa. This town can't keep any secrets from insiders. Ilsa was the only one who didn't know you were gunning for her. I—I only added a little ground almond to your plate and the hot chocolate. Just enough to make you sick. I didn't think you would react so badly."

Felix's face crumpled. "I had to protect Magda. You were asking too many questions. You were always poking around."

Magda's laugh was cruel. "And yet here you are, still alive. You should've learned your lesson, Annee."

Before I could respond, Magda lunged for me. I twisted out of her grasp, fumbling with my phone in my pocket. It slipped from my hand, clattering to the floor, and Magda's eyes flashed as she dove for it.

But I didn't wait to see what she would do. I bolted for the window, wrenching it open with trembling hands. Behind me, Felix shouted something, but Magda's footsteps were closer. I climbed out onto the roof, the icy shingles slick beneath my feet.

The cold night air hit me like a slap, but I didn't stop. The glow of the Christmas decorations on the roof provided just enough light to navigate the terrain. I crouched behind a large inflatable snowman, pressing myself against the cold surface as I tried to quiet my ragged breaths.

Inside, I heard Magda scream in frustration. "Find her, Felix! She can't have gone far."

Icy panicked tears streamed from my eyes as I heard her voice, so close. I prayed Paul had heard everything and that he was on his way.

The distant sound of sirens broke through the night. They were faint at first but grew louder and louder. Paul. He must have heard. He was coming.

Then movement caught my eye. Magda shoved the window wide and climbed out onto the roof. My stomach dropped. She was headed straight toward me, her red scarf snapping in the wind.

"You ruined everything!" she shouted, boots sliding on the icy shingles.

The sirens grew deafening as a pair of police cars skidded into the driveway below. She lunged forward, but her foot slipped. For one terrifying moment, she was airborne—then she went tumbling right off the roof. A chorus of gasps rose from the officers below.

Instead of hitting the hard ground, she landed with a heavy thump in the snowbank at the edge of the lawn, half-burying herself in the drift. The inflatable snowman she'd clipped on the way down sagged drunkenly to one side, wheezing out air.

Cora's officers were on her in seconds, pulling her upright as she sputtered and shrieked, red scarf now crusted with snow.

"Bonne Annee!" Paul's voice rang out, panicked and desperate.

"Here!" I called, my voice cracking.

He looked up, spotting me on the roof. Relief washed over his face as he ran to the side of the house. "Stay there, I'm coming up."

Moments later, Paul was at my side, pulling me into his arms. "You're okay," he whispered, his voice shaking. "You're okay."

Below us, Cora's officers hauled Magda and Felix into custody. Magda's defiant screams echoed through the night, but Felix's sobs were louder, his guilt finally breaking through.

As the officers led them away, Paul tightened his hold on me. "It's over," he said softly. "You're safe now."

I nodded, my exhaustion crashing over me. It was over. But the memory of Magda's cold smile and Felix's trembling hands would stay with me, as a chilling reminder.

Chapter 37

C'est la Cerise sur le Gâteau:
*It's the Cherry on the Cake (it's the final detail to finish
something satisfactorily)*

O ver the past few weeks, Hazelton had transformed from a festive holiday town into a place of quiet tension. The twelfth day of Christmas had arrived, and while some in town celebrated Epiphany and Three Kings Day with their decorations of crowns, stars, and camels, the atmosphere remained heavy. For me and the small group of friends who had spent the past few weeks unraveling the mystery of Charlie's death, this day marked something else entirely—justice was finally about to be served.

Felix and Magda were facing trial, their assets frozen while they awaited judgment. Evergreen, Alejandro's former employer and the company that had quietly taken over Hazelton Farms, had slipped past accountability once again. They claimed ignorance of Felix and Magda's actions and were cleared of any criminal involvement, though the sale still stood. The farm would be demolished within weeks to make way for a new project, and with it, a wave of new people and businesses would come to town, likely changing the face of Hazelton forever.

Ilsa had been cleared, but she'd made the decision to leave town. She put Charlie's house up for sale and resigned from any future involvement in the Christmas market. Her absence would be felt, but Jasper had stepped up, convincing the town council to keep the market alive next year. "For Charlie's sake," he had said, and no one had dared to argue.

The future of Hazelton hung in the balance, but tonight wasn't about the past or the changes looming on the horizon. Tonight was about the Epiphany and about new beginnings. I had gathered the people closest to me to celebrate.

Paul arrived first, carrying a bottle of sparkling wine. Just like in *Christmas in Connecticut*, he was my Mr. Jefferson Jones, and he wasn't giving me the old Magoo (like Sinkewicz). And to quote my favorite line from the movie, we were having a romance. I tried not to overthink it, and it was easy. That was really something, because nothing ever had seemed easy to me before.

Alejandro followed, looking lighter somehow, as if the burden of the past few weeks had finally eased. Everyone knew about Evergreen now; he was no longer alone in the fight. Mackenzie, with her infectious laughter, brought a cake she'd decorated with golden stars. Katie came with a plate of her famous pastries, declaring she'd "gone a little overboard" as she set them on the table. Emerson and Sylvester arrived together, Emerson immediately slipping into his usual sarcastic commentary while Sylvester greeted everyone warmly, already discussing his ideas for a new restaurant in Hazelton. He seemed genuinely excited about staying connected to the town, even as Emerson reminded him that they both had busy lives to return to.

As the table filled with steaming dishes, the spirit of Three Kings Day truly came alive. The aroma of spices, roasted pork, and sweet coconut lingered in the air, weaving itself into the fabric of the celebration. Puerto Rican traditions had made their way to Hazelton tonight, and I couldn't have been more grateful for the warmth they brought.

At the center of the table sat a glistening platter of lechón asado, the roasted pork shoulder seasoned to perfection with garlic, oregano, and a hint of citrus. Its crispy, caramelized skin crackled under the knife, revealing tender, juicy meat that everyone was eager to try. Next to it, a bowl of arroz con gandules stood proudly, the seasoned rice speckled with pigeon peas and flecks of pork, its smoky sofrito base filling the room with its unmistakable fragrance.

"I can't believe you made pasteles," Sylvester said, lifting one of the green banana-wrapped bundles with reverence. The labor-intensive dish was a staple for such occasions, its masa made from grated green bananas and yautía, stuffed with pork, and wrapped in banana leaves. When unwrapped, the pastel revealed a soft, savory interior that tasted like the holidays themselves.

Mackenzie, always a fan of fried food, reached for the tostones. "I could eat a whole plate of these," she said, dipping one into a small bowl of garlicky mayo-ketchup sauce. Katie, meanwhile, was busy serving herself guineítos en escabeche, tangy green bananas marinated in a vinegar-based sauce with onions and peppers, a side dish that perfectly complemented the richness of the pork and rice.

For dessert, the centerpiece was a rosca de reyes, a golden, ring-shaped bread decorated with candied fruits and powdered sugar. Hidden inside was a small figurine of the baby Jesus, and we laughed as Mackenzie cautiously cut her slice, terrified of being the one to find it. Alongside the bread was a shimmering plate of tembleque, a coconut pudding dusted with cinnamon, its creamy sweetness melting on the tongue. Flan de coco sat nearby, its glossy caramel topping glinting in the light of the Christmas tree.

And, of course, no Puerto Rican celebration would be complete without coquito. The creamy, coconut-based drink—spiked with a generous pour of rum—was passed around in small glasses, its nutmeg and cinnamon flavors warming us from the inside out. Even Alejandro, who rarely indulged, raised his glass with a small smile.

"This is what Three Kings Day is all about," Sylvester said, his voice warm as he looked around the table. "Family, food, and a little bit of magic."

As the night stretched on, laughter echoed through the house, and the worries of the past few weeks seemed to melt away. The glow of the decorations and the warmth of the food made it feel like a tropical paradise. Conversation flowed, laughter bubbled up, we were our version of normal once again.

At one point, Emerson leaned over, handing me a folded piece of paper. "By the way," he said, smirking, "you're going to be very busy this year."

I frowned, unfolding the paper to find a printed copy of an article. My eyes widened as I read the headline: "A Feast for the Mind: How Literary-Themed Dining Events Are Revitalizing Small-Town Culture." It was all about my bookstore and events.

I turned to Emerson, stunned. "You wrote this?"

Emerson shrugged, feigning nonchalance. "Figured it was time to give you some positive press."

Sylvester grinned from across the table. "Looks like the Steele family is making a name for itself here."

I couldn't help but smile, warmth spreading through me. The support from everyone here, even from those I didn't expect, meant more than I could express.

After dessert, as the group lingered over coffee and wine, I pulled Alejandro aside. "I know you're planning to get back to your projects," I began hesitantly, "but there's something I'd like your help with."

He raised an eyebrow, curious. "What's that?"

"My mom," I said softly. "I need to know what really happened to her. I know it's been years, but—"

"Say no more," Alejandro interrupted, his tone firm. "I'm in."

I smiled, feeling a mix of relief and gratitude. For the first time in years, it felt like I might finally get answers.

As the night wound down and my friends began to leave, I stood at the doorway, watching them go with a heart full of hope. Hazelton was changing, but it wasn't just the town—it was me. The past weeks had been a whirlwind, drawing me closer to the people I cared about, reminding me of my strength, and giving me a sense of purpose that I'd never had before.

As the last car disappeared down the snowy lane, I glanced up at the bare branches of the tree by the driveway. Two ravens perched there, their dark forms steady against the cold winter night. They had been with me through so much, like quiet neighbors who always seemed to know more than they let on. Wise and watchful, they felt like a part of Hazelton itself, steadfast and patient. I wondered if they might stay until spring, keeping an eye on the changing seasons and, perhaps, on me. With a small smile, I stepped back inside, comforted by the idea that I wasn't alone—not in this town, not in this moment.

I turned off the lights, leaving only the soft glow of the Christmas tree behind me. I patted Oscar on the head and whispered to myself, "What a night to remember." It felt like the perfect gathering—a night to celebrate not only the end of the Christmas season, but the possibilities of new beginnings. A true Bonne Année.

From Annee's Kitchen

Hazelton is a place where food brings people together. Whether it's a bustling holiday dinner, a quiet tea by the fire, or a market treat enjoyed on a snowy evening, the dishes we share carry memories and meaning. I've gathered some of the recipes that played a part in these recent events—meals that comforted, delighted, and, in more than one case, kept secrets simmering beneath the surface.

They aren't fancy, but they are full of flavor and heart. Some are old family staples, others are twists on traditions, and a few are special creations made just for gatherings, such as the Poe Dinner or the Nutcracker Party. I hope you'll try them in your own kitchen, and maybe even share them with the people who bring warmth to your table. After all, stories and recipes both are better when passed along.

Enjoy!

Annee

Poe's Thanksgiving Dinner

*This was the menu at the Poe Dinner, the gathering
that set everything in motion. Inspired by Edgar Allan
Poe, the dishes were playful nods to his stories, dark
and dramatic enough for a Thanksgiving table that
turned unforgettable.*

"NEVERMORE" BLACKENED SHRIMP COCKTAIL
(SERVES 6–8)

SPICY SHRIMP WITH A TANGY BLACKBERRY COCKTAIL SAUCE.

INGREDIENTS
- 1 1/2 lbs large shrimp, peeled and deveined
- 2 tbsp olive oil
- 1 tbsp blackening spice (paprika, cayenne, garlic powder, onion powder, thyme, salt, pepper)
- 1/2 cup ketchup
- 3 tbsp blackberry preserves
- 2 tbsp prepared horseradish
- 1 tbsp lemon juice

INSTRUCTIONS
1. Toss shrimp with olive oil and spice blend.
2. Sear in a hot skillet until pink and charred at the edges, 2–3 minutes per side.
3. Whisk ketchup, blackberry preserves, horseradish, and lemon juice into sauce.
4. Chill both shrimp and sauce before serving.

Serving Note: Plate the shrimp in small glasses with the sauce at the bottom and shrimp hooked around the rim.

RAVEN'S WING STUFFED MUSHROOMS (MAKES 12 CAPS)

PORTOBELLOS FILLED WITH WILD RICE, CRANBERRIES, AND SAGE.

INGREDIENTS

- 12 medium portobello mushroom caps, stems removed
- 1 cup cooked wild rice
- 1/4 cup dried cranberries
- 1/4 cup onion, finely chopped
- 2 tbsp fresh sage, minced
- 2 tbsp olive oil
- 1/4 cup breadcrumbs
- Salt and pepper to taste

INSTRUCTIONS

1. Preheat oven to 375°F (190°C).
2. Heat olive oil in a skillet. Sauté onion and chopped mushroom stems until softened.
3. Stir in wild rice, cranberries, and sage. Season with salt and pepper.
4. Fill mushroom caps with mixture, sprinkle with breadcrumbs.
5. Bake 20 minutes until tender and golden.

Serving Note: Arrange the mushrooms in a spiral, so they look like raven's wings on a platter.

"DARK SHADOWS" ROAST TURKEY (SERVES 10–12)

CLASSIC BIRD WITH A CRANBERRY-BALSAMIC GLAZE.

INGREDIENTS

- 1 whole turkey (12–14 lbs)
- 1/4 cup olive oil
- 2 tbsp fresh rosemary, minced
- 2 tbsp fresh thyme, minced
- Salt and pepper to taste
- 2 cups cranberry juice
- 1/2 cup balsamic vinegar
- 2 tbsp honey

INSTRUCTIONS

1. Preheat oven to 325°F (165°C). Rub turkey with olive oil, herbs, salt, and pepper.
2. Roast in a large pan, basting occasionally, until internal temp reaches 165°F (about 3 hours).
3. In a saucepan, reduce cranberry juice, balsamic, and honey until thick.
4. Brush glaze over turkey during final hour.

Serving Note: The glaze creates a deep sheen. Carve the turkey tableside for dramatic effect.

"MOURNFUL MIDNIGHT" MASHED POTATOES (SERVES 8)

ROASTED GARLIC AND A WHISPER OF TRUFFLE OIL.

INGREDIENTS

- 3 lbs Yukon Gold potatoes, peeled and cubed
- 1 head garlic, roasted until soft
- 1/2 cup butter
- 3/4 cup heavy cream
- 1 tsp truffle oil (optional)
- Salt and pepper to taste

INSTRUCTIONS

1. Boil potatoes until fork tender. Drain.
2. Mash with roasted garlic cloves, butter, and cream.
3. Stir in truffle oil. Season to taste.

Serving Note: Place the potatoes in a black ceramic bowl to match the Poe theme.

"OBSIDIAN" GRAVY (SERVES 8)

PAN DRIPPINGS, BLACK GARLIC, AND A SPLASH OF PORT WINE.

INGREDIENTS

- 1/4 cup pan drippings from roast turkey
- 2 tbsp flour
- 2 cups chicken or turkey stock
- 2 cloves black garlic, mashed
- 1/4 cup port wine

INSTRUCTIONS

1. In a saucepan, whisk flour into drippings until smooth.
2. Slowly add stock, whisking until thickened.
3. Stir in black garlic and port. Simmer 5 minutes.

Serving Note: Pour into a silver gravy boat. Its deep color will make it stand out on the table.

"HARVEST MOON" PIZZA (SERVES 4)

CHARCOAL CRUST, ROASTED BUTTERNUT SQUASH, WILD MUSHROOMS, MOZZARELLA, GRUYERE, FRESH HERBS, AND BALSAMIC DRIZZLE.

INGREDIENTS

- 1 prepared pizza dough (charcoal-infused if available)
- 1 cup roasted butternut squash cubes
- 1 cup wild mushrooms, sautéed
- 1 cup shredded mozzarella
- 1/2 cup shredded Gruyere
- 1 tbsp fresh thyme leaves
- 2 tbsp balsamic glaze

INSTRUCTIONS

1. Preheat oven to 450°F (230°C).
2. Roll dough onto a baking sheet. Top with squash, mushrooms, cheeses, and thyme.
3. Bake 12–15 minutes until crust is crisp and cheese bubbly.
4. Drizzle with balsamic glaze before slicing.

Serving Note: This rustic dish as a nod to autumn harvest, so cut the pie into small squares for sharing.

"RAVEN'S NEST" STUFFING (SERVES 6–8)

GLUTEN-FREE BREAD, CHERRIES, CHESTNUTS, AND CURRANTS, BAKED GOLDEN.

INGREDIENTS

- 6 cups gluten-free bread cubes
- 1/2 cup onion, diced
- 1/2 cup celery, diced
- 1/4 cup dried cherries
- 1/4 cup currants
- 1/2 cup chestnuts, chopped
- 2 cups chicken broth
- 2 tbsp butter

INSTRUCTIONS

1. Preheat oven to 350°F (175°C).
2. Sauté onion and celery in butter until soft.
3. Stir in cherries, currants, and chestnuts.
4. Toss with bread cubes and broth.
5. Transfer to baking dish and bake 30 minutes, until golden.

Serving Note: Arrange the stuffing in a deep dish so the fruit and chestnuts peek out like a bird's nest.

"SHADOWY GREENS" SALAD (SERVES 6)

KALE, SPINACH, ROASTED BEETS, PUMPKIN SEEDS, AND
BLACKBERRY VINAIGRETTE.

INGREDIENTS
- 4 cups kale, torn
- 2 cups spinach leaves
- 2 roasted beets, diced
- 1/4 cup pumpkin seeds
- 1/4 cup crumbled goat cheese
- 1/4 cup blackberries
- 3 tbsp olive oil
- 1 tbsp balsamic vinegar
- 1 tsp Dijon mustard

INSTRUCTIONS
1. Toss greens, beets, seeds, and cheese in a bowl.
2. In blender, combine blackberries, olive oil, vinegar, and mustard. Blend until smooth.
3. Drizzle dressing over salad just before serving.

Serving Note: The deep red of the beets against dark greens makes this salad as striking as it is tasty.

"MACABRE" BRUSSELS SPROUTS (SERVES 6)

*CARAMELIZED WITH BALSAMIC AND TOPPED WITH
CRISPY PANCETTA.*

INGREDIENTS

- 1 1/2 lbs Brussels sprouts, halved
- 2 tbsp olive oil
- 1/4 cup balsamic glaze
- 1/4 cup pancetta, diced and fried crisp
- Salt and pepper to taste

INSTRUCTIONS

1. Preheat oven to 400°F (200°C). Toss sprouts with olive oil, salt, and pepper.
2. Roast 25–30 minutes until caramelized.
3. Drizzle with balsamic glaze and top with pancetta.

Serving Note: The dark caramelized edges fit the Poe-inspired menu perfectly.

"LENORE'S FALLEN APPLES" TART (SERVES 8)

*RUSTIC APPLE TART WITH A GLUTEN-FREE CINNAMON-OAT
CRUST AND DARK CARAMEL DRIZZLE.*

INGREDIENTS

- 1 1/2 cups gluten-free oats
- 1/2 cup rice flour
- 1/4 cup brown sugar
- 1/2 cup butter, melted
- 4 apples, thinly sliced
- 1 tsp cinnamon
- 1/4 tsp nutmeg
- 1/2 cup dark caramel sauce

INSTRUCTIONS

1. Preheat oven to 375°F (190°C).
2. Mix oats, rice flour, sugar, and butter to form crust. Press into tart pan.
3. Toss apples with cinnamon and nutmeg. Layer over crust.
4. Bake 35–40 minutes until apples are tender.
5. Drizzle with caramel before serving.

*Serving Note: Share while slightly warm. The tart will perfume the room with
cinnamon and caramel.*

"THE BLACK CAT" FLOURLESS CHOCOLATE CAKE (SERVES 10)

DUSTED WITH A POWDERED SUGAR SILHOUETTE.

INGREDIENTS

- 8 oz dark chocolate
- 1/2 cup butter
- 3/4 cup sugar
- 3 eggs
- 1/2 cup cocoa powder
- Powdered sugar, for dusting

INSTRUCTIONS

1. Preheat oven to 350°F (175°C). Grease an 8-inch round pan.
2. Melt chocolate and butter together. Whisk in sugar and eggs.
3. Stir in cocoa powder.
4. Pour into pan and bake 25 minutes until set.
5. Cool, then dust with powdered sugar using a stencil.

Serving Note: For a playful gothic touch, use a stencil of a cat or raven to powder the cake.

"BLOOD-RED" POMEGRANATE SORBET (SERVES 6)

SERVED IN DARK CHOCOLATE CUPS.

INGREDIENTS

- 2 cups pomegranate juice
- 1/2 cup sugar
- 1 tbsp lemon juice
- 6 small dark chocolate dessert cups

INSTRUCTIONS

1. In saucepan, heat juice and sugar until dissolved. Stir in lemon juice.
2. Chill mixture, then churn in ice cream maker.
3. Freeze until firm. Scoop into chocolate cups.

Serving Note: The jewel-toned sorbet in chocolate cups will look striking against white dessert plates.

"POE'S PUNCH" (SERVES 6)

DARK RUM, BLACKBERRIES, POMEGRANATE, AND CINNAMON.

INGREDIENTS

- 1 cup dark rum
- 2 cups pomegranate juice
- 1/2 cup blackberry puree
- 1/4 cup cinnamon syrup
- 2 cups sparkling water

INSTRUCTIONS

1. Stir together rum, juices, and syrup.
2. Chill, then top with sparkling water before serving.

Serving Note: Pour the punch into a crystal bowl with floating orange slices for drama.

"RAVEN'S BREW" COFFEE (SERVES 4)

DEEP ROAST WITH OPTIONAL VANILLA OR RASPBERRY LIQUEUR.

INGREDIENTS
- 4 cups strong brewed coffee
- 2 tbsp sugar (optional)
- 1 oz vanilla liqueur (optional)
- 1 oz raspberry liqueur (optional)

INSTRUCTIONS
1. Brew coffee. Sweeten to taste.
2. Add liqueur if desired.

Serving Note: Pour the coffee into heavy stoneware mugs to keep it hot while guests linger.

"MIDNIGHT MULLED WINE" (SERVES 6)

WARM AND SPICED WITH CLOVES, ORANGE PEEL, AND STAR ANISE.

INGREDIENTS
- 1 bottle red wine
- 1/4 cup honey
- 2 cinnamon sticks
- 3 whole cloves
- 1 star anise
- Peel of 1 orange

INSTRUCTIONS
1. Combine all ingredients in saucepan.
2. Heat gently until steaming, but do not boil.
3. Simmer 15 minutes, strain, and serve warm.

Serving Note: Keep the mulled wine on the stove the entire evening, ladling it into mugs as the room fills with spiced fragrance.

Tamales with Alejandro

Cooking tamales with Alejandro was about more than food—it was about memory, tradition, and connection. The slow process of making masa, soaking husks, and wrapping each tamal mirrored the way his family once gathered together in the kitchen. Tamales are festive food, tied to holidays and celebrations, but also an act of care. They're messy, demand patience, and are deeply satisfying.

TAMALES (PORK WITH RED CHILE SAUCE)

MAKES ~24

INGREDIENTS

- 4 cups masa harina (corn flour for tamales)
- 2 ½ cups warm chicken broth
- 1 cup lard or vegetable shortening
- 2 tsp baking powder
- 2 tsp salt
- 24 dried corn husks, soaked in hot water until pliable
- Filling
- 2 lbs pork shoulder, cooked and shredded
- 4 dried ancho chiles
- 2 dried guajillo chiles
- 2 cloves garlic
- 1 tsp cumin
- 1 tsp oregano
- 1 cup reserved pork broth

INSTRUCTIONS

1. Soak chiles in hot water 20 min. Blend with garlic, cumin, oregano, and broth to make sauce. Simmer with pork until coated.
2. Beat lard until fluffy. Add masa, baking powder, salt, then slowly broth until dough is soft but holds shape.
3. Spread 2 tbsp masa on corn husk, add spoon of filling. Fold sides, then bottom up.
4. Steam upright in large pot 1–1.5 hrs until husks peel away easily.

Sugar Plum Fairy Tea

From the day of Isla's arrest, this menu leans into holiday whimsy with peppermint and sugar plums. It's a lighter menu, but no less memorable.

CANDY CANE SCONES (MAKES 8)

CRUMBLY AND DELICATE, WITH JUST THE RIGHT HINT OF PEP-PERMINT, TOPPED WITH CRUSHED CANDY CANES.

INGREDIENTS

- 2 cups flour
- 1/4 cup sugar
- 1 tbsp baking powder
- 1/2 tsp salt
- 1/2 cup cold butter, cubed
- 2/3 cup heavy cream
- 1 egg
- 1/2 tsp peppermint extract
- 1/4 cup crushed candy canes

INSTRUCTIONS

1. Preheat oven to 400°F (200°C).
2. Mix flour, sugar, baking powder, and salt. Cut in butter until crumbly.
3. Stir in cream, egg, and peppermint. Fold in half the crushed candy canes.
4. Shape into a circle, cut into 8 wedges. Sprinkle with remaining candy canes.
5. Bake 15–18 minutes until golden.

SUGAR PLUM TARTS (MAKES 12)

*BUTTERY LITTLE PASTRIES FILLED WITH SPICED PLUM COMPOTE,
DUSTED WITH POWDERED SUGAR LIKE SNOW.*

INGREDIENTS

- 1 sheet puff pastry, thawed
- 6 plums, diced
- 1/4 cup sugar
- 1 tsp cinnamon
- 1/4 tsp nutmeg
- Powdered sugar

INSTRUCTIONS

1. Preheat oven to 375°F (190°C).
2. Simmer plums, sugar, cinnamon, and nutmeg until thickened.
3. Cut puff pastry into 12 squares. Fill with plum mixture, fold corners.
4. Bake 15–20 minutes until golden. Dust with powdered sugar.

PEPPERMINT HOT CHOCOLATE (SERVES 6)

RICH, VELVETY COCOA WITH CANDY CANE STIRRING STICKS, TOPPED WITH WHIPPED CREAM.

INGREDIENTS

- 4 cups whole milk
- 8 oz semisweet chocolate, chopped
- 2 tbsp cocoa powder
- 2 tbsp sugar
- 1/2 tsp peppermint extract
- Whipped cream, for topping
- 6 candy canes

INSTRUCTIONS

1. Heat milk in saucepan until steaming. Stir in chocolate, cocoa, sugar.
2. Whisk until smooth. Add peppermint extract.
3. Pour into mugs, top with whipped cream, and serve with candy canes.

WHITE AND DARK CHOCOLATE MICE (MAKES ABOUT 20)

SHAPED LIKE TINY MICE WITH LICORICE TAILS AND CHOCOLATE CHIP EYES—AN ODE TO THE NUTCRACKER'S MOUSE KING.

INGREDIENTS

- 12 oz white chocolate, melted
- 12 oz dark chocolate, melted
- Licorice laces
- Mini chocolate chips

INSTRUCTIONS

1. Line tray with parchment. Spoon small mounds of chocolate for bodies.
2. Use smaller drops for heads. Attach licorice tails and chocolate chip eyes.
3. Chill until firm.

CRANBERRY ORANGE TEA CAKES (MAKES 12)

MOIST, CITRUSY, AND PERFECT FOR CUTTING THROUGH ALL THE SWEETNESS.

INGREDIENTS

- 1 1/2 cups flour
- 1/2 cup sugar
- 1 1/2 tsp baking powder
- 1/2 tsp salt
- 1/2 cup butter, melted
- 2 eggs
- Zest of 1 orange
- 1/2 cup orange juice
- 1 cup fresh cranberries

INSTRUCTIONS

1. Preheat oven to 350°F (175°C).
2. Mix flour, sugar, baking powder, and salt. Add butter, eggs, zest, and juice. Stir until smooth.
3. Fold in cranberries. Divide into muffin tin.
4. Bake 18–20 minutes until golden.

French Christmas Party

*A French-inspired holiday menu is all about warmth, richness,
and a touch of indulgence. This cozy Christmas gathering collection
pulls from French classics that felt both celebratory and comforting:
a rich pâté, a slow-simmered beef stew, creamy potatoes, and a festive
dessert centerpiece. These dishes are meant to be shared at a long,
laughter-filled table, paired with good wine and even better company.*

PÂTÉ EN CROÛTE (PÂTÉ IN PASTRY)

SERVES 8–10

INGREDIENTS

- 1 lb ground pork
- ½ lb ground veal (or substitute chicken or turkey)
- ½ lb bacon, finely chopped
- 1 small onion, finely diced
- 2 cloves garlic, minced
- 2 tbsp cognac or brandy
- 2 tsp thyme leaves
- 1 tsp ground allspice
- 1 tsp salt, ½ tsp black pepper
- 1 sheet puff pastry, thawed
- 1 egg, beaten (for egg wash)

INSTRUCTIONS

1. Preheat oven to 375°F (190°C).
2. In a large bowl, mix pork, veal, bacon, onion, garlic, cognac, thyme, allspice, salt, and pepper until well combined.
3. Roll pastry out slightly larger than a loaf pan. Line the pan with the pastry, leaving edges overhanging.
4. Fill with meat mixture, pressing firmly. Fold pastry edges over the top, sealing tightly. Brush with egg wash.
5. Bake 50–60 minutes, until pastry is golden and internal temp is 160°F.
6. Cool slightly before slicing.

BOEUF BOURGUIGNON (BEEF STEW WITH RED WINE)

SERVES 6–8

INGREDIENTS

- 3 lbs beef chuck, cut into 2-inch cubes
- 4 oz bacon, chopped
- 2 carrots, sliced
- 1 onion, diced
- 2 cloves garlic, minced
- 2 tbsp tomato paste
- 2 cups red wine (Burgundy if possible)
- 2 cups beef stock
- 2 tbsp flour
- 2 tbsp butter
- 1 bouquet garni (thyme, parsley, bay leaf tied together)
- ½ lb pearl onions, peeled
- ½ lb mushrooms, quartered
- Salt & pepper

INSTRUCTIONS

1. Cook bacon in a Dutch oven until crisp. Remove.
2. Brown beef in batches in bacon fat. Remove.
3. Add carrots, onion, garlic. Cook until softened. Stir in flour, then tomato paste.
4. Add wine, scraping browned bits. Add stock, bouquet garni, beef, and bacon back in.
5. Simmer covered for 2–3 hours until beef is tender.
6. In a skillet, sauté mushrooms and pearl onions in butter. Add to stew.
7. Season and serve with crusty bread.

GRATIN DAUPHINOIS (CREAMY POTATO GRATIN)

SERVES 8

INGREDIENTS

- 2 lbs Yukon Gold potatoes, thinly sliced
- 2 cups heavy cream
- 1 cup whole milk
- 2 garlic cloves, minced
- 1 tsp nutmeg
- 1 ½ cups Gruyère cheese, grated
- Salt & pepper

INSTRUCTIONS

1. Preheat oven to 375°F.
2. Heat cream, milk, garlic, nutmeg, salt, and pepper until just warm.
3. Layer potatoes in a buttered baking dish. Pour cream mixture over.
4. Top with Gruyère. Cover with foil. Bake 45 minutes.
5. Remove foil, bake another 15 minutes until golden and bubbling.

BÛCHE DE NOËL (YULE LOG CAKE)

SERVES 10–12

INGREDIENTS

- 4 eggs, separated
- ½ cup sugar
- ½ cup flour
- 2 tbsp cocoa powder
- 1 cup whipped cream (for filling)
- 1 ½ cups chocolate buttercream (for frosting)
- Powdered sugar (for garnish)

INSTRUCTIONS

1. Preheat oven to 350°F. Grease and line a jelly roll pan with parchment.
2. Beat egg yolks with sugar until pale. Beat whites until stiff peaks. Fold whites into yolk mixture.
3. Sift flour and cocoa, fold in gently.
4. Spread batter in pan. Bake 12–15 minutes.
5. Invert onto towel dusted with powdered sugar. Roll while warm.
6. Unroll, fill with whipped cream, re-roll. Cover with buttercream, dragging fork for "bark" effect.
7. Garnish with powdered sugar "snow."

Feast of the Seven Fishes

Paul's family welcomed me into their Christmas Eve tradition: the Feast of the Seven Fishes. A meal rich with history, it carried me from one family's table to another, weaving me into a larger story of love, loss, and community.

FRIED CALAMARI (SERVES 6)

CRISP RINGS OF SQUID, GOLDEN AND TENDER, SERVED WITH MARINARA.

INGREDIENTS

- 1 1/2 lbs squid, cleaned and sliced into rings
- 1 cup flour
- 1 tsp salt
- 1/2 tsp black pepper
- 1/2 tsp paprika
- Oil for frying
- 1 cup marinara sauce, warmed

INSTRUCTIONS

1. Heat oil to 350°F (175°C).
2. Mix flour, salt, pepper, and paprika. Dredge squid rings in mixture.
3. Fry in batches until golden, 2–3 minutes. Drain on paper towels.
4. Serve hot with marinara.

BAKED CLAMS (SERVES 6)

*CLAMS TOPPED WITH BREADCRUMBS, HERBS, AND PARMESAN,
BAKED UNTIL GOLDEN.*

INGREDIENTS

- 24 littleneck clams, shucked
- 1/2 cup breadcrumbs
- 1/4 cup Parmesan cheese
- 2 cloves garlic, minced
- 2 tbsp parsley, minced
- 2 tbsp olive oil
- Lemon wedges for serving

INSTRUCTIONS

1. Preheat oven to 375°F (190°C). Place clams on baking sheet.
2. Mix breadcrumbs, Parmesan, garlic, parsley, and olive oil.
3. Spoon mixture over clams.
4. Bake 12–15 minutes until golden.
5. Serve with lemon wedges.

LINGUINE WITH WHITE CLAM SAUCE (SERVES 6)

PASTA TOSSED WITH GARLIC, OLIVE OIL, AND CLAMS IN A LIGHT BROTH.

INGREDIENTS

- 1 lb linguine
- 3 tbsp olive oil
- 4 cloves garlic, thinly sliced
- 1/2 tsp red pepper flakes
- 2 dozen clams, scrubbed
- 1 cup dry white wine
- 2 tbsp parsley, chopped

INSTRUCTIONS

1. Cook linguine until al dente. Drain, reserving 1/2 cup pasta water.
2. Heat olive oil in large skillet. Sauté garlic and red pepper until fragrant.
3. Add clams and wine. Cover, cook until clams open (about 5 minutes).
4. Toss with pasta, parsley, and reserved water if needed.

SHRIMP SCAMPI (SERVES 6)

SHRIMP SAUTÉED IN BUTTER, GARLIC, AND LEMON, FINISHED WITH PARSLEY.

INGREDIENTS

- 2 lbs large shrimp, peeled and deveined
- 4 tbsp butter
- 3 tbsp olive oil
- 4 cloves garlic, minced
- 1/2 cup white wine
- 1 lemon, juiced
- 2 tbsp parsley, chopped

INSTRUCTIONS

1. Heat butter and oil in skillet. Add garlic, cook 1 minute.
2. Add shrimp, cook until pink, 2–3 minutes.
3. Stir in wine and lemon juice, simmer 2 minutes.
4. Garnish with parsley and serve immediately.

WHOLE ROASTED BRANZINO (SERVES 4–6)

DELICATE MEDITERRANEAN FISH ROASTED WITH HERBS AND LEMON.

INGREDIENTS

- 2 whole branzino (about 1 1/2 lbs each), cleaned
- 2 lemons, sliced
- 4 sprigs rosemary
- 2 tbsp olive oil
- Salt and pepper to taste

INSTRUCTIONS

1. Preheat oven to 400°F (200°C).
2. Stuff fish cavities with lemon slices and rosemary.
3. Place on baking sheet, drizzle with olive oil, season with salt and pepper.
4. Roast 20–25 minutes until fish flakes easily.

BACCALÀ STEW (SERVES 6-8)

SALTED COD SIMMERED WITH TOMATOES, OLIVES, AND POTATOES.

INGREDIENTS
- 1 lb salt cod (baccalà), soaked overnight and drained
- 2 tbsp olive oil
- 1 onion, chopped
- 2 cloves garlic, minced
- 1 can crushed tomatoes (28 oz)
- 2 potatoes, peeled and diced
- 1/2 cup green olives
- 1/4 tsp red pepper flakes

INSTRUCTIONS
1. Heat oil in pot. Sauté onion and garlic until soft.
2. Add tomatoes, potatoes, and red pepper. Simmer 10 minutes.
3. Add cod and olives. Simmer until potatoes are tender and cod flakes, about 25 minutes.

ANCHOVY CROSTINI (SERVES 6)

TOASTED BREAD TOPPED WITH BUTTER AND ANCHOVY FILLETS.

INGREDIENTS

- 1 baguette, sliced
- 1/4 cup butter, softened
- 1 tin anchovy fillets, drained

INSTRUCTIONS

1. Toast baguette slices until golden.
2. Spread with butter, top each with an anchovy fillet.
3. Serve warm or at room temperature.

Puerto Rican Holiday Menu

The season always brings me back to my roots. These are the dishes tied to my Puerto Rican heritage, shared around Three Kings Day. Food has always been part of my story, and in this menu, tradition mingles with celebration, memory, and family.

LECHÓN ASADO (SERVES 10–12)

SLOW-ROASTED PORK SHOULDER, SEASONED WITH GARLIC, OREGANO, AND CITRUS, WITH SKIN ROASTED UNTIL CRISP.

INGREDIENTS

- 1 whole pork shoulder (8–10 lbs), skin on
- 8 cloves garlic
- 2 tbsp salt
- 2 tbsp oregano
- 1 tbsp black pepper
- 1/4 cup olive oil
- 1/2 cup sour orange juice (or mix orange + lime juice)

INSTRUCTIONS

1. Mash garlic with salt, oregano, and pepper to make a paste. Stir in olive oil and citrus juice.
2. Score pork skin in a crosshatch. Rub seasoning paste over the pork, working into slits.
3. Refrigerate overnight.
4. Roast at 325°F (165°C) for 4–5 hours, until tender and skin is crisp.

ARROZ CON GANDULES (SERVES 6–8)

THE NATIONAL DISH OF PUERTO RICO: RICE WITH PIGEON PEAS, FLAVORED WITH SOFRITO.

INGREDIENTS

- 2 tbsp olive oil
- 1/2 cup sofrito (onion, garlic, peppers, cilantro blend)
- 1/4 cup tomato sauce
- 1 can gandules (pigeon peas), drained
- 1/4 cup pimento-stuffed olives
- 2 cups long-grain rice
- 3 cups chicken broth
- 1 packet sazón seasoning

INSTRUCTIONS

1. Heat oil in a pot. Add sofrito and tomato sauce, cook 2 minutes.
2. Stir in gandules, olives, rice, broth, and sazón.
3. Bring to a boil, reduce heat, cover, and simmer 25 minutes, until rice is tender.

PASTELES (MAKES ABOUT 12)

MASA MADE FROM GREEN BANANAS AND YAUTÍA, FILLED WITH
PORK AND WRAPPED IN BANANA LEAVES.

INGREDIENTS

- 3 lbs pork shoulder, cubed
- 2 tbsp adobo seasoning
- 2 tbsp olive oil
- 1 onion, diced
- 1 bell pepper, diced
- 1/2 cup sofrito
- 2 tbsp tomato paste
- 1 tbsp capers
- 10 green bananas, grated
- 2 yautía (taro root), grated
- 1/2 cup achiote oil
- Banana leaves, cut into squares

INSTRUCTIONS

1. Season pork with adobo. Brown in oil, then add onion, pepper, sofrito, tomato paste, and capers. Simmer until tender.
2. Grate bananas and yautía. Mix with achiote oil to form masa.
3. Place a spoonful of masa on banana leaf, add pork filling, top with more masa. Fold and tie securely.
4. Boil wrapped pasteles in salted water for 1 hour.

TOSTONES (SERVES 4–6)

*TWICE-FRIED PLANTAINS, CRISP ON THE OUTSIDE,
TENDER INSIDE.*

INGREDIENTS
- 3 green plantains
- Vegetable oil for frying
- Salt, to taste

INSTRUCTIONS
1. Peel plantains and cut into 1-inch chunks.
2. Fry in oil at 350°F (175°C) until lightly golden, about 3 minutes. Remove and flatten with the bottom of a glass.
3. Return flattened plantains to oil and fry until crisp. Drain on paper towels.
4. Sprinkle with salt.

GUINEÍTOS EN ESCABECHE (SERVES 6)

GREEN BANANAS MARINATED IN TANGY ESCABECHE SAUCE.

INGREDIENTS

- 6 green bananas
- 1/4 cup olive oil
- 1 onion, thinly sliced
- 1/2 cup white vinegar
- 1/2 cup roasted red peppers, sliced
- 1 bay leaf
- Salt and pepper

INSTRUCTIONS

1. Boil green bananas until just tender. Peel and slice into rounds.
2. In a skillet, heat oil and sauté onion. Add vinegar, peppers, bay leaf, salt, and pepper.
3. Toss bananas in the marinade. Chill at least 4 hours.

ROSCA DE REYES (SERVES 10–12)

*A RING-SHAPED SWEET BREAD, TOPPED WITH CANDIED FRUITS
AND HIDING A SMALL FIGURINE.*

INGREDIENTS
- 4 cups flour
- 1/2 cup sugar
- 1 tbsp yeast
- 1/2 tsp salt
- 1/2 cup butter, softened
- 4 eggs
- 1/2 cup warm milk
- Candied fruits for topping
- 1 small figurine or dried bean

INSTRUCTIONS
1. Mix flour, sugar, yeast, and salt. Add butter, eggs, and milk. Knead until smooth.
2. Let rise 1 hour. Shape into a ring, tucking the figurine inside.
3. Brush with egg wash, decorate with candied fruits.
4. Bake at 350°F (175°C) for 30–35 minutes.

TEMBLEQUE (SERVES 6)

COCONUT PUDDING, DUSTED WITH CINNAMON.

INGREDIENTS

- 4 cups coconut milk
- 1/2 cup cornstarch
- 3/4 cup sugar
- 1/4 tsp salt
- Ground cinnamon, for garnish

INSTRUCTIONS

1. Whisk cornstarch with 1 cup coconut milk until smooth.
2. In a saucepan, heat remaining milk, sugar, and salt. Stir in cornstarch mixture.
3. Cook until thickened, about 5 minutes.
4. Pour into molds, chill until firm.

FLAN DE COCO (SERVES 8)

COCONUT FLAN WITH CARAMEL TOPPING.

INGREDIENTS

- 1 cup sugar (for caramel)
- 1 can sweetened condensed milk
- 1 can evaporated milk
- 1 cup coconut milk
- 3 eggs
- 1 tsp vanilla extract

INSTRUCTIONS

1. Melt sugar in a pan until golden, pour into a round baking dish.
2. Blend condensed milk, evaporated milk, coconut milk, eggs, and vanilla. Pour over caramel.
3. Bake in a water bath at 350°F (175°C) for 50–60 minutes.
4. Cool, then invert onto a plate.

COQUITO (SERVES 8)

PUERTO RICAN COCONUT EGGNOG WITH RUM.

INGREDIENTS

- 1 can sweetened condensed milk
- 1 can evaporated milk
- 1 can cream of coconut
- 1 cup white rum
- 1 tsp vanilla
- 1 tsp cinnamon
- 1/2 tsp nutmeg

INSTRUCTIONS

1. Blend all ingredients until smooth.
2. Chill overnight for flavors to meld.
3. Serve cold, shaken well.

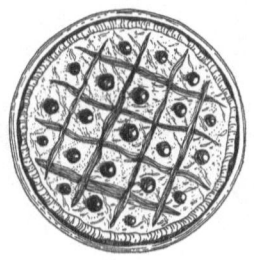

Closing Note

Food, like stories, has a way of bringing people together, even in the middle of mystery. From the shadows of the Poe Dinner to the sparkle of the Nutcracker Party, from the traditions of Puerto Rican cooking to the long history of the Feast of the Seven Fishes, each menu carried more than flavor. They carried memory, comfort, and connection.

Thank you for sharing these dishes and this journey with me. May these recipes find a place at your own table, reminding you that every meal tells a story.

www.ingramcontent.com/pod-product-compliance
Lightning Source LLC
Chambersburg PA
CBHW061640190726
48289CB00006B/1673